The Baron Takes a Bet

Gambling Peers, Book 2

Matilda Madison

ARE YOU SIGNED UP FOR DRAGONBLADE'S BLOG?

You'll get the latest news and information on exclusive giveaways, exclusive excerpts, coming releases, sales, free books, cover reveals and more.

Check out our complete list of authors, too!

No spam, no junk. That's a promise!

Sign Up Here

www.dragonbladepublishing.com

Dearest Reader;

Thank you for your support of a small press. At Dragonblade Publishing, we strive to bring you the highest quality Historical Romance from some of the best authors in the business. Without your support, there is no 'us', so we sincerely hope you adore these stories and find some new favorite authors along the way.

Happy Reading!

CEO, Dragonblade Publishing

Additional Dragonblade books by Author Matilda Madison

Gambling Peers Series
A Duke Makes a Deal (Book 1)
The Baron Takes a Bet (Book 2)

Chapter One

HOLLY WINCOMBE, NEE Smyth, had never once considered that she would be a widow after only being married for seven days.

Staring at the Mora grandfather clock that stood against the plum-colored wall of the Kingston House parlor, she tried to relax her shoulders. Her entire body was tense and her hands gripped tightly together, resting on her black-crepe-covered lap. She and her siblings, Jasper and Katrina, silently waited for their lawyer, Mr. Franklin Armstrong, to arrive.

Though she had only been married to the baron for a week before his passing, Holly wore her mourning dress with a heavy heart. John Wincombe, 6th Baron of Bairnsdale, had been one of her dearest friends. Even during the last moments of his life, his only concern had been for Holly and her siblings. He had insisted on their marriage to secure her family's future, and after months of refusing him, she had finally ended up marrying him on his death bed. Holly hadn't been able to deny the dying man his wish to help them.

Besides, she and her siblings were in desperate need of whatever help they could get.

"How long will we have to be in mourning?" Jasper asked, toeing the fringe of the oriental rug beneath his foot.

Holly tried not to glare at her adolescent brother, who had

returned from Eton for the funeral. His walnut-colored hair, not unlike hers, had grown out since he had visited for Christmas and was arranged in a devil-may-care fashion. As most seventeen-year-old boys were, he was preoccupied with his own feelings above all else.

"As long as we must. The baron was family," Katrina, his twin, said, turning to her sister. "Right, Holly?"

But before Holly could answer, Jasper leaned forward from his chair to continue.

"Wincombe wasn't family. They were barely married a week."

"Yes, to save us from destitution, Jasper. Or have you forgotten who's been funding your education these past few years?"

"Oh yes, a fine reason to marry someone," he retorted, folding his arms across his chest as he slumped back. "So you can pawn off your brother—"

"Jasper!"

"—and let him rot in some dingy school."

"Eton is not some dingy school," Katrina argued. "And you're being unfair to Holly. She did the only thing she could, and we should be grateful that the baron was kind enough to propose to her."

Jasper's face darkened. His eyes flickered to Holly though he continued to address Katrina.

"She wouldn't have had to marry him if she just let me help."

"And what could you have done?" Katrina pressed. "We have no money, no income—"

"Well, if you two would ever stop treating me like a child—"

"Hush the both of you," Holly said, her tone low as her gaze returned to the clock. "Mr. Armstrong will be here any minute, and I will not have him witness our family squabble."

Both siblings instantly quieted. Katrina began picking at her thumbnail while Jasper continued toying with the carpet with his foot. But a minute hadn't passed before Jasper tried once more.

"If you just sold the blasted farm—"

"Jasper," Holly bit out, her tone one of warning.

The youth sighed loudly and stood, walking around the settee towards the window. Evidently, he was too annoyed to continue sitting in silence, but Holly wasn't concerned about his foul mood. She had more important things to worry about.

Since the death of their mother several years ago, Holly has had to become her siblings' surrogate parent and caretaker. Their father, a member of the landed gentry who had been nearly sixty-two when he married, succumbed to old age before their mother's death from fever several years ago. It had been traumatizing to suddenly be the sole caregiver to two young children, but Holly had swallowed her grief and met the challenge head-on. Life was full of unexpected challenges. Holly knew that all too well.

Their family home, Felton Manor had been floating purely on credit the last few years. Holly's mother had tried her hardest to pay off the debts Holly's father had left, though her economizing was never enough to get them ahead of the bills. Her mother had kept their debt a secret and Holly had not learned the extent of their poor situation until her mother's death. She had told her siblings about their financial woes, which had only garnered her tears from Katrina and foolish ideas from Jasper.

Holly wasn't in the mood to entertain one of his ridiculous whims. In the past twelve months, her brother had become increasingly argumentative about his position in the family. He had recently come to the realization that once he came of age, he would technically be the head of their household, even though Holly had maintained their family on her own for years. Jasper believed she should rely more on him, but as his only suggestion was to sell off Felton Manor, Holly refused to listen. Her brother was to inherit Felton Manor on his eighteenth birthday, barely two months away, and he had promised to sell it the moment it came fully into his possession. Holly was still searching for a way to keep it. She could stand to lose a great deal in life, but she absolutely refused to lose her home.

Even if that meant marrying a dying man for money.

Holly inhaled deeply as she began to rub her index fingertips over her thumbnails. It hadn't been as vulgar as it sounded. John had been a good friend for years and he was aware of the family's dire financial strains. He had proposed to her a handful of times in the past year to try and help her with her burden, but Holly had always refused, believing she could eventually find a way to manage it all on her own. But when she had to sell the last of their livestock that past fall, Holly knew her time was running out.

Just then, a middle-aged butler, Mr. Jorden, entered the room. Holly straightened her spine.

"Mr. Armstrong has arrived, my lady," Mr. Jorden said, followed by an unreasonably tall and thin man.

Mr. Armstrong was a pale fellow with thick black hair atop his oval head. He wore a pair of thin-rimmed spectacles and nodded at Holly and her siblings before entering the room. Walking around the short coffee table between the settee and a couple of chairs, he sat, his knees high over the table. He was obviously too long-framed for the delicate furniture, but he didn't comment as he brought the leather satchel he had been carrying onto his lap.

"My lady. It is a pleasure seeing you again," he said, searching his bag.

Though he appeared to be a bit scattered, Holly had no choice but to trust him. After all, he had been one of the witnesses at her wedding and had been entrusted with John's last will and testament.

"Mr. Armstrong," Holly said with a tight smile. "Was your journey pleasant?"

"Eh, it wasn't terrible," he said, pulling out a thin leather book. Opening it on the table revealed several dozen papers that didn't appear to be bound. "Finding the new baron was more troublesome though."

Holly frowned. She had learned bits and pieces of John's heir over the years. His name was Mr. Gavin Winscombe and he had worked for a time in banking, which was odd for a man set to inherit a title. She also knew John's nephew also loved to travel and was often out of the country. He supposedly possessed a touch of wanderlust.

Leaning slightly forward, Holly spoke.

"Was he not in London?"

A part of her had expected that Gavin would come to Kingston House for the burial of his uncle, but he hadn't. There was little love lost between the two men, from what John had said. Still, it irked her that Gavin hadn't had the decency to at least pay his respects to the man whose home he would inherit.

"Well, he had only just returned, you see," Mr. Armstrong said, flipping through his pages. "He has been on the continent for six months and only arrived in London the day before last. I was practically camped out on his front steps until he returned."

That explained why he wasn't at the funeral. Holly supposed she couldn't fault his absence since he had been out of the country.

"Oh. Perhaps, all things considered, that is rather fortuitous. John always said they weren't very close," she said, swallowing a lump in her throat. Lord, how it pained her to talk about her dearly departed friend. "Did you explain to the new Lord Bairnsdale the, um, situation here?"

Initially, she had been worried that he would think poorly of her when he discovered the circumstances of their marriage, but John had assured her that his nephew would understand why they married and that he would adhere to the promises John had made.

Mr. Armstrong was bent over the table, but his eyes lifted, catching her gaze.

"I did."

Holly waited for him to elaborate, but he didn't as his sight fell back to his pages. Her sister gently elbowed her side to prompt her to speak.

"Did Lord Bairnsdale come with you?" Holly asked.

"No."

"Oh."

"I came with him."

Holly sighed, annoyed. Why was this man being intentionally obtuse?

"Well, then where is he?"

"He asked if it would be all right to inspect the stables for a bit." Mr. Armstrong's brow lifted as he found the paper he was searching for. "I couldn't think why it would be a problem."

Holly could. There were pressing matters to attend to. Lord Bairnsdale had an entire lifetime to examine his new home. Was he not aware that it was discourteous to keep people waiting?

"And you explained to him that my marriage to John was indeed a legitimate one? That John insisted on it?"

Having married John on his deathbed, Holly knew a dozen arguments could be used to delegitimize their union—especially the consummation, or rather, lack thereof.

"Do not worry, my lady. Everything is set up to the former baron's explicit instructions," Mr. Armstrong said.

Holly leaned back slightly and bit the inside of her cheek as nausea churned in her stomach. What would this nephew think of her? Would he believe she had coerced a dying man into marrying her? Everyone knew John had been asking for her hand for nearly a year. There were witnesses all over Lincolnshire who could attest that John loved her and that their relationship, while not romantic, was sincere. But the new baron was largely a stranger here. Would he give credence to the accounts?

She tried to calm herself. Her anxiety over the situation was making her paranoid.

"Here he comes," Jasper said, breaking through Holly's worrying.

Turning around at the waist, she saw her brother leaning against the windowsill, arms still folded across his chest. He seemed to glower as he watched the unseen baron amble across the property.

"Well?" Katrina said. "What does he look like?"

Jasper peered closer to the window.

"Like a man, though he's a bit far away." He squinted as his voice trailed off. "So, who can tell." Katrina sighed loudly, and Holly bit her lip to stop herself from smiling. Though she frequently butted heads with Jasper, he often made her laugh with his dry humor. He glanced at Katrina, who was not amused in the least. "What?"

Katrina stood up and walked around the settee.

"Of course he looks like a man, but what of his hair? His height? Does he walk with purpose? Possibly a limp?"

"Why would I care about the man's hair?"

"It's not about whether you care or not, it's about describing him," she said as she peered out the window. Her shoulders slumped. "Drats. Where did he go?"

"Come away from there," Holly said. "We don't want him to find us with our noses pressed against the glass as if we were spying on him."

"But we *are* spying on him," Jasper said.

Katrina quickly returned to her seat. Jasper did not leave the window, however, and Mr. Armstrong cleared his throat.

"Now, as you know, upon your marriage to the baron, all of your debts were acquired by his estate, as well as your dowry," the lawyer said. "Um, a pair of sheep, was it?"

Holly exhaled slowly. That was all the property the Smyths had left, except for their home.

"Yes, all but Felton Manor," she said, her heart pinching slightly. "That was reserved for my brother in my parents' will and will be inherited by him upon his eighteenth birthday."

"A broken-down pile of rocks, how generous," Jasper murmured. Holly gave him a sharp glare, but he was unfazed. "Why not just sell it? We can divide the proceeds three ways, like I said six months ago—"

"We are not selling Mama and Papa's house," she said defiantly.

"I'm just going to do it in a few months anyway."

"Then I won't be able to stop you, but I will not be responsible for losing our family home. As long as the decision remains mine, it remains with us," Holly said, trying to control her temper. She turned back to the lawyer. "Please continue, Mr. Armstrong."

"Right, well, as you also know from your original agreement, you *were* entitled to a third of the baron's property and assets that aren't entailed. Unfortunately, Kingston House is entailed, but the late baron did make a string of additions to his will in the days after your marriage. A cat, for example, by the name of Pauline Musgrove, has been left in your care. John's journals however, have been left to his nephew."

Holly stared at the lawyer. Did he say *were*? As in, past tense?

"Excuse me?" Katrina said. "Did you say cat?" She turned to her sister. "Why would he name a cat Pauline Musgrove?"

"He named it after his neighbor from when he was a boy," Holly said, turning expectantly to the lawyer. "I'm sorry, you said something about our original agreement?"

"His neighbor?" Katrina continued. "Why ever would he do that?"

Holly sighed as she recounted the story.

"Because she was a recluse and so was the cat. Now, Mr. Armstrong—"

"A recluse? But—"

"Katrina, please," Holly said, cutting her off. Her sister's mouth snapped shut. "Mr. Armstrong, you mentioned an original agreement?"

"Ah, yes, the conversation you had with the baron before your marriage? I'm referring to that."

"Oh," Holly said, an uneasy sensation settling into her spine.

"Where is the cat?" Katrina asked.

"She lives in London and apparently is intolerant of loud voices. It's marked down right here," Mr. Armstrong said, pointing to the paper he held.

"The cat is at the baron's residence, Bairnsdale Terrence. Now, that property is also entailed, but there are a number of things within the home that the baron insisted you have. He reworked a bit of his will before he died."

Holly lifted a brow.

"Did he?"

"But why would he keep a cat in London and not bring it with him here?" Katrina pressed.

"He didn't like the cat."

"Well then why have it?"

"Because he felt sorry for the thing," Holly said exasperatedly. "Mr. Armstrong, I'm sorry, I wasn't aware that John had changed anything. I mean to say, I was with him the last week of his life and I barely left his side."

"Ah, yes, but you did. The Thursday before his passing, you went to wash and rest," Mr. Armstrong said, his head lifting with his tone. He had been there as well. "He requested an audience with me to make sure that the marriage contract was solid. He was adamant that I was to do everything to make sure that it was unbreakable."

Holly's shoulders dropped as she breathed a sigh of relief. John had always tried to take care of her, and at that moment, she was even more sorry that he was no longer with them.

"He was a fine gentleman," she said.

"Yes, although you may think differently after I explain about this next part," Mr. Armstrong said lowly, shuffling his papers.

Holly peered at Katrina, who shrugged her shoulders.

"I'm sorry," Holly said. "What next part?"

Mr. Armstrong took a deep breath and observed her.

"Lady Bairnsdale, have you ever heard of the term proxy marriage?"

Chapter Two

THE MORNING SKY was overcast, and Gavin Winscombe wondered if it would rain before night fell as he strode across one of the two vast, flat wheat fields harvested the previous fall. He had been eager to stretch his legs after the two-day journey from London and to give Kingston House a quick survey, a place he had rarely visited before but had known his entire life would be his home.

The house was a sizeable Tudor-style brick manor, nearly three hundred years old, and it had been kept in pristine condition. Uncle John had apparently spared no expense in its maintenance. Almost a dozen chimneys poked up from the red clay roof, and the dark, nearly black, planks of lumber that stood out against the red brick gave it a rather charming contrast. Gavin had been informed by Mr. Armstrong, his late uncle's lawyer, that the house had recently undergone several renovations whilst repairing most of the façade to its Tudor-era style. Essentially, it was a contemporary home dressed in medieval clothes, providing all the comforts of modern times, which pleased Gavin immensely. Though he had traveled far and wide, experiencing at times the barest of creature comforts, he had always been most pleased to return to the civility of London.

An ancient, yew hedge lined the crushed white stone of the drive, crunching quietly beneath Gavin's boots as he headed for the front entrance upon leaving the stables. They had been updated as well, and Gavin couldn't help but smile, feeling his luck at having inherited a property that didn't seem to need any work. He doubted he would find many issues with Kingston House.

Save the baroness, of course.

The news that his uncle had passed away was hardly a surprise, seeing how frail he had appeared during their last meeting the previous autumn. However, learning that Uncle John had married only days before his death had shocked Gavin for several reasons. For one, his uncle was a confirmed, life-long bachelor. It had long been believed that Uncle John didn't have a "taste for ladies," as his Aunt Marnie had always put it. She had disowned her brother decades ago and had tried very hard to persuade Gavin to join her in her condemnation, convinced that such a life was immoral. But the harder she tried to convince him, the more Gavin thought such things didn't matter. Still, such was the nature of his relationship with Aunt Marnie. If she hated something, Gavin would be far more inclined to like it on principle. Or maybe out of spite.

Aunt Marnie had taken Gavin in at age ten after a particularly lethal strand of scarlet fever had claimed his father's life. For that, she would always hold a particular place in Gavin's heart, but they seemed to disagree on nearly every topic.

Uncle John was supposed to take Gavin in to teach him about the barony he was set to inherit. But Aunt Marnie had told him that her brother didn't want him, and Gavin had been sent to live with her. Gavin had been somewhat bitter about being left in the hands of his miserable, morally righteous aunt.

Aunt Marnie had complained about everything during Gavin's time with her, but mostly about how finically stringent her brother was, which led to two very distinct personality traits in Gavin. The first was to never rely on anyone for money. The other was to always find the good in every situation, if only to spite his sourpuss aunt. She hadn't liked that he went into banking either, but he wasn't ashamed to be in the rare group of first-class men who had decided to have careers. His father had not left him much of an inheritance, and since he had no intention of turning to his uncle, hat in hand, and begging for an allowance, earning his own income had been the only option. Besides, he'd like that his work made him independent, requiring nothing from the uncle who had never had time or affection to spare for him.

A sense of abashment came over Gavin. He wouldn't be bitter about the past, even if he still believed it had been unfair. The money his uncle had sent to Aunt Marnie had provided him with food and clothing, as minimal as it had been, and paid for his education. There were thousands of men who were not as fortunate as he.

Sticking his hand into his coat pocket, Gavin pulled out a small, brown envelope with the words *Gibraltar's* stamped on it. Opening the flap, he tipped it into his hand until a pebble-sized, pale-yellow candy fell into his palm. Popping the sweet into his mouth, he climbed the front steps of Kingston House, finding it humorous how addicted he had become to these little confectionaries. Upon his arrival home in London, he had discovered the treats waiting for him, without a note saying who they were from. Someone who knew him personally, he assumed. Only his closest friends knew his ridiculous, somewhat embarrassing habit of always having sweets on his person. He had picked it up while attending Eton.

Taking a deep breath, Gavin lifted his fist to knock when the door suddenly opened, revealing a portly man with large, almost bulbous eyes. He was dressed in claret and black livery and motioned to a line of servants, from footmen to maids to the cooks, lined up against the wall.

"Lord Bairnsdale," the round man said with a deep bow. "Forgive the household for not meeting you outside. With the impending rain, we didn't wish to sully to floors with mud."

"Impending rain? It's just a bit overcast," Gavin said at the same time a roll of thunder sounded above them. Glancing up at the ceiling, with its dark wood beams, he smiled again and returned his attention to the butler. "But then, who am I to argue with locals?"

The butler seemed to be debating the question.

"Uh, well, My lord…"

"No, never mind it," Gavin said, waving his hand. "What is your name?"

The butler squared his shoulders and puffed out his chest.

"Dougherty, my lord. Underbutler."

"Underbutler? And where is your superior?"

"Mr. Jorden is with the baroness and Mr. Armstrong. If you will," he said, bowing and stretching his arm out. "I thought to introduce you to the staff first, so you could attend to the rest of your business uninterrupted today."

Gavin couldn't argue with that and nodded.

"Very well."

Mr. Dougherty bowed yet again and led him to the line of servants.

"This is Mr. Caplan, Mrs. Sheen, Mr. James…"

Gavin nodded at each servant, saying each name in his head three times as he did to remember them. It was a trick his father had taught him once as a lad.

Although Gavin had a cook, butler, and housekeeper at his London residence, Kingston House had nearly two dozen employees. He doubted there would be much room for solitude in a place like this, which unnerved him slightly. He had always been relatively comfortable with being alone. As soon as his income with the bank had allowed for it, he'd set up his own household separate from Aunt Marnie. He still supported her quite handsomely, of course—setting her up in a respectably sized home for a single, elderly woman, with a full staff and all her bills sent directly to him—but he'd ensured that she lived at a reasonable distance from his own London home.

And it wasn't just Aunt Marnie from whom he appreciated a

bit of distance. Gavin had always enjoyed social settings like balls and soirées, but he would disappear without so much as a farewell whenever he decided he wanted to leave. He wasn't sure why he wasn't good at goodbyes, but he avoided them at all costs. It was why he never took on a permanent lover. He was always more comfortable with courtesans. Theirs was a transaction, a primal chore that required seeing to. No drama, no fuss, no commitment—just a fair exchange of goods for services. The business was business, even if Silas Winters, the Duke of Combe, thought otherwise.

Gavin smirked at the thought of his friend, whose recent second marriage had turned him into a damn convert on the ideas of romantic love and familial contentment. He was happy for Silas, who had suffered greatly in his first marriage, but Gavin had always been able to use that first marriage as proof that a man was wiser to stay alone. While their mutual friend Derek had argued that one needed a wife to procreate, Gavin saw no need to do so. Yes, he was the last living heir to the barony, but what of that? He felt no particular compulsion to see the line continued. Perhaps it had run its course.

After the staff introductions, he followed Mr. Dougherty into the parlor, where he was met by not two but five people, all of whom stopped speaking immediately upon entering the room.

Mr. Armstrong sat across the way from two ladies dressed in black gowns who were far more attractive than Gavin had anticipated. He had assumed his uncle had married some plain-faced spinster who hadn't been able to snag a husband due to a lack of attraction, but as he beheld the woman in front of him, he saw that this was not the case.

Though they were sitting, the two ladies appeared to be the same height, though the one closer to him had a slightly rounder face, appearing somewhat innocent compared to her more angular-faced, blue-eyed counterpart. Both had rich walnut-colored hair pulled back and twisted into near-matching styles, though the blue-eyed lady wore a grey teardrop pearl pendant around her neck. She was decidedly less angelic looking of the two, but there was something about her that commanded all of his attention.

"The Baron Bairnsdale," Mr. Dougherty said with a low bow. "May I present the Lady Bairnsdale, Mr. Armstrong, Miss Katrina Smyth, and Mr. Jasper Smyth."

"A pleasure," Gavin said with a bow, but when he raised his head, neither lady had moved. In fact, the lady with the pearl necklace only stared, her mouth slightly open, her expression suddenly panicky. He quickly surveyed the room and realized that everyone was staring at him.

The pearl-wearing lady returned her attention to Mr. Armstrong without so much as a hello.

"There has to be some sort of mistake," she said, her voice deeper than Gavin had expected but quite lovely. "John wouldn't have done something like this. Certainly not without at the very least explaining his reasons to me. But even then, I cannot believe he would have done so, because he would know that I would never agree to it."

"But you did agree, my lady," Mr. Armstrong insisted nervously. He reached for several papers and held them up. "This is your signature, is it not?"

So, this was his late uncle's wife, Gavin thought. Even frowning, she appeared far too pretty to be wed to an elderly, dying man. He could only assume her motive had been to gain some sort of inheritance.

"Yes," she said. "But half this document is in Latin, as you know very well since you were the lawyer who presented it to me to be signed. I was under the impression that it was marrying me to John. When you explained the terms, I distinctly remember you saying the *sixth* baron."

"But the paper says seventh."

"But *you* said sixth. I heard you. You said John's name."

"Yes, because he was the representative. I'm very sorry, my lady, but it is indeed all here," the lawyer said, shaking his papers.

"You can petition for a dissolvent, I suppose."

"Yes. Yes, do that, straight away."

"But seeing as you were married by a Catholic priest, it will take more than a few months. Possibly years."

"Years?" She nearly choked. "No. No, absolutely not. I will not abide by this."

"Er, hello," Gavin said, taking a step forward, finished with being ignored. "I don't mean to intrude, but what exactly is the issue here?"

Once again, everyone turned to look at him, but no one spoke. A wave of impending dread swamped Gavin. He stared back at all of them. Something was wrong, and if the way they were looking at him was any indication, it involved him.

He took a step towards Mr. Armstrong.

"May I?" he asked, motioning towards the papers the lawyer held.

"Oh yes," he said, handing them to Gavin.

The papers were drawn in exaggerated penmanship, with flourishing letters and flowery prose. Gavin squinted, reading a line twice before realizing it was Latin. He frowned.

"And what exactly am I looking at?"

"A marriage certificate, my lord," Mr. Armstrong said before coughing and adding quietly, "Yours, actually."

Gavin paused. He couldn't have heard that right. His gaze lifted; his eyes locked on the lawyer's face.

"Excuse me?"

"It's a marriage certificate. Yours and the baroness's, to be precise."

Gavin didn't move. Why in the world would this man say something so ridiculous? He wasn't married. After a moment, he turned to see the baroness staring at him with something akin to fear. What the devil was going on?

"I don't understand," he said.

"It seems," she said, finally addressing him. "That your uncle didn't marry me for himself but as a stand in for you."

"For me?" Gavin repeated. "How?"

"Well, my lord," Mr. Armstrong said, pointing to a line on the paper, "do you see this, here?"

"Yes."

"I believe that is your signature, is it not?"

Gavin squinted. Sure enough, it was his signature, but he couldn't for the life of him remember when he signed it.

"It is, but how…"

"Your uncle said that you came to visit him, some time before you left for the continent last fall. Is that so, sir?"

"Yes, I was here last autumn."

"And you submitted to signing several pages when you came, did you not?"

Gavin's mind reeled as he remembered the visit. It had been a short trip. He hadn't even spent the night, returning to London as quickly as possible to continue packing for his trip to the continent. Uncle John had given him a ridiculous number of papers to sign, something about inheriting a soon-to-be-defunct whiskey distillery or something preposterous. He remembered being annoyed over having traveled so far for something absurd, but his uncle had insisted on finishing the large pile of paperwork before he left.

"Yes, but I certainly didn't sign a marriage certificate."

Mr. Armstrong visibly winced.

"Well, actually, sir… you did. The late baron explained to me that you had given your consent to have him stand in during a proxy wedding, as you were set to leave for the continent. I wondered at the time if he was being entirely truthful as to the degree of your consent, since I knew he was… ah… withholding some information from the baroness… but his instructions to me were quite clear, and I followed them to the letter. The document had your signature, and the marriage was duly recorded."

"But I never gave my consent to *that*."

The lawyer shook the pages in his hands.

"I believe you, sir, but the marriage happened all the same.

These documents are perfectly legal—and binding. I'm afraid that the late baron was successful in his quest."

"His quest being to marry me off?" Gavin asked, his tone filled with incredulity.

"Well, um… Yes."

"But that means…"

Gavin's gaze fell on the distraught widow. Well, not a widow, technically.

"That means," she said slowly. "That we are married, my lord."

Chapter Three

"No, no, no," the new baron said, shaking his head. Then, to Holly's surprise, he laughed before continuing his chant. "No. No, Mr. Armstrong. No."

"Unfortunately, yes," Mr. Armstrong said apologetically, pointing at a line on the paper that the new baron held. "You see? Right here. *Lex loci celebrationis contractus*. Now that first half is in reference to the common laws of marriage in England, but that last bit is in reference to the contract where it was signed. The sixth baron stood in as you during the wedding to Miss Holly Smyth. It was a proxy marriage."

"No," Gavin said again, even more firmly this time. It seemed the new baron was done with this jest. "No. In order for it to be a proxy marriage, both parties must be aware of it, and I was not. I never agreed to this."

"Neither did I," Holly said quickly, catching his eye. "I wouldn't have gone through with it if I knew."

"Are you sure?" Jasper said from the window. "You were willing to marry the baron just to pay off our debts—"

"Jasper!" Katrina nearly shouted as she turned around. "That's completely unfair and you know it!"

"That is not why John and I married. And I certainly wouldn't have condoned marrying a stranger who knew nothing about me," Holly said before realizing they were about to have an all-out family argument in front of strangers. With the suspicious glare the new baron gave her, it was clear that she needed to get a hold of the situation. "Jasper, Katrina, will you please leave so I might have a moment to speak with the baron and Mr. Armstrong privately?"

"But we have a right to know what's going on," Jasper said, coming forward.

"And I will inform you, just as soon as I have this mess settled. Now please, go."

Katrina stood dutifully and left the room while Jasper huffed loudly and stalked behind her. She would have to deal with her brother later, but for now, she had to fix this. Turning back to face the new baron, she gave him a proper look.

He was just her height, if not a hair taller, with hazel eyes and a square face, his jaw sharp and rather attractive in an indeterminable way. His shoulders were broad, giving the appearance of solid strength beneath his finely cut clothes. Though it was evident by his speech and posture that he had grown up within the peerage, there was something slightly different about him. Perhaps it was his seeming laissez-faire nature or the way he was calmly arguing with Mr. Armstrong about this marriage sham. Any other peer would be livid to arrive at his newly inherited home to find himself shackled to a spinster, but the new baron appeared more amused than irate, almost as if he didn't believe it was happening.

A faint scent of lemon and mint hovered about him, Holly noted as she stepped up to interrupt the two men.

"I'm not sure what John was thinking to have dreamt up such a ridiculous scheme," Holly said. "But I assure you I had no part in it."

The new baron opened his mouth but appeared to think better of it and closed it. He eyed her hesitantly, and she was sure he didn't believe her. Oddly, it irked her that this man didn't trust her, but why would he? They had never met before, and John had warned Holly that his nephew was contemplative and reserved, slow to accept anyone into his confidence.

Taking a small step forward, she brought her hands together, almost in a pleading way.

"I promise you, I had no idea what John's plan was."

His hazel eyes stared intently at her, and to her surprise and discomfort, she felt the slightest flutter in her chest. He was rather handsome, in a sweet sort of way. But she was sure it was simply the symmetry of his face that made her feel suddenly odd. Frowning slightly, she pulled back a fraction.

"Then may I ask you something?" he asked, his tone even as he addressed her. She nodded. "Why did you marry my uncle, when he was so close to death?"

Holly gave Mr. Armstrong a glance, wondering if she should continue. She had assumed he had already explained all this. Apparently not, however.

Taking a deep breath, she dropped her hands to her waist and spoke.

"John and I were very dear friends for the past several years. Ever since…" Holly nearly spoke about her mother's death and her failed engagement, but she simply shook her head and continued, not wishing to be pitied by a stranger. "He asked me to marry him several times over the years, becoming more persistent just these past twelve months. I knew he meant it to be a marriage of convenience and I understood his reasoning to do so, but I always refused until last month."

"Why did he want to marry you?"

Holly tried not to appear affected, even though it wasn't a terribly flattering question.

"John was aware of my family's misfortunes and wanted to help. But his charity was too akin to pity and I couldn't bear it. Until the last time he asked."

"What changed?"

Holly sighed, shifting uncomfortably beneath his questioning.

"He said it was his dying wish. I couldn't refuse that," she explained. The memory of her dear friend, lying on his back in his bed chambers, resurfaced in her mind. He had been so frail, and it had broken her heart when he begged her. "I could rarely deny him anything, really, but in his last days, his only concern was for my siblings and myself and I couldn't... I didn't want him to be cross with me." She sniffled, giving a half-hearted laugh. "It was a foolish reason, I suppose."

A wayward tear rolled down her cheek, and she was mortified to have exposed her emotions so blatantly. When a handkerchief appeared in her blurry vision, she glanced up and saw the concern in his hazel eyes. She took it and dabbed her cheeks quickly before handing it back to him.

"That makes sense enough," he said gently, tucking the handkerchief back into his pocket as he turned to Mr. Armstrong. "But I'm still confused about why he would set up a proxy marriage."

Holly faced the lawyer as well, who suddenly appeared slightly red beneath the collar of his shirt.

"I don't understand it either," she said. "John swore that as his widow, I would be entitled to certain protections. There was certainly no need to marry me to his nephew."

"Well, who knows why great men do anything?" Mr. Armstrong asked, a thin sheen of perspiration appearing at his hairline. "Now, on to finances. I believe the former baron promised to fully restore Felton Manor, buy back the manor's livestock, allot you an annual allowance of..." The lawyer scanned the paper in from of him. "...five thousand pounds—"

"Five thousand pounds yearly?" Lord Bairnsdale asked, his brow raised with surprise.

Mr. Armstrong nodded before continuing.

"—as well as finishing paying for Mr. Smyth's tuition to Eton, sponsoring Miss Smyth's season, and paying off the remainder of your family's debts. But as you are not a widow but rather currently the baroness, your access to the estate's accounts will be at the discretion of your husband."

The word husband hung in the air like a guillotine and the

realization that she was now at the mercy of this man made Holly's head swirl. How could John have done this?

"Um," Holly started, feeling suddenly dizzy.

"But there are several items at Bairnsdale Terrace that he had wanted the baroness to have, exclusively," the lawyer continued. "The cat, for example."

"The what?" Lord Bairnsdale asked, frowning.

Ignoring the question, Mr. Armstrong went on. "But your uncle was very insistent that you retain his journals, my lord. He wished that you would read them once, and then destroy them. I was instructed to take them with me to London last time I was here, and I have placed them at Bairnsdale Terrace."

"Why would he want me to destroy them?"

But the lawyer didn't answer. Instead, he faced Holly.

"Have I covered all the points that were discussed with you in the original agreement, my lady?"

A bolt of shame coursed through her as the new baron watched her. Yes, John had promised her that Felton Manor would be restored. The roof had nearly collapsed last spring under the weight of an oak tree that had fallen on it, making the entire third floor uninhabitable. The stables had needed to be re-established for nearly a decade.

There were also her brother's increasing debts that Holly suspected were coming from his inexperience at the faro tables and the need to set her sister up for a remarkable season. Holly had thought all of this would be taken care of by John's estate, as he had promised, but now she was at a loss. She only wanted to restore Felton Manor and fund her sister's season. Then, once Katrina was married and Jasper was handed a viable, working farm to provide him an income, she could settle quietly somewhere, knowing that she had done her best to see that her siblings were leading happy, stable lives.

What she *really* wanted was to go back to her peaceful existence before her mother's death and before she assumed all the responsibilities that kept her awake at night. But that was an impossible wish. The best she could hope for was to find a way to live peacefully—and the only way she could do that was by relying on herself and herself alone.

She felt her cheeks warm beneath the heavy gaze of Lord Bairnsdale. She turned her attention to the lawyer.

"Yes, Mr. Armstrong."

"Yes indeed," the lawyer said. "And of course, as the baroness, you are entitled to a great deal more than you would be if you were merely a widow."

Holly's eyes widened. Was that why John had arranged a proxy marriage? So that she had more justification to use his coffers? Had he not trusted his nephew to take care of her and to follow through on the promises John had made?

A long sigh sounded beside her.

"Ah," Lord Bairnsdale said. "I see."

Facing the gentleman, she saw a shadow pass over his face.

"Do you?" she asked.

"My uncle didn't believe that I would honor his wishes and therefore decided to set a trap for me. Very clever." He exhaled slowly. "Very well. He wins. I'll honor all his promises to Miss Smyth here. Now how do we get out of this, Mr. Armstrong?"

"Um, well..." he started nervously. "You don't."

"Surely there must be something, Mr. Armstrong," Holly said. "John wouldn't destine the both of us to a life of... of..." She shook her head, unable to say a word. "You must do something."

"I'm afraid the contract is ironclad."

"It can't be annulled? Neither of us were aware of John's plan."

"No, it appears you weren't. And that alone might get you out of the marriage contract set forth by the laws of England, but I must remind you, you were married by a *Catholic* priest."

"What difference does that make?" Holly asked, unfamiliar with Catholic customs. She had been raised in the Church of England. In fact, she had been somewhat surprised to learn that not only was John Catholic, but he was one of only a handful of peers whose ancestors had been able to retain their title and religion from the English civil war. "I'm sure there are annulments in the Catholic church."

"There are, but they take a long time and must be granted by the pope himself," Mr. Armstrong said, standing up. "However, I will do my best to see what can be done."

"And in the meantime?" Lord Bairnsdale said.

"In the meantime," Mr. Armstrong replied, shaking his head. "I suppose you may pretend that you aren't married."

Holly scowled.

"That's it? Pretend like we aren't married?"

"Yes. I'll send word as soon as I figure out what can be done, but I really must be off. London business waits for no man. Good day," he said with a stiff bow before exiting the room, leaving Holly alone with her husband.

Husband. What an absurd thing John had done. What would have possessed him to do such an asinine thing as to marry her to his nephew, a man Holly knew next to nothing about?

Feeling as though she had to defend herself, Holly spoke.

"I know that this isn't exactly what you were expecting upon your arrival."

He glanced at her.

"What do you suppose I was expecting?"

"Well, whatever it was you were expecting, I'm sure it wasn't a wi—"

"A wife?"

She smiled painfully at him.

"There's no need to use that word. We are not married and therefore not husband and… that," she said, unable to speak it. "But I assure you that you will find nothing but a helping hand where I am concerned when it comes to resolving the matter. I don't want any part of this."

His stare turned intent. "So you agree with Mr. Armstrong? That we should just… continue on, pretending like you're a widow and I'm unattached?"

"I don't see why not. Everyone in the neighborhood believes that I married John. If we keep the truth a secret and keep our distance, everyone will continue believing that I'm merely a widow," she said. "My siblings and I will return to Felton Manor at once and—"

"I thought Armstrong said it needed to be restored?"

She hesitated.

"It does, but we have taken refuge on the first floor."

Lord Bairnsdale frowned.

"Refuge? Is it unsafe?"

"No," she lied. "It's perfectly fine."

He stepped towards her, his hands behind his back, and Holly inhaled. The cool scent of lemon and mint filled her senses once more, yet she could swear he smelled sweet. For the briefest of moments, she felt a vibration go through the center of her body as if she was physically reacting to his scent.

"I should like to see it."

Holly swallowed, unsure.

"Excuse me?"

"I should like to see your home. This Felton Manor."

She frowned.

"No, that won't be necessary."

"But I insist."

His hazel eyes sparked with challenge, and Holly felt torn. She felt an unwanted wave of warmth come over her at the concern she heard behind his words—but at the same time, she felt the unprecedented need to put him in his place, far away from her.

She folded her arms across her chest and tilted her head. She would explore that warm feeling later. For now, better to put it out of her mind.

"No."

A tension snapped and sizzled between them, and Holly had to concentrate very hard on her breathing to focus. His eyes squinted slightly, and he began to walk around her, causing her to spin around to keep him in view.

"Then you will have the neighbors believe that I turned out my uncle's week-old widow the moment I arrived at Kingston House?" he asked. "They'll think I'm some sort of devil."

She shrugged.

"People may think what they like."

"About me, you mean."

Holly stared at him.

"What else might we do? I certainly cannot live here."

"Why not?"

"Because it's improper."

He laughed.

"How so? We're married. Husband and wife."

Holly balked. Not only at the idea of remaining at Kingston House but the use of that word. *Wife*. Had he lost his mind? How could they get an annulment quietly and efficiently if he went around talking like that? They were alone at the moment, but what if a servant overheard?

"I would ask that you keep that to yourself. We aren't telling anyone about this," she said forcefully. "And I am not your w-wife."

He tipped his head to the side, walking behind the settee. She turned again to compensate.

"Well, technically you are."

"What do you want, Lord Bairnsdale?"

He shrugged.

"To inspect your house."

"I already told you, it's fine."

"And yet, I don't believe you."

"Well, perhaps you should trust people more."

"You are not people, *Lady Bairnsdale*." The use of that title made her uncomfortable. She swallowed again. "You are someone who I don't trust in the least."

His honesty unnerved her, but she couldn't deny his reasoning. She didn't trust him either, even if John had believed him a suitable husband for her. Oh, *what* had John been thinking?

"That may be, but I will have you know something. I won't be bullied into doing as you say simply because a piece of paper states that you should have some sort of power over me. Do you understand?"

He clicked his tongue, and Holly inhaled a waft of lemony mint again.

"Of course," he said, and she exhaled a breath she hadn't realized she was holding. The tense pain in her shoulders throbbed as she nodded at him, turning to leave the room when he softly added, "…my lady."

The inflection in his voice caused her to pause momentarily, but she recovered quickly and continued out the door into the hallway.

Heaven help her.

Chapter Four

THE BARONESS AND her siblings returned to Felton Manor that evening, leaving Gavin alone to inspect and explore Kingston House in uninterrupted silence. It was just as well, as he was adjusting to the idea of being married.

Married. What a preposterous thing his uncle had done.

While he hadn't been exceptionally pleased with the idea of marriage at first, against his will as it so happened, there was something intriguing about it. Gavin had rarely even considered the idea of marriage before, but now he approached it as if it were some rare specimen.

Once during a voyage down the eastern coast of the Southern Americas, Gavin had encountered a naturalist, Dr. Herman Pike, who was in search of new flora and fauna to study. He had been a calm, if rather dull older gentleman, until he began to speak about his passion on plants. Gavin had assisted him during an exhibition and found similarities between himself and the doctor, particularly how they met with surprises. He was approaching this marriage much the way Dr. Pike approached a new plant. It wasn't exactly frightening, and it certainly didn't make him upset, but more curious than anything else.

Uncle John apparently had very little faith in him to fulfill his promises to Holly and her family. Well, they'd see about that, he thought as he climbed the wooden staircase within Kingston

House.

Contemplative, he toured the second-floor gallery. The portraits of family members long since dead stared down at him as he pondered about the wife he had been bequeathed. Gavin knew it wasn't right to think of her in such a way, but he could hardly deny it. He had inherited her just as much as he had inherited Kingston House and while a small, inconsequential part of him seemed quite taken with the idea, he needed to remember that it was an outrageous scenario.

Holly Smyth didn't belong to him, and he didn't belong to anyone. Gavin had always been deliberately untethered. Certain of his own uncertainty and aware that the only thing that seemed to be guaranteed in life was being alone, which he hadn't ever considered a bad thing. It simply was what it was.

Still, it gave him a perverse, if surprising amount of pleasure to pretend that Holly could belong to him, even if only for a little while.

Pushing the obstinate thoughts from his mind, he returned his attention to Kingston House. It was a stylish home, well-kept and remarkably tasteful for a man known throughout London society as an eccentric. Uncle John had been a dandy in his younger days, but it seemed that his love for overtly furnished rooms and large, colorful pieces hadn't spilled over into his country estate. Gavin knew that the London home was ostentatiously covered in gold-pressed wallpaper, tulipwood furnishings, and crimson velvet fabrics. From the window drapes to the ornate carpets, the furnishings at Bairnsdale Terrace were dripping with intricate designs, clashing colors, and tastelessly expensive styles. Gavin had only been there once, but when he visited, it had felt like he had fallen into a pirate's chest.

Kingston House wasn't nearly as gauche. The walls were surprisingly simple, painted with various pastel shades and decorated with tasteful paintings, mostly depicting men and women in country settings. It was strange that a man could have such contradictory tastes. But then that might explain Holly.

Patience would eventually reveal Holly's true nature. She didn't initially appear to be some sort of conniving social climber, eager to take all she could from a dying man, yet she wasn't a meek country miss, haplessly going about life either. She seemed to fall somewhere in between, logical enough to understand her dire situation but genuine enough not to want to take advantage of a friend.

She was a bit of a conundrum, and he was baffled that someone so seemingly reasonable and attractive should still be unwed. Well, not any longer—but it made him wonder why no other nearby man had proposed to her. Perhaps the burden of her family had scared off other suitors. Though with her rational mind, striking blue eyes, and oddly soothing velvet voice, Gavin was confused as to why anyone wouldn't be willing to pay a king's ransom to be with her. But maybe the situation at Felton Manor was more calamitous than she let on. Either way, he wished to inspect the house she currently resided in and headed out to do so the very next day.

Gavin knew she had been lying about the state of Felton Manor, but he was still surprised at what he found as his horse came over the crest of the hill, some five miles north from Kingston House. To his horror, a massive oak tree was leaning against the large, square, grey stone house. Though it was spring, the leaves on the fallen tree were brown and still clinging to the branches, giving Gavin the impression that it had been at least six months since the tree had come down and yet it hadn't been removed.

What in the hell was going on?

Why hadn't Holly had it taken down? Had his uncle known about this? She hadn't spent the winter here, living in such conditions, had she? The image of her huddled next to a fire suddenly flashed in his mind and unnerved him. Not just because Holly was now under his protection, but as a decent human being. Why hadn't she sought out any help?

Climbing off his horse, Gavin stalked across the gravel drive towards the front door and knocked rapidly. When no one opened the door, he tried again. He was contemplating shouldering the door open by force when it finally opened, revealing a wide-eyed Miss Katrina.

"Lord Bairnsdale," she said, curtsying slightly behind the partially open wooden door. "Um, uh… Can I help you?"

"May I come in?"

She peered over her shoulder, seemingly unwilling to let him enter.

"Well, you see, Holly—my sister, that is—um… I don't think…"

"It's quite alright," Gavin said, dropping his voice. "Holly is expecting me."

Katrina bit her lip, seemingly surprised by his use of her sister's Christian name. Nodding slowly, she stepped back, opening the door for him to enter.

The foyer was sizeable for a country farmhouse, and though it wasn't nearly as grand as Kingston House, Gavin instantly saw the attraction to this place. Stacks of books lined the hall, leading one to assume this was a house where reading was encouraged. The walls were adorned with dozens of oval portraits of family members, and though it was drafty, Gavin felt that a tremendous amount of heart had lived within these walls throughout the years. He was sure it was why Holly seemed so set on keeping it, even thought it was very clear that the house was in dire need of extensive repairs—and not solely to the roof.

Dry rot was eating away at the bottom corners of the paneled walls and the first-floor ceilings seemed to be bowed. It would take a considerable amount to fix even the most obvious issues. Not to mention the not so obvious ones. Gavin wondered if selling it would be the best move, before the entire place fell down around them. Or perhaps he could tear it down and rebuild it? Gavin began considering numbers when he heard a heated exchange of words drifting out from what he assumed was the dining room as he followed Miss Katrina deeper into the house.

"—I need a hundred quid to pay a mate of mine in school."

"We don't have a hundred quid, Jasper. And have you lost your mind, asking me for such an exorbitant amount of money?"

"We just inherited a third of Kingston House, didn't we?"

Gavin's jaw set, unimpressed with the youth's vulgarity. He seemed oblivious to the situation he and his sisters were in.

"No, and had you listened to me the first two times I explained it, you would understand that we haven't inherited anything. Which puts all of us in a precarious situation."

The young man sighed loudly.

"The house is falling apart! Just sell the heap of junk already. It's not worth fixing. Besides, I've an opportunity to join Clemet Club—as a lifetime member, mind you—if only I can settle my debts."

"I will do no such thing. And what in the world is the Clemet Club?"

Gavin knew. The Clemet Club maintained itself to be a gentlemen's club, but no gentleman in London would claim that nowadays. At one point it had been a place that catered to men of the peerage, but time had changed it. Now it was little more than a building that admitted anyone, should they be able to afford the outrageous buy ins. A man named Joseph Kilmann operated it, and he was just as ruthless as his name suggested.

"It's a place where likeminded gentlemen go to discuss business and politics and the like."

Holly paused.

"Are you seriously trying to sell me on a gentleman's club? When we are drowning in debt?" She scoffed. "Absolutely not, Jasper."

"Fine, have it your way," Jasper bit out. "I'll just carry my debts until I can sell the place myself."

He stalked off, bumping into Gavin's shoulder as he did. Gavin's hands came up and steadied the young man, whose brow was furrowed with bitter anger over what he clearly perceived as dire injustices. Wrenching out of his grasp, he continued down the hallway, out the front door.

"Lord Bairnsdale?" Holly's voice carried in over Gavin's shoulder.

Turning back towards her, he stepped into the dining room but stalled when his eyes fell on her. Holly was dressed in a simple, unadorned dark-blue muslin gown. The neck scooped low, and the sleeves were sheer, though Holly was wrapped in a dark green shawl. He hadn't expected to see her in such a rich color, and how he stared at her must have alerted her because she bent her head down, almost embarrassed.

"I didn't expect to see anyone today," she said, motioning towards her gown with her hands. "I had all my gowns dyed black when John passed away, but this one didn't take. It became a grey color and I had the bright idea to cover it with blue, but... well..." She shook her head. "What are you doing here?"

Gavin swallowed, remembering why he was there.

"I came to inspect your house."

"I told you there was no need."

"Yes, except that obviously wasn't true given that there's an oak tree on it," he said, remembering his anger when he first saw it. "Why haven't you had anyone take down?"

Holly's mouth tightened as if the undeniable statement irked her.

"People require payment, my lord."

"Gavin."

Her eyes squinted.

"There's no need for such informalities."

"It won't scandalize me, I assure you," he said. "And since you and your siblings will be staying at Kingston House for the foreseeable future—"

"Excuse me?" she said, walking around the small dining room table. "We are not moving to Kingston House."

"Oh yes, you are."

"No, we are not."

"How long has that thing been on this house? Six months? It's a wonder you haven't frozen to death."

"We've fared very well, thank you very much, and it is not so cold—"

"Where are your servants?" he asked, his temper rising once more, looking around. While tidy at first glance, the house showed clear signs that it was overdue for the kind of deep, thorough cleaning he wouldn't think Holly and her sister could manage on their own. "Where are your footmen? Or maids?" He turned back to face her, and Holly's cheeks turned pink as her mouth set in a hard line. "Tell me you have at least a cook?"

"It is not your concern."

Gavin remained still, trying hard to reel in his temper. It didn't make sense that her stubborn refusal should annoy him so much, but he couldn't stop himself. His concern for her shouldn't be so great after only meeting once before, but he felt deeply that he was responsible for her. And whether it was because of his uncle's lack of faith in him or because they were technically married, he knew with absolute certainty that her concerns were now his. This woman was reliant on him, whether she wanted to be or not, and he would not fail her.

Aside from his aunt, no one had ever relied on Gavin, and though he had always been sure that it would be burdensome, he found that instead, he felt necessary. Almost needed. It was somewhat unnerving, but also satisfying.

What an odd sensation to be depended on. But he pushed the thought from his mind, deciding to decipher it at a later time. For now, he needed to focus on the matter at hand, which was convincing her that she couldn't possibly remain in this house a day longer. He leveled her a stern stare.

"You're not staying here."

"I said it is of no concern of yours, and might I remind you—"

"Oh, please, Holly," the timid voice of Katrina came from the doorway. Both Gavin and Holly turned to face her. "It would be very nice not having to wake every hour to make sure the fires are still lit."

How had Holly and her sister maintained this large house without any assistance? He faced Holly once more and the shame that crossed her face made him uncomfortable, but his anger at the situation suddenly subsided. He could bully her into coming to Kingston House, but there was something sensitive in her eyes, something akin to embarrassment. Gavin didn't want to add insult to injury and he resolved to handle her and the situation with a more delicate touch.

"Katrina—" Holly started, but Gavin cut in.

"Please tell me this much," he said, his tone gentler than it had been. Holly watched him, startled by his sudden plea. "Was Uncle John aware of this tree situation?"

Her mouth moved, seemingly unsure how to answer, and it surprised Gavin how interesting he found it. He waited for her to answer.

"Not exactly," she said slowly. "He knew a branch had come through one of the upstairs windows. But I didn't want to worry him."

"He never came to visit?"

"John took ill around the same time as the tree fell and was bedridden from that point on. His health began to deteriorate rapidly over the winter. He never left Kingston House again."

"Hmm, I see. And would he have been worried had he known the truth?"

"Yes, of course."

"Then as a favor, to honor his memory, can't you let me house you and your siblings, until it is repaired?"

Her face scrunched up suddenly as if she were trying to stop herself from crying.

"We aren't feeble, incapable people. It's just that bad luck seems to catch us at every turn."

He nodded, knowing it was rarely easy for people to ask for help. Still, she *hadn't* asked. In fact, she had refused all his offers. He admired resilience, but this felt like it was edging into stubbornness, particularly since the house seemed in such poor condition as to put her health and safety at risk.

"I would greatly appreciate the opportunity to prove my uncle wrong," he said, taking a single step forward. Their eyes met. "He didn't think I was capable of honoring his wishes. If I could be allowed to demonstrate my true character while also seeing to the comfort of his closest friend, I would like to do so. Please. I would view it as a personal favor."

Holly stared at him, and he could see her resolve to break.

"It would only be temporary, until the tree can be removed and the roof repaired. Though how I'm to find the money to pay someone…"

"I'll cover the cost," Gavin said. When she seemed on the verge of protesting yet again, he added, "As a loan."

"A…a loan?" she repeated. He nodded. She took a moment to think this over, and then sighed in resignation. "Very well, then. A loan. One that my family will pay back immediately upon turning this farm back into a profitable one. I promise."

"We'll have Mr. Armstrong draw up papers if you like."

"Yes."

"Then you will come to Kingston House?"

She gave him a stiff nod.

"Oh, thank goodness," Katrina said, taking off like a shot down the hallway before suddenly reappearing. "May we leave now?"

"Er, I suppose," Holly said, and her sister disappeared again. Now alone, she crossed her arms, less a belligerent pose than a defensive one, as if she was covering and protecting her heart. "I hope you don't think I'm ungrateful. It's just that I've been the sole protector of this house and my family for several years now, and every time someone has offered to help, it has come with a price."

He frowned, curious. He didn't like the sound of that, but it resonated with him. He himself did not like to ask for help, simply because he had learned at a young age that he could never rely on anyone else.

"How so?"

Holly let out a humorless huff of breath.

"If it isn't the local gentry trying to get me to sell off our lands, it's someone else paying only half price for our livestock." Her gaze fell to the floor. "I was never taught how to run a profitable farm. I had to learn all my mistakes on my own. Turn after turn, it seems I can never manage to get ahead." She sighed, her eyes lifting to meet his. "Ever decision I make always turns out to be the wrong one."

Gavin was surprised that she would confess something so personal.

"Surely not every decision?"

Holly shrugged.

"Nearly. It was my idea to pay off our family debts as soon as possible. To do so, I had to sell half our livestock to our neighbor, Mr. Granger. He promised to sell them back to me once I could turn a profit with what we had, but I never could, and he eventually had to sell them. Then a harsh winter followed by a wet summer drove our wheat to rot, and I had to sell off the rest of our stock to get by. The house has been falling apart for ages and every chance I have to better our situation..." she said quickly, the words tumbling out as if she had been holding them in for years and was relieved to finally have them released. "Well... it never works."

Holly shook her head, looking embarrassed that she'd spoken so frankly.

"I beg your pardon. I shouldn't have bored you with such personal issues." She forced a smile that didn't reach her eyes. "I won't make you wait long. We will be ready to leave in a few minutes. Excuse me," she said, moving past him, but Gavin's hand came up as she reached him, and he gently placed his fingers on her forearm.

She froze, and for a moment, so did he. A shot of electricity seemed to zap between them, and just as quickly as he had reached for her, he dropped his hand. It was a moment before he spoke.

"Bad luck isn't something you should blame yourself for," he said, his tone low.

She nodded jerkily and disappeared into the hallway, leaving Gavin alone. Moving his thumb over the pads of his fingers, he wondered if she had felt that strange galvanic current, too.

Chapter Five

THOUGH HOLLY FELT uneasy moving into Kingston House full-time, she had to admit the comfort of a home being run efficiently by a proper staff was enough to make her never want to leave. She no longer had to rise every hour, on the hour, to maintain the fires so that she and her siblings wouldn't freeze in their sleep, as she had at Felton Manor. After only a week at Kingston House, Holly felt surprisingly relaxed. The nervous strain that had become a permanent pain in her shoulders had lightened, and she felt far more rested than she had been in months, if not years.

Except for the constant arguments she was having with Jasper.

Her brother had been close to furious when he learned they were to be staying at Kingston House. He thought he should have a say in where his family lived. His pride was hurt, Holly knew it, but she hardly had time to console him over it. Unlike her brother, she had to do what was in the family's best interest, not just act for her own benefit.

"Best interest?" he had countered their first night at Kingston House. Jasper had found her in her bedchambers. "Have you lost your mind? Taking charity from this bloke?"

"We don't have much of a choice, in case you didn't notice. And don't act as though we haven't been taking charity already, what with John paying your way through Eton. Plus, who do you think has been paying our bills, keeping our creditors away?"

Jasper's brow scrunched together.

"It was different when it was John. He was a family friend."

"If anything, that made it worse."

"Why?"

"Because you aren't supposed to be a burden to your friends," Holly said.

"Regardless, John should have left you a sum, so that you could manage things on your own."

She agreed, actually—but it was a moot point. "It doesn't really matter now, does it?"

"Still. A widow is expected to be taken care of. This is nothing more than… than…"

He had puffed out his chest.

"Than what?" she argued.

"Than begging on the street."

Holly's eyes widened as her temper flared.

"You ungrateful child," she snapped. "If you'd like to know exactly what begging on the street feels like, then I suggest you continue losing at card games and milking our family's coffers for your own gratification. You've no care for anyone in this family except yourself, and I have had it."

"That's not true," he countered, blinking at her harsh criticism. "I care. I care a hell of a lot more than you think. And I can manage us."

"Oh? Then, by all means, Jasper, how would you like to fix the house? How do you think we should remove the tree that's been on our roof for half a year?'

He gave her a smug look.

"We hire someone, obviously."

"With what money?"

"The money from your inheritance."

Holly rolled her eyes, her hand coming to her forehead.

"I've told you, we don't have any sort of inheritance. I was married by proxy. Legally, I am married to the current baron."

Jasper sighed.

"Then I don't know!"

"No, you don't, yet you're more than willing to criticize me without offering any sort of support."

Jasper's mouth slammed shut, his eyes blazing. Then, he inhaled and puffed his chest out slightly.

"I am the man of this family, and I should have some say in how it operates."

Holly let out a frustrated laugh.

"Oh, you think so, do you? Tell me, how often have you gambled away monies that could have been better used in our home? Do not pretend that John didn't send you extra coin, even though I told him he shouldn't. Katrina is about to be presented to society and she hasn't had any new dresses in over two years. Yet you ask me for a hundred pounds to pay off your debts at a school paid for by the patronage of this very house?" Holly shook her head. "You've no right to tell me that you could manage us better, particularly when you've been funded for as long as you have. Frankly, it's insulting. Lord Bairnsdale has very graciously offered to let us stay here while Felton Manor is being renovated—out of his own pocket, I might add. Once the renovations are complete, we will return to our home, and you will inherit an estate thanks to everyone around you. Everyone *except* you." She glared at her brother, shaking her head. "I loathe to think what Mama would say of your behavior."

Jasper dropped his gaze, evidently ashamed of himself, but the redness of his cheeks spoke to his mounting anger.

"It's not fair that I shouldn't be allowed to make decisions for myself. As a man, I have the right—"

"Start behaving like one, and perhaps I'd take your opinion into consideration," she bit out, unwilling to let him finish. She was exhausted from fighting him about everything. Particularly when he had zero foresight. "Now, please leave."

He had left in a huff, and by the following morning, he was

back on his way to Eton. Holly's temper had eventually subsided, and she was sorry that their last exchange had been so heated, but her brother did aggravate her to no end. His entitlement and indifference to consequences made her worry about his future. At least with him back at school, she no longer had to argue and defend her every move. Now, she needed to direct all her attention on the repairs that would go into Felton Manor and how she would fund Katrina's upcoming season.

Before everything had happened with John, Holly had planned to have several of her own gowns redone to match the latest fashions, but when he passed, she had dyed all of her dresses black for her mourning period. Of course, not being well versed in coloring clothes, the dye didn't take very well. This had resulted in ruining two gowns and mudding the rest. Now, she only had one decent dress that she had managed to turn deep blue. Gavin had offered to send Holly and Katrina to a modiste in London, but—

No. Not Gavin. Lord Bairnsdale. Holly had started thinking of him as Gavin, and she needed to correct herself.

He seemed to be everywhere she went. It made sense, of course, since he lived at Kingston House as well, but every room she entered, he was there, and if he wasn't, he would eventually show up. It didn't help that her sister was always wandering about the grounds on solitary ambles, having taken it upon herself to learn every inch of their new home, leaving Holly inside by herself. She had tried to avoid him at first, not particularly pleased with being alone with him. The memory of his hand reaching for her in Felton Manor had caused her great worry. Would he try to do so again? Even though they were technically married, he had to know that any physical touch between them was out of the question. If an annulment was going to happen, they needed to keep their distance.

Not that Holly couldn't control herself. She was more than capable of keeping her hands off him. But there was something curious about Gavin Winscombe that made her think about things she had never dared to before.

He was an attractive man, that much she couldn't deny, but there was something more to him than just his pleasing face. There was an underlying solidity to him, as if nothing in the world could shake him or push him off balance. If he ever became upset or angry, moments later it would melt away and he would become completely disarming and earnest. She had first noticed it the second week since arriving at Kingston House, when he had found her in the library, pouring over the latest fashion plates from London that had come with the latest letter from her dear friend Clara, the new Duchess of Combe. She would often send Holly and Katrina pamphlets with the latest dress styles as both sisters had a fondness for fashion.

He walked into the room, carrying himself like a man aware of the world. Holly's eyes lifted from the pages on the table before her to take in the sight. It wasn't a leisurely walk, nor guarded, but rather a self-assured gait that projected confidence.

Catching her gaze, Gavin smirked, holding his large hands up as if he was surrendering to the authorities.

"Don't mind me, I promise I'm not here to bother you. I'm just looking for a book."

Holly didn't believe him for a second. Whenever she smelled mint and lemons, Holly knew he would appear and try to talk to her. She had resisted at first, being wary of him, but his quiet confidence had slowly drawn her out. And as indifferent to mint as she had always been, she found it rather annoying now. Her heart would jump slightly at the scent, and it was aggravating to know why.

"You don't bother me, I assure you," she lied.

"Really?" he said, paused, and then shook his head as if he had more to say but was choosing to refrain.

Holly's brow arched as he turned his back to her.

"What?"

"I didn't say anything."

"No, but you were thinking something."

He peered over his shoulder, and the way the corner of his eyes crinkled when he smiled made her core shake. She remained still, unwilling to show any outward reaction.

"Perceptive," he said, reaching for a book. He moved his fingers over the spine and pulled it down before facing her. "I was just surprised that you chose to keep your seat. You usually go scurrying from the room whenever I enter."

She scowled.

"I don't scurry."

The side of his mouth quirked, and he made a clicking noise with his teeth.

"I've seen you scurry."

"Mice scurry, my lord. Ladies simply leave."

"Still with 'my lord,' then?" He said, flipping through the pages of his book. "My, what a formal marriage we live in."

Holly's mouth flattened, and she exhaled out of her nostrils.

"We won't be married for long."

"Well, one hopes," he said, snapping the book shut. "But I've been doing some reading on the topic."

"The topic of marriage?"

"Annulments, actually. I'm afraid our Mr. Armstrong is in for a rather brutal workload. It seems that Catholics don't like to undo things."

"He will manage to get us out of it, I'm sure," she said, standing up. She would have no peace to finish inspecting these dress designs in the library, not with this man smirking at her as if he knew some secret. "Is there something else I might help you with?"

Gavin tilted his head, his hazel eyes looking her up and down before he spoke.

"Are you a gambler?" he asked. "I mean to say, have you ever gambled before?"

"No," she said pointedly. "Why do you ask?"

"No reason," he said, a self-satisfying grin on his lips. Holly turned to leave when he spoke again. "Good day, Holly."

Thankfully, she was already halfway out of the room when he said her name. Her eyes closed at the sound of his voice, and she did indeed scurry away, needing to be out of his presence immediately.

There was something startlingly familiar about Gavin, she thought as he made her way to her rooms. She felt a sort of kinship with him, as ridiculous as that sounded. It was more than just his ability to look on the bright side of things. There was a loneliness behind his smiling eyes that she recognized in herself and though she would never admit it, she found an odd comfort in knowing that he felt lonely as well.

But Holly could not, *would not* let him distract her. The coming season was at the forefront of her mind, and she decided to discuss the dress matter with Katrina over breakfast the following day.

The dining room was a long, somewhat narrow, south-facing room with pale pink wallpaper decorated with a bluebird and cherry blossom pattern. It was one of Holly's favorite rooms and had been the first one she had redecorated last summer when John had insisted that she help him.

It had been an odd request and Holly hadn't wanted to be too opinionated, but John had very much wished for her to style it in her own tastes, insisting that he always trusted her style, and eventually Holly had relented.

It had been a great deal of fun, choosing wallpapers and fabrics, not worrying about the cost of any of her choices. Out of all the rooms in Kingston House, the dining room was certainly one of the most cheerfully decorated.

That morning, a seasonal serving of strawberries and cream, poached eggs, toast, pound cakes, tea, and cocoa had been laid out on the white linen table. A fresh bouquet of orange tulips had been cut from the spring garden. It made Holly sorry that she hadn't been able to have something so lovely at Felton Manor for so long, but she was grateful to be a part of it here.

She sat at the table across from Katrina, who was flipping

through the same fashion pamphlets that Holly had dropped off in her room last night. Apparently, her sister hadn't put them down since.

"I quite like this one," she said, pointing to an illustration of a white bodice gown with a periwinkle blue underskirt and a sheer overlay. "But this one is lovely too. This Miss Piedmont certainly is a talent."

"Miss Piedmont?" Holly repeated with a frown. She had deliberately tried to push Katrina toward Mrs. Bean's plates as they were less expensive.

"Yes. It must have fallen out of your letters. I found it on the ground, peeking out from beneath the table in the library."

"Oh," Holly said, pouring herself a cup of tea. "Well, Miss Piedmont is quite costly."

"But look at this one. It's exquisite."

Holly glanced up as Katrina held up the pamphlet.

"Yes, it is. But maybe you can try something from Mrs. Bean's collection."

Katrina frowned.

"But hers are so old fashioned." She looked down at the other pages that covered the table. "Can we not afford a dress or two from Miss Piedmont's shop, now that you're the lady of the house?"

The familiar pinch in Holly's shoulders returned.

"It's not that simple. The baron is already helping restore Felton Manor. I should hate to ask for more, particularly when there are a number of other dressmakers who make good enough gowns."

"But 'good enough' isn't going to get me a husband of standing. And the baron did promise to honor his uncle's wishes."

"Yes, but I'm… afraid to ask, I suppose."

"Why should you be afraid to ask for money?" Katrina asked, taking a sip of her tea. "It is yours too, isn't it?"

Holly gave her sister a wry smile.

"Keep that opinion to yourself when searching for a husband

this season, my dear," Holly murmured. "Besides, we have plenty of material to create a trousseau for you."

Katrina took another sip, somewhat dejected.

"I was looking forward to going to a real London modiste."

"At the very least, you will have London-made gowns," Holly said. Was a modiste really necessary at all? Perhaps they could skip that expense altogether. "Supposedly, Mrs. O'Kirk, the housekeeper at Bairnsdale Terrace has a very steady hand."

"The housekeeper?"

"Yes." Katrina remained silent, causing Holly to glance up. She saw her sister's brow scrunched together as she chewed on the inside of her bottom lip. "What is it?"

"It's just…" she started but shook her head. "Never mind. I'm sure it will be grand."

Holly gave her a reassuring smile but understood her hesitation. Even though she was bright and beautiful, reassembled gowns wouldn't give Katrina much edge compared to all the ladies paraded about London. Every season, the events seemed to become more and more spectacular, and they were both aware of how important it was for Katrina to make a match.

Just then, Mr. Jorden arrived, holding a tray of letters that he presented to Holly. She scooped them up.

"Thank you, Jorden," she said.

He nodded and turned, leaving just as quietly as he had come. The first letter in her pile was Clara. She read it eagerly.

Evidently, Clara's sister-in-law, Lady Violet Winters, was hoping to reach London before the season so that she might attend to her wedding dress, which was being made by the most exclusive modiste in London. Lady Violet had recently become engaged to the Earl of Trembley's youngest brother, Fredrick. Clara was writing to ask if Violet could be escorted by Holly and the new baron to London as the dowager duchess was away in Italy for the season and Clara and Silas were needed in Bristol to secure some building for one of her father's inventions.

Of course, Holly would welcome Violet and immediately

sent off a missive saying yes. The second letter she read, however, robbed her of all her joy.

The spindly handwriting of Mrs. Charlotte Payne stared up at her, and the letter became suddenly heavy in her hands. She wanted to avoid it, to throw it away and not read whatever condolences were given in its contents, but knowing Charlotte the way she did, she knew it would announce a day of a visit, and it was always better to be prepared rather than surprised.

Holding her breath, she tore open the letter.

Dearest Holly,

Bertram and I called on Felton Manor the day before but found you weren't in residence. We will be around Kingston House at noon.

Sincerely,

The Paynes

Holly reread the letter several times before dropping it to the table, only to see her sister's concerned expression.

"Charlotte?" she asked, apparently aware of Holly's discomfort.

"Is it that obvious?"

Katrina stood, finished with her meal.

"You only ever look like that when Charlotte or Bertram are brought up."

"They'll be here before noon," Holly said, just as Mr. Jorden reappeared.

"Mr. Mannion is here," he said quickly. "I tried to stop him, but—"

"Where is he?" A bellow from the hallway echoed through the dining room. A short, red-faced man with thinning grey hair and bright blue eyes entered the dining room. He pointed his finger directly at Holly. "I demand you hand him over!"

The Mannions and the Smyths were longtime neighbors who had always gotten on quite well, though the relationship had diminished in recent years. Old Mr. Mannion had been angling to buy Felton Manor for months to expand his farm and while he had been polite and charming at first, he had become increasingly less so since Holly's first refusal. He had continued to offer, each time decreasing his price until it had become close to insulting. Holly hadn't seen him since their last tense encounter, when he offered her a hundred pounds for their entire property, citing that the tree that had fallen on the manor had eviscerated the property's worth, as if the house was the only part of the property that had any value. It was a ridiculous idea, since it was the land he wanted anyway—if she *had* sold it to him, he would have just knocked the house down anyway.

"Who?" Holly asked, standing, hoping that he wasn't searching for Jasper.

A whiff of mint suddenly filled the air.

"Don't pretend that you don't know who I speak of," Mr. Mannion spat. "Your brother will pay for this, that bast—"

"Excuse me."

Gavin's calm, strong, masculine voice seemed to echo throughout the room, catching everyone's attention. Mr. Mannion whipped around.

"Who are you?"

The slightest uptick in his right brow made Holly concerned. She wondered what Gavin's reaction would be to such rudeness, but he seemed unfazed.

"As it's my home," he began. "I believe I should be asking that question."

"Your home?"

"Yes."

"Then you are—"

"The Baron of Bairnsdale," he said with the barest of nods. "And you are?"

The short man inhaled sharply and approached Gavin to bow.

"Mr. Stephen Mannion. Your neighbor, and possibly your

enemy, if you're housing that," he pointed his finger again at Holly. "Woman's brother."

A pregnant pause followed. Holly saw Gavin's eyes lock onto Mr. Mannion as a flash of warning crossed his face. He exhaled before he spoke.

"I can assure you that Mr. Jasper Smyth isn't in residence," Gavin said quietly, his hazel eyes on Mr. Mannion's hand. "I can also assure you that if you insist on pointing your finger at that woman, I will have no choice but to remove it."

A tense silence fell around all of them. Katrina's mouth fell open as Holly's gaze shifted from one man to the other. Mr. Mannion's hand dropped slowly as he cleared his throat with an insulted cough.

"You don't understand."

"I understand that anything can be understandable, given the context," Gavin said, the quip appeasing him more than anyone else judging by the slight pull at the corner of his mouth. Holly herself felt a small smile creep across her own lips. "What I won't stand for is disrespect in my home."

Mr. Mannion began to stutter and spit.

"That boy has ruined my daughter!"

"Oh no," Holly said, stepping forward, but Gavin held his hand up to indicate that she should stay put.

Irritated but intrigued, she stilled and allowed him to continue.

"That is a serious accusation, Mr. Mannion. Are you sure?"

"She told me as much!"

"When was this supposed ruining?"

"The night before last. He came to bid farewell to my Daphne."

Holly turned to Gavin. Jasper had left days ago. He knew it but apparently wished to learn more.

"How long was he at your home?" he asked.

"A quarter of an hour."

Holly and Gavin shared a look.

"Alone?" Gavin asked.

"Yes. Well, not quite," Mr. Mannion said, stomping his foot. "My wife was there in the parlor with them."

"And she witnessed this?"

"Yes. Well, no," he said. "I mean, she was there, but she went into the hall to give them some privacy. Daphne only told us this morning that the blackguard had behaved inappropriately—and I demand he marry her."

Gavin's eyes shifted to Holly's, and she silently cursed. She wondered if she would ever not have a headache where her brother was concerned.

"I see. Well, I'm sorry to inform you, but Mr. Smyth left several days ago to return to Eton. He hasn't been here for nearly a week."

The old man's eyes bulged.

"Are you calling me a liar?"

"I'm very sorry, Mr. Mannion," Holly said slowly. "But my brother did return to school."

"He was in my very parlor, the night before last!"

"Even if he had been," Gavin began, his tone growing sterner. "I find it hard to believe a youth like Jasper would have the talent to defile your daughter, with your wife only a few steps away, in under fifteen minutes, without your wife being any the wiser until this morning."

"I demand that he be held accountable!"

"I don't see what you could possibly want," Holly said.

"Well, now, I'm not an unreasonable man, as you well know, Miss Smyth," Mr. Mannion said, shaking a finger once more at Holly. "But I cannot let such an injustice pass without restitution."

"Put. Your finger. Down, Mr. Mannion," Gavin said with a hint of threat in his tone. The man dropped his hand to his side instantly and Holly felt a bloom of warmth in her chest. She ignored it. "And she isn't Miss Smyth. She's a baroness and should be addressed as such." He glanced at her. "Isn't that correct?"

Holly swallowed, uncomfortably aware that Gavin had left out "dowager." If they were going to let everyone believe that she truly had married John and not Gavin, then that would make her the *dowager* baroness. She should correct him, but then it wouldn't be an honest correction. She was technically married to Gavin, so the title of baroness was accurate.

Perhaps she should merely ignore it and move on.

"Yes," Holly said softly, before looking to Mr. Mannion. "And what restitution would you be looking for?"

"Well, only what's owed to me. Perhaps, your farm? Trivial, really, compared to the injustices my family has suffered, but again, I am not an unreasonable man," Mannion said, his tone dropping. "Is it not in your brother's possession yet?"

Holly felt a sickening feeling settling in her stomach. So that is what this was all about. Wishing to be rid of this meddling man once and for all, she squared her shoulders and held her chin up high.

"Unfortunately, we sold the manor, Mr. Mannion," Holly said, stepping forward. "Day before last."

She ignored the curious looks from her sister and Gavin.

"Sold it?" The old man scoffed. "To whom?"

"I'm afraid I cannot disclose that, but we had to. To pay off Jasper's debts, you see."

"...Debts?"

"Yes. Massive debts, I'm afraid. He's a terrible spendthrift, my brother. And gambler too, actually, but not a very good one."

"Holly—"

"There's no need to hide it, Katrina," Holly said, turning back to Mr. Mannion. "We shan't stand in the way of Jasper and Mr. Mannion's daughter. If you insist upon this marriage, Mr. Mannion, I'm sure I can convince my brother. No doubt they will be able to spend your daughter's dowery on a least a portion of his debts. Lord knows the money we earned from selling Felton Manor barely covered a quarter of it—"

"Um, well, now, let's not be too hasty," the old man said,

suddenly holding up his hands. "I'm sure there has been a mistake."

"Oh?" Holly said with feigned interest.

"Yes. Yes, as you said, my lord," Mr. Mannion said, addressing Gavin. "Mr. Smyth couldn't possibly have ruined my daughter in just fifteen minutes, with my wife so near at hand no less. In fact, I believe this to be one of my daughter's imaginative stories." He took a step backwards. "Yes. Yes, that's it and I would greatly appreciate it if everyone here could feign ignorance of her silly claim."

Holly smiled sweetly at him.

"Of course," she said as Mr. Mannion quickly left.

Katrina immediately came up to her sister.

"Oh Holly, why did you say that? Now everyone will think Jasper is no good. His reputation will be tarnished."

"I had no choice. Can you believe that man? Trying to soil his own daughter's reputation to gain the manor," Holly said, returning to the table to gather her correspondence.

"Why did you tell him that you sold it?" Gavin asked, coming towards her, at the edge of the dining room table.

"So that he might leave me alone."

"You could have told him that your debts were paid and that you had no reason to sell Felton Manor now." Holly looked up at him as she picked up her letters. "Why not tell him the truth?"

"Because I don't consider my debts paid."

He tilted his head.

"You don't?"

"No. If anything, they've just been transferred to you." Gavin's brow creased and Holly knew he was about to argue. Looking down at the pile of letters she held in her hand, she saw a letter addressed to Gavin and picked it up quickly to hand to him. "It seems your mail has gotten mixed up with mine."

Without her usual attention to detail, she quickly separated her letters and handed Gavin his, leaving the room as fast as she could. She needed to prepare for the Paynes' arrival, especially since she knew they liked to show up early. Hopefully she would be able to meet with them without Gavin's presence as he had plans of going to Felton Manor to inspect the tree.

Holly was quick to go through her daily morning tasks. It was Thursday, and she was set to make lists for the larder. Also, as it was the last day of the month, the following Sunday meant that she would have to go out to see tenants, a task that she had performed for the past several months.

Yet the soft threat Gavin had issued Mr. Mannion hadn't left her. She wasn't sure if she should be offended by his outrageous words or if she should be grateful that he had been so swift to stand up for her. Holly had rarely, if ever, had anyone to protect her, and she was surprised by just how nice it felt to be defended.

Even though she would never admit it aloud.

Returning to her rooms to write replies to her correspondences, she wondered if she would have enough time to do so before the Paynes' arrival. She was in something of a hurry, since the morning had gotten away from her and the conversations she had had with the kitchen staff had taken longer than usual.

Rushing to finish, Holly reached across the desk and carelessly knocked over her inkwell.

"Oh no!" she said quickly, standing up, but it was too late.

Blackish blue ink completely covered her hand and sleeve. She would need to wash it off instantly with lye if she didn't want it to stain.

"Drats," she said to herself as she ran from the room to return to the kitchens.

She was definitely going to be late greeting the Paynes now.

Chapter Six

SINCE BEFORE MOVING Holly and her sister into Kingston House, Gavin had made it his responsibility to have Felton Manor made livable again. Not because he wanted them to leave or because he desired to prove his uncle wrong. Well, he did wish to do that, but his ultimate goal in restoring Felton Manor was because it had been evident that Holly desired it. The way her shoulders would tense up whenever he mentioned the old farm displeased him greatly, and he had the unrelenting urge to smooth away her anxieties and eliminate all the worries of her world—even if she continued to argue against him any time he offered to make things easier for her.

He understood her hesitation, himself familiar with the desire to control all aspects of his life without needing to rely on anyone. Holly hadn't been able to depend on any one person in a long time. But he would simply have to show her that she could trust him to take care of her problems, even if she didn't relish the idea.

He first needed to figure out all that was wrong with Felton Manor and what needed to be tackled first. Gavin began visiting stonemasons and laborers in the local village during the past week, searching for men who could be hired to do the work. He even planned to buy back some of the livestock Holly had sold to Mr. Granger. It would take time for the farm to be profitable, but he didn't mind waiting. Holly had made it clear that everything she received from Gavin was a loan and that he would be paid back in full. Who was he to keep her from doing so?

The tree removal was the most pressing issue, and it would be the most dangerous part, but Gavin was sure once the pricing had been settled on, the house repair would be completed by the beginning of autumn.

Gavin had unwittingly surprised Holly with the ledger he had begun to use to record all the expenses. The colorless cheeks and haunted expression on her face when he showed it to her one afternoon had gutted him. He hadn't intended to make her feel bad. It was his way as a banker to keep ledgers on all expenses, and he had only wanted to show her that the damage wasn't nearly as bad as he first surmised. But the rate at which the debt had accumulated clearly scared her. Holly had become withdrawn for a day or so, her shoulders drawn up in a tense strain whenever he saw her.

Eventually, it disappeared, but Gavin knew he had to handle the situation more delicately. He continued recording the expenses, since he had promised her he would do so, but he did not show the ledger to her again. And soon, he would be adding another item to the list—the cost of hiring a foreman. Since he would be escorting Holly and her sister to London to attend the upcoming season, he needed to find a trusted man to oversee the reconstruction while they were away in town.

It would be a good, distracting time for Holly to be in London, as she could pick out all new furnishings and décor for the house. It would give Mr. Granger and Mr. Lemon time to finish their work, and once that was complete, they could return to Felton and Holly herself could interview the tenants who would allow her to start paying him back as she was so insistent on doing. Or, if he could get her to accept that there was no need for repayment, she could keep the money for herself and have the independence she seemed to crave without the stress and burden of the debts that had weighed on her for so long.

Gavin had gone out that morning to speak with Mr. Timothy Lemon, a foreman who was willing to lead the job at Felton House. He was a tall, middle-aged man with four sons who worked with him on the farm. He had agreed to oversee Felton Manor for a reasonable sum, and Gavin trusted him, having inspected the man's house which he had built himself.

Walking through the front door of Kingston House just before noon, he was handing his overcoat to Dougherty when he heard a smatter of conversation from the parlor. Though he had planned to head to his offices, he followed the unknown voices instead and, coming into the parlor, saw an unfamiliar young couple seated on a sofa. It was clear that the butler had just seen them in, and turning at the sound of his footsteps, Mr. Jorden bowed at Gavin.

"The Paynes, my lord."

Ah, yes. The letter Holly had handed him that morning. He had read it before realizing that she probably hadn't intended on giving it to him in her rush to leave the dining room. Still, he had read the short note and knew they were expected at noon.

Gavin mustered up a polite smile. Dressed in a bright orange gown with white blossoms stitched into the hemlines, Mrs. Payne sat beside her husband, her tightly curled hair framing her heart-shaped face. Mr. Payne wore a blue coat with a cream-colored waistcoat and a small orange flower tucked into his breast pocket, complementing his wife's dressings, and he stepped forward to greet Gavin.

"Lord Bairnsdale, may I introduce myself. I am Mr. Bertram Payne and this is my wife, Charlotte," Mr. Payne said, bowing his head at Gavin.

Gavin would have to entertain these people until Holly or Katrina appeared. He came around the chair opposite them.

"The pleasure is all mine. Please, sit," he said, and they did so. "Um, Mr. Jorden if you could bring us some refreshments and possibly inform the baroness?"

The butler nodded and disappeared.

"May we offer our deepest sympathies to you, my lord," Mr. Payne said once they were alone. "We are so very sorry for your loss."

"Thank you," Gavin said, though he felt a trifle uneasy accepting condolences when his uncle had been such a minor part of his life. "Were you friends of my late uncle?"

"Oh yes," Mrs. Payne said, bobbing her head up and down. The pitch of her voice was high yet soft. "We were often guests here at Kingston House. The late baron was always so generous to his friends and neighbors." She frowned sadly. "I can't imagine it's been easy on poor Holly."

"I'm sure it's been dreadfully difficult for her these past few weeks," Mr. Payne said with a nod. "How is dear Ducky fairing?"

The nickname piqued Gavin's interest.

"Ducky?"

"Oh, yes," Mrs. Payne said with a quick smile, her curls gently bouncing off her cheeks. "It's a nickname we have for her."

"I see. And why Ducky?"

"Well, you see, when we were younger, Holly fell into a duck pond."

Gavin waited for her to continue, but she didn't, nor did her husband. He blinked.

"Is that all?"

"Well, it was a duck pond," she said slowly as if he wasn't following. "So, we call her Ducky. Affectionately, of course."

The wit of these country folk was either the driest ever, or there was just a simplicity to it that he didn't quite grasp. Those matching outfits seemed suddenly more annoying. Nodding, he spoke.

"Yes, well, the baroness is faring well enough, given the circumstance," Gavin said. "I'm sure you know she was very close to my uncle."

"Yes, she was. You must understand, Holly is one of our dearest friends," Mrs. Payne said, her fingers curling around her husband's arm. "We all grew up together."

"Is that so?"

"Yes."

"Well, I assure you both that she is faring quite as well as could be expected."

"I'm so glad," Mrs. Payne said, a pitying expression crossing his face. "Especially after everything she's been through. It's good for her to have some sort of comfort." Gavin's brow lifted, questioning. "I only mean, it was kind of you to let her remain in Kingston House, considering the condition of Felton Manor."

"Yes, unlucky that," Mr. Payne said, shaking his head. "But then, when hasn't Ducky been unlucky?"

Gavin's attention focused on the man who spoke so familiarly about Holly. He seemed to pity her, and for some reason, it grated Gavin's nerves that a couple who wore matching outfits would pity someone as capable and resilient as Holly.

"How do you mean?"

"Oh, only that Ducky has always had her fair share of trouble," Mrs. Payne said just as Mr. Jorden returned, followed by two maids. One carried a tray of beverages, while the other had a tiered platter full of tiny sandwiches and pastries.

"The baroness will be down momentarily, my lord," Mr. Jorden said, his voice dropping as he leaned in. "There was an ink issue."

"Ink?" Gavin repeated somewhat confused and Mr. Jorden nodded. "Very well then," he said, facing the Paynes once more. "Ah, what sort of trouble were you talking about?"

"Well, her father died when she was still very young," Mrs. Payne said, reaching for a sugared teacake. "And didn't leave much for the family to live on. Lady Eloise, Holly's mother, was the daughter of an earl and though most believed her marrying landed gentry a step down, she was really quite pleased to live in the country. But she was a nervous sort of woman. Suffered greatly from anxiety."

"Until she passed, seven years ago," Mr. Payne said, stirring his tea. "That was unfortunate as well."

"Yes, and then there was the… well…" Mrs. Payne stopped suddenly, peering at her husband. She swallowed, seemingly having spoken out of turn. "Well, nothing."

Gavin wouldn't normally have pressed the apparent hesitation, but he noticed something pass between the couple and was curious.

"What is it?"

"Well, Ducky and I were once engaged, if you can believe it," Mr. Payne said, a small laugh escaping him as his gaze dropped. He squeezed his wife's hand. "For a short time."

Gavin stared at the thin man. He wasn't sure why, but he suddenly had a bad taste in his mouth. He reached into his pocket and pulled out one of his minty lemon confectionaries and unwrapped it, popping the sweet in between his teeth as he stared at Mr. Payne.

"Is that so?"

"Yes, although it was quite an uneventful period in our lives," Mr. Payne said, reaching for a tiny cucumber sandwich. "My darling Charlotte here encouraged me to make Ducky an offer."

Gavin frowned, looking at the man's wife.

"Why was that, Mrs. Payne?"

"Well, Ducky needed some help and I thought it was a good idea. I thought my Mr. Payne would be able to support her."

"Yes, and my Mrs. Payne was so desperate to help out our friend. So, I proposed and Ducky accepted, but she ended it several days later," Mr. Payne said, looking at his wife. "She knew my heart would only ever belong to Charlotte."

Mrs. Payne blushed as she gazed adoringly at her husband and Gavin had to stifle a groan. Good god, where in the world was he that people expressed themselves so loudly.

"Poor Ducky," Mrs. Payne said, facing Gavin once more. "She never gets her fair shake, does she?"

"No, she doesn't. Which is unfortunate. Such wit, gone to waste," Mr. Payne said.

Gavin squinted at the man.

"Waste?"

"Well, her marriage to John wasn't very effective. Now she's a widow and likely won't marry again until after her best years are behind her," he said, leaning forward to pick up a teacake, which he dipped into his teacup before taking a bite. "It's a shame, really."

Gavin lifted one brow as he watched the man, annoyed that he had effectively denounced Holly's entire life as a waste. Who did he think he was making such a proclamation?

"Poor dear," Mrs. Payne said. "It really is a pity her marriage was so short. People in town are already saying it was a sham."

"A sham? How so?"

"Well, everyone knew how close her and John were, but to marry a man on his deathbed? It smacks of desperation."

Gavin's irritation was growing. Holly was *not* desperate. Her situation may be, but she as a person was not.

"But no one is surprised," Mr. Payne chimed in again. "She is the unluckiest woman in Lincolnshire."

"It's true," Mrs. Payne agreed. "Poor unlucky Ducky."

It seemed the most either of these two could say was poor Ducky this and poor Ducky that. It was annoying. In fact, it was more than annoying, and Gavin had a distinct desire to rob them of the ability to say such things, to push their perspective of Holly in a different direction.

Before he knew what he was doing, Gavin leaned back in his chair and spoke.

"Well, *poor Ducky* might have applied to the baroness had she married my uncle," he heard himself say, knowing he would eventually regret it, though, for his life, he couldn't imagine when he might. "But I'm afraid that's not what happened."

"What do you mean?" Mrs. Payne asked, eyes wide.

"I mean the baroness is actually *my* wife."

The shock that appeared on both their faces was gratifying enough, but what surprised him was his deep satisfaction from saying it out loud.

Holly was *his* wife.

"Your wife?" Mr. Payne said.

"Yes. Proxy marriage, as it was, since I was overseas."

"A proxy marriage?" Mrs. Payne repeated, eyes wide. "Why, aren't those for soldiers during war time?"

Gavin shrugged.

"I always found them to be rather romantic myself actually," he lied. "I insisted on it, because I couldn't bear to be unwedded from her the day I decided I wanted her as my wife."

"Oh, my," Mrs. Payne replied, falling back. "Well, that is quite romantic."

Just then Holly entered the parlor, only to hesitate suddenly when she saw Gavin seated across from her guests. Gavin stood, unsure how she would take the next thing he would say, but then he couldn't let these people pity his wife.

"Ah, darling," he said, causing her to give him a startled stare. "I've just met your dear friends. It seems they were under the impression that you had married my uncle." He chuckled, looking back at the Paynes as if they had just told him the sky was orange instead of blue. "But have no fear. I corrected their mistake."

For several moments Holly just stared at him.

"W-what?" she asked as he held out his hand to her.

Thankfully, she took it. He frowned as he noticed the slightly blue tint to her skin, but drew her close as Mrs. Payne spoke.

"Holly, you never told us that you were engaged," she said, suddenly beaming after the shock had to warn off. "I had heard rumors that you and John were married, but this makes far more sense."

Holly's eyes went wide.

"Does it?"

"Of course, my love," Gavin said, guiding her to the settee beside him. "How could it not?"

She turned to him, her lips parted slightly as her teeth clenched and hissed below her breath.

"What are you doing?"

But Gavin only winked before turning back to the couple.

"Yes, Holly and I have been able to keep our correspondence a secret these past six months. She is a most proficient letter writer." He held up her hand, inspecting it. "Ink?"

She nodded, blushing slightly. Gavin chuckled and held her hand up to their guests.

"You see? But I'm sure you are aware of my wife's writing skills. Aren't you, Mrs. Payne?"

"Oh yes, of course," Mrs. Payne spoke, though her expression said otherwise.

"Yes. It was during my time abroad, reading her letters, that I realized what a prize of a woman she was, and how fortunate I was to know her," Gavin continued, ignoring the growing ferocity in Holly's glare. "I believe I proposed around January, though I had half a mind to do so before sending that Christmas letter. Do you remember, darling?"

Holly's face was perfectly blank, but the unchecked fury in her blue eyes only served to amuse Gavin. She was furious, and he didn't doubt that he was in for a tongue-lashing once their guests left, but he couldn't help it. He wanted her friends to see that she wasn't some unfortunate thing. In fact, she was a baroness, wealthy and beautiful, with a voice that seemed to wrap around his shoulders whenever she spoke.

"I… I don't remember," she said after a moment.

"Ah, no need to be shy, my love," Gavin said, turning back to face the Paynes. "These are close friends, after all."

"Well, that is… something isn't it?" Mrs. Payne said, evidently confused why her friend hadn't confided in her with such an important secret.

"Indeed, it is," Mr. Payne said, taking a small sandwich from the tiered plater, obviously unaffected by the news. "I believe the last time I visited the late baron, he mentioned that you were in Greece, my lord?"

"Yes, I was."

"I've never had to good fortune to travel abroad. If you don't mind me asking, what is Greece like?"

They all continued to chat for another twenty minutes before the Paynes finally stood, expressing their thanks for the hospitality, felicitations on their marriage, and condolences once more for their loss. Holly maintained a calm composure until they left. Once the Paynes were gone however, she turned on Gavin, practically shaking with rage.

"What on earth were you thinking?" She asked, furious. "Telling them we were married? And that foolish story about writing letters. Are you mad?"

"We *are* married. And I didn't like the way they held their noses in the air about you."

"That's just how their noses are."

"Well, they wouldn't stop blathering on, and… I didn't like it."

Holly paused at his confession. She frowned.

"What were they blathering on about?" she asked. When he didn't answer right away, her shoulders dropped. She apparently knew they had been talking about her. She cleared her throat and asked, "What did they say?"

"Nothing worth repeating."

"Tell me."

"I don't really see a reason to—"

"Please."

Gavin closed his mouth, pressing his lips firmly together. Exhaling loudly, he yielded, unable to disregard a direct plea from her.

"It was irritating, really. They kept saying poor Ducky—"

"Ducky?" she said, cutting him off. Her shoulders hitched up with tension once more. "Oh lord, they told you about Ducky?"

Her hands went to either side of her head, and her fingers pressed into her temples as if she were trying to ward off an impending headache.

"Well, it's hardly something to be embarrassed about—"

"You fall into a pond as a child and see what the brilliant minds of this village can't think up. One misplaced step and all of a sudden I'm unlucky Ducky for the rest of my life."

"Foolish nickname. It certainly wasn't as brilliant as they seemed to consider it."

There was a pause between them. For some reason, Holly looked at him as if she were seeing him for the first time.

"No," she said, her voice soft. "No, it wasn't brilliant at all."

"Rather the opposite actually," Gavin said slowly, staring at her. "I hardly think one misstep as a child should follow you your entire life. Especially when it's obvious you dislike it so much."

"It's not that I dislike it," she said, looking down. "It's just the unlucky part. Ducky I can handle, but unlucky Ducky I've always felt was... well, slightly cruel. Particularly because of all the bad luck that happened afterward. It was as if I was doomed by a self-fulfilling prophecy."

Gavin watched her momentarily, confused that he should suddenly feel grateful for her telling him something so personal. She had been hurt by the constant reminder that she was unlucky, and as preposterous as luck was, he didn't wish her to believe it of herself.

He moved closer to her a brought a hand up beneath her chin. She lifted her head, and though he could sense her sudden desire to pull back, she didn't.

"You aren't unlucky," he said, his tone rough.

Her blue eyes shined at his words. Her mouth opened slightly, catching his attention, and for the briefest of moments, he wondered what it would be like to brush his mouth over hers.

Dropping his hand immediately, he looked away to clear his throat. No. He shouldn't kiss her. Holly was not the type with whom he could play those sorts of games. She was the kind of woman who would only love one person, wholly and most keenly. And whoever that man might be, Gavin knew it wouldn't be the man she had been tricked into marrying. And since the only thing keeping their marriage from being legitimized was consummation, well, he simply had no choice but to not kiss her.

"You shouldn't have told them we were married. Now our annulment will be in jeopardy," she said after a moment, her voice rather huskier than a moment ago.

God, how it pierced him.

"Have no fear about that," he said. "Our marriage was done without either of our consents and as confounding as the Catholic church can be, it certainly won't hold in a court of law. And when it does go through, we will be able to part ways." He gave her a reassuring smile, though he wasn't pleased. "But until then, I won't have my wife disparaged as some sort of bad luck charm."

Holly's eyes opened, her gaze locking onto his.

"You can't stop people from seeing me how they do, especially the Paynes."

"I can and I did."

Holly frowned.

"Yes and now everyone in town will know that we're married. And regardless of what you say, I'm sure that will make our annulment harder." Holly sighed. "Whatever possessed you to tell them the truth?"

For a moment neither spoke and silence hung between them. But after a moment, Gavin shook his head.

"They pitied you," he said lowly. "I didn't like it."

Holly stared at him as if unable to comprehend his words and what they meant.

"No one likes being pitied, but some of us have no choice."

"I don't pity you, Holly."

"Are you sure? Everyone seems to."

"No," he said, inching ever slightly closer to her. "I don't."

His tone was serious, and his eyes fell on her lips. For a moment, he had the urge to move his hands down her arms, perhaps pull her into his chest in some sort of comforting grasp, but instead, he swallowed.

"I'm sorry for telling your friends the truth about our situation."

Holly seemed conflicted as she gazed back at him.

"It's all right, I suppose. But I warn you, all of England might know before the weeks' finished. Charlotte is a notorious gossip."

"I'm not particularly put off by that idea."

"What idea?"

"All of England knowing that you're my wife."

Her mouth opened slightly as a small crease pinched between her brows. Gavin found that he rather enjoyed the way her eyes widened at his words and his body seemed to react to her in a visceral way, particularly when he called her his wife.

Holly must have felt something, too, for the next moment, she took a step back and turned, leaving him alone in the parlor. Gavin watched her as she left, unsure of what to do next. A part of him wanted very much to follow and see where this thread of near constant yearning might lead, but the lessons of his youth remained steadfast.

When he wanted something, Gavin made it a point to avoid it. The slightest chance of not getting what he desired caused him to want to pursue every possible avenue to get it. But their marriage wasn't something he could have. Not for long, anyway. He couldn't let himself forget that.

FOR THE NEXT several days, Holly avoided him while he took great pains to learn all that he could about her. He made a few inquiries with the staff, but everyone who worked beneath Kingston House's roof only had high praise for Holly. It wasn't that he was searching for uncouth details about her, but he had never met a woman without any apparent faults or, at the very least, a past. Why he was so intent on knowing about her, he couldn't comprehend, but his gut urged him on.

One afternoon, when the skies had turned dark, canceling his plans to inspect the brewery that sat on the property's northern edge, he overheard Holly and her sister in the family parlor. He had planned to write his friend Derek Trembley to see about a card game when they reached London, when all of a sudden he heard Holly's throaty, surprising laugh, causing him to stop dead in his tracks.

What a voice, he thought as he unwittingly followed the sound. It had surprised him the first time he heard her speak and had become the singular thing he most anticipated when he woke up each morning.

She was laughing about something Katrina was saying. Suddenly an idea popped into his head. He hadn't asked Katrina about Holly. Who better was there to help him learn everything about his wife?

Spotting a maid down the hallway, he hurried towards her, though she appeared uncertain at his approach. She curtsied quickly.

"May I help you, my lord?" She asked.

"Might you draw the baroness out of the room for a moment?" he asked, hoping to question Katrina. "I would like a private moment with Miss Smyth."

The young maid's eyes widened, and her cheeks turned bright red. She began shaking her head violently.

"Oh, no, sir, please."

"What?" he asked, confused, before it dawned on him what she might be thinking. *Dear lord.* "Oh, no, no, you misunderstand. I don't wish—"

"What's all this?" Holly's voice sounded from behind them.

Gavin turned to see Holly dressed in one of her grey gowns. The mirth in her eyes hadn't yet disappeared.

"There's a problem with the laundress," Gavin said quickly, glancing at the maid. "It seems a dying issue has happened."

Holly's hands instinctively smoothed over her skirts. Aware that she was worried about her clothes, she took a step forward, addressing the maid.

"Is that so?"

"Ah, yes," Gavin interrupted. "But I'm afraid you'll have to check on it yourself. Miss… um…"

"Harriet," the maid supplied.

"Yes, this young woman is helping me find a book."

Holly frowned.

"A book?"

Gavin nodded and gave the maid a pleading glance. Though her brow furrowed, she nodded.

"Yes ma'am."

"Very well, excuse me," Holly said, rushing down the hallway, leaving Gavin and the maid behind.

Surprisingly, the young woman turned on him.

"I know you're the new master, my lord, and I'm to be obeying you, but I won't have you lift a finger against Miss Katrina. I know what your London lords are about—"

"You are aware that I could fire you for such audacious behavior. Correct?"

The maid swallowed and nodded, but she still stood her ground.

"I promised my mother I would never be privy to a person's ruining."

"How very noble," he said dryly. "But I'm not in the market to ruin Miss Katrina. I only wish to question her—and so you will see for yourself, since having you around will make it easier. Shall we?"

Gavin turned, entering the library, to see Katrina sitting on a winged back chair, examining dozens of small squares of cloth, each different color. She was holding up a sheer tangerine piece over a cream-colored square when she saw him. Her hands dropped to her knees, and she stood up, curtseying.

"My lord," she said. "Is everything alright?"

"Yes," he said, shaking his head as he headed towards the bookshelf, followed by the maid.

Gavin reached the bookcase and scanned the leather books' spines. Mind-numbing books such as *The Complete Works of the*

Native Flora and Fauna of the Americas stared back at him. No, this wouldn't do.

Turning back, he caught Katrina's eye as she watched him.

"Your sister has been avoiding me, and I'm afraid I've upset her somehow," he said, folding his hands behind his back. "Most probably when I informed the Paynes of our marriage."

Katrina's eyes widened slightly as if she were surprised he would broach such a topic.

"Oh, um, yes, she mentioned that."

"I wonder if it's because she wasn't still, possibly, infatuated with Mr. Payne."

A laugh escaped Katrina's lips.

"Oh, no," she said, placing the pieces of fabric on the table as she stood up. "Holly doesn't have feelings for him. I mean, that is to say, she may still hold some soreness about the event."

"Their engagement, you mean?" he asked, and she nodded. "I believe it was broken off because Mr. Payne was in love with someone else?"

"Well, it was a well-known fact that Mr. Payne was fond of Charlotte, and I believed Charlotte felt sorry for Holly. She has a well-off family, you see, and she had no shortage of suitors. But Holly... everyone knew that we were struggling. Charlotte didn't wish for Holly to become destitute. She persuaded Mr. Payne to propose. I believe your uncle helped facilitate it."

"Did he?"

She nodded.

"But after Holly said yes, she could see plain as day how it affected poor Charlotte, not to mention she felt rather embarrassed by the idea of taking Mr. Payne's charity—though it didn't quite feel like charity, if you ask me. Anyway, she didn't want to be the eternal cause of Charlotte's suffering, so she stepped aside to allow them to marry. It was really quite heroic."

"But not at all helpful to her own cause."

"No. But then that's Holly. If she's not sacrificing her happiness for someone, it's because she's doing it for someone else, if that makes sense."

"It does," he said thoughtfully. "How did someone as attractive as your sister stay unattached for so long?"

Katrina perked up.

"You find her attractive?"

Gavin shrugged.

"As attractive as any young lady, I suppose."

Katrina's shoulders dropped slightly. It was clear this wasn't the answer she'd hoped for, but Gavin didn't care to entrust his entire attraction to Holly to her sister. Even if they were married.

"Bad luck I suppose, but don't mention that to her. She hates the term. And really, it wasn't so much luck as circumstance, but when hurdle after hurdle appears, one can't help but get a little superstitious about it. If she didn't have to take care of Jasper and I, she might have made a fortuitous match. The farm being in the state that it is didn't help her cause, either. Bringing it back to the point of profitability would require a great expense, or so I'm told." Katrina peered down at her fingers, intertwined before her. "It's rather unfair that Holly should have to deal with it all, if you ask me."

"What is?"

"Sacrificing all of her own joy for others. Particularly Jasper. He's set to inherit it all and yet he doesn't care one iota about it."

"Unfair indeed," Gavin said. "Tell me more about how my uncle tried to facilitate a match between Holly and Mr. Payne."

"Well, your uncle was terribly fond of Holly and thought it was rather cruel for someone like her to go through life alone. He and Charlotte worked on Mr. Payne together to encourage him to propose. But in the end, Holly refused to see it through. Perhaps that was why he did what he did with your marriage license—making sure the truth wouldn't come out until it was too late for Holly to stop it from happening. Still, it was rather devious of your uncle to marry the two of you by proxy."

"Yes," Gavin said. "Yes, it was."

"Um, my lord, may I ask you something?" Katrina asked,

shaking him from his thoughts.

"Of course."

"Holly would be furious to know I asked, but… we are in rather desperate need of dresses. You see, Holly dyed all hers and I have none for the upcoming season. I was hoping, well…"

Gavin waved his hand.

"Say no more. Once we are in London, you and your sister will have several appointments to attend and each of you will have a proper wardrobe made for the coming season."

"Oh, thank you!" Katrina said.

Just then, Holly returned. Glancing between her sister and Gavin, her expression grew suspicious.

"There wasn't any issue with the laundry, my lord," she said. She looked at Katrina. "Why do you look so pleased?"

"Oh, no reason," her sister said, unable to completely hide her own smile.

Chapter Seven

L ADY VIOLET WINTERS arrived at Kingston House two days before the house's departure for London. The dark-haired beauty, who had led a very privileged life, had surprised Holly in many ways, but then she did recall Clara's letters, stating that while Violet could be prone to dramatics, she possessed an overall genuine and kind soul. Katrina had taken an instant liking to her, and they became fast friends.

With Katrina's debut set for mid-May, Holly hoped to have begun reconstructing some of her old gowns herself while still at Kingston House, but found Gavin insisting that they leave for London at once.

"It'll be better if we leave tomorrow instead of next week," he said one morning to Holly over breakfast. "The sooner we arrive, the better."

"I suppose so. This way Mrs. O'Kirk will be able to begin the task of stripping gowns herself, as opposed to me starting to do so."

"There's no need," Gavin said, leaning back from his empty plate. "There are plenty of fabric stores in London."

Sticking his hand in the breast pocket of his coat, he pulled out a small sweet, unwrapped it from its parchment paper, and popped it into his mouth. It was something that Holly had become accustomed to. After every meal, he would reach for one of his candies.

"There may be," Holly said. "But we haven't the capital."

"My uncle made it very clear in his will that you should have all that you needed for Katrina's season, Holly. I'm sure that included clothing."

Holly opened her mouth to argue, but she wasn't sure why she would. Katrina would fare far better in newly made gowns, and Holly had far fewer qualms about accepting assistance when it came to what was best for her sister.

"Very well. Katrina will have a few new gowns made."

"You will as well."

Holly as she frowned at Gavin. Why would she need anything new?

"I'm in mourning."

"Mourning is reserved for parents, spouses, siblings and the like," Gavin said, flipping the candy in his mouth with his tongue. "Not uncle-in-laws."

"John was my friend."

"And by the time Katrina makes her debut it will have been three months since his passing, more than an appropriate amount of time for a friend to have put off mourning."

Holly bristled. She wouldn't be dictated to by Gavin, even if he did make a valid point. It didn't matter. She would mourn for as long as she wanted.

"Thank you for the offer, but I really must insist on keeping my dresses as they are."

A slight, annoyed frown crossed Gavin's lips as he gazed back down at his paper, and though he didn't speak, Holly understood that their conversation was far from over.

"Where in London will we be staying?" Katrina asked, her cheerful tone sounding a little forced. Holly assumed she was trying to break the tension. "I'm terribly frightened. I've never been to London before."

Gavin's head lifted; his brow scrunched together as if she had spoken in an unknown language.

"Excuse me? What do you mean you've never been to London?"

"Just that," Katrina said, glancing at Holly. "We've never been."

Gavin followed her gaze, and Holly felt her cheeks warm.

"Why would we go to London?" she asked, somewhat defensively. "It's outrageously expensive and without many friends, the social aspects never held much fascination."

"Drury Lane? The Opera? The British Museum? None of these tempt you?"

"It's not a matter of if they tempt me, it's the practicality. It would have been wasteful to attend the season when neither of my siblings was of age to participate."

"What about you?"

Holly's frown deepened.

"Oh yes, I should have gone to London, unchaperoned and without a sponsor to what? Stroll the Serpentine?" She shook her head. "It was an impossibility."

"London should never have been out of your reach," he said. The gentle declaration settled around the room. Holly glanced at him, unsure what to make of his statement. Evidently, even Gavin was uncomfortable with having said such a thing, for he was on his feet the next minute. "If you ladies will excuse me, I have some business to attend to," he said with a quick nod before exiting the room.

Holly watched him depart, her eyes on the doorway until the fading sound of his footsteps disappeared utterly. Turning, she saw a wide-eyed Katrina and a smirking Violet.

"What was that all about?" Holly asked no one in particular.

Katrina's brows hitched up as a realization came over her face. She reached for Holly's wrist with both of her hands and squeezed.

"Do you think that the baron might... well, fancy you?"

Holly rolled her eyes and tried to pull her arm free of her sister's hands.

"Really, Katrina."

"I agree with Katrina. The baron seems practically smitten with you," Violet said.

"Smitten?" Holly repeated, somewhat flustered. She tried to ignore the fluttering of her pulse at the idea of Gavin being interested in her. It was implausible of course. They were still practically strangers, but she had to confess that a small part of her had recently begun to consider what it might be like if Gavin actually fancied her. But she wouldn't admit that out loud. "Do be serious."

"We *are* being serious," Katrina continued. "Why, he told me just the other day that he found you attractive."

To Holly's dissatisfaction, her heart did that wobble that always seemed to happen when Gavin walked into the room. She bent her head slightly in her sister's direction and tried to sound as uninterested as possible.

"Did he?" Holly asked.

"Yes," Katrina said before her smile faltered. "Well, he did say you were as attractive as any young lady." Holly pulled her arm away wholly. "But I think he meant it!"

"Yes, what a daring thing to admit," Holly said sarcastically. "Really, Katrina, I know you want to romanticize our situation, but the baron and I are simply bound by an illegal contract."

"But you're married."

"And seeking an annulment."

Katrina huffed and sat back against her chair, her arms folding across her chest, while Violet continued to smile.

"Very well," Holly's sister said. "But he is right. You deserve some new gowns."

"I'm perfectly content with my own dresses, thank you very much," Holly said.

Katrina gave her sister a concerned look before standing up and leaving the dining room without so much as a goodbye. Violet shrugged and followed Katrina, leaving Holly to watch as they both disappeared around the corner. Was she being too cynical about the entire matter? John had wanted her to have fine things, and though she had refused him, as it was socially unacceptable, this arrangement she found herself in now seemed to free her from the constraints that usually surrounded social gift-giving.

Gavin wished to order her new gowns. Who was she to argue? Perhaps she should allow him to follow his uncle's wishes, but the years of living shilling to shilling had made Holly wary. She couldn't help but think of a dozen other places the money could go.

She should speak to Gavin about it.

Standing up, she went to find him but found his office empty. Frowning, she turned only to nearly run into Mr. Jorden.

"Oh!" She said, her hands coming up to her heart. "Mr. Jorden, I'm sorry."

"Not at all, my lady. Are you in need of assistance?"

"Yes, actually, I was wondering where the baron has gone to?"

"He's gone to inspect the brewery building."

Holly frowned. The brewery building had been built nearly two years earlier after John had visited Whitbread's Brewery and become fascinated with the process. Of course, as was typical with John, he soon grew bored of it, and it hadn't been used since the previous spring.

"Why?" she asked.

"He had the idea of opening it up again. He said if the building was in proper working order and if it could produce a half decent ale, then he would rent the space to a few local taverns."

Holly nodded slowly, pleasantly surprised at the entrepreneurial spirit. Most ladies would probably be displeased with Gavin's involvement in commerce, seeing it as beneath someone of his station, but Holly admired it. He had a mind for making money, and as someone who had often suffered from lack of funds, that was a trait that she admired.

"Oh. Very well. I'll go and meet him there."

"Would you like an escort, my lady? The ground is wet and I'm afraid it isn't very pleasant out."

It had rained for nearly five days straight, and while she was sure the break in the weather would be brief, she did not need assistance. She had grown up in these fields, and no amount of mud could stop her.

"No thank you Mr. Jorden. I'll wear my boots, though."

"Very good, my lady."

Holly changed into her sturdy leather boots, the one piece of her wardrobe she had never skimped on. She tied the laces tightly and, wearing her oldest pelisse coat, she headed out the front door of Kingston House.

Though the air was damp, the gentle warmth of spring hung all around her. Beneath her careful steps, the mud tried to suck her feet in, but her strong legs wouldn't allow it. Holly never admitted it, for it was decidedly provincial, but the smell of earth was her favorite scent in the world. It reminded her of a time when she wasn't burdened, when she and Clara would run through the fields as children.

The walk across the western field took nearly twenty minutes until the land curved downhill. There, sat on the edge of a wood, stood a large, three-story brick building with two large barn doors facing south. A dirt road had been created to reach it from the main thoroughfare, and while it was a relatively new building, its abandoned state made it appear far older than it was.

Holly reached the building reasonably quickly, and taking a deep breath, she heaved one of the heavy, large barn doors open. The building was mostly one large room, with mezzanines built along the sides of the walls on each floor. It was an open floorplan mainly consisting of stairs going up and down, surrounding a large copper broiler in the middle of the room. It was vast, and though Holly had no idea how it worked, she knew that John had been particularly proud of that piece.

"Hello?" she called out, her voice echoing back as she glanced around. The only light was from the open door and the windows placed near the roof.

"Yes?" a masculine voice answered.

To her left, Gavin came out of a small room off to the side without his jacket and sleeves rolled up to his elbows as he carried a dirty rag and some metal bit. He stopped when he saw her, and for an instant, neither moved.

What a strange place, Holly thought vaguely as she stared at Gavin. A slash of sunshine sliced between them from the door behind her, and the dust danced in the beam of morning light. There was no dining room, parlor, or ballroom, yet Holly had never felt relatively so calm in a single place.

But then, perhaps it was simply because she wasn't surrounded by servants or crumbling walls. She was alone with a man who technically was her husband, a man she barely knew.

Except that she did know him. She knew he was an even-tempered man who always seemed to be grinning. He was someone who was eager to honor the wishes of his relative, even though their relationship hadn't been very close. She was curious about that. She was also curious why he had no qualms about financing her family's home repairs or buying her sister gowns for her upcoming season. But then, that was why she had sought him out. They needed to discuss some things.

"Can I help you?" he asked, his tone curious.

She cleared her throat and took a step to her right.

"I wanted to discuss somethings with you, before we left for London."

Gavin stalled for a moment before coming froward. He leaned against a railing that outlined the floor they were on, near the stairs leading downward.

"What things?" he asked.

She inhaled.

"I want to first thank you for being so accommodating. I know you didn't have the best relationship with your uncle and I just want to say that I think it is kind of you to want to honor his wishes, despite your history."

Gavin didn't move.

"What did he tell you of our relationship?"

Holly paused, remembering what John had said about his nephew.

"Only that you didn't approve of his sort. He said some people only knew what they were taught and that I shouldn't be too hard on you, if ever we were to meet," she said. "But I guess he knew we would meet one day."

Though the lighting wasn't great, Holly could see a blush touch the bridge of Gavin's nose. He folded his arms across his chest.

"He didn't want you to be hard on me?" he asked, and she nodded. "Why would he say that?"

Holly swallowed as she walked around the room.

"I may have been unkind when he first explained the situation. You must know, I was terribly protective of him."

"Yes, so I've gathered," Gavin breathed. "Uncle John was lucky to have someone like you. Unfortunately, he explained our relationship perfectly. I was raised to disparage people like him. My aunt in particular made it a point to criticize his lifestyle, and for a long time I thought she was correct."

"Do you still?"

"No," he said. "I've learned some time ago that the only judgment I can pass on someone is kindness."

"That's not really a judgement."

"Exactly."

Holly tilted her head.

"Is that why you're so eager to meet his requests? To make amends to him in some way?"

Gavin shrugged.

"Possibly. But having gotten to know you and your family, I believe Uncle John was, at the very least, a good judge of character when it came to his friends."

Holly smiled in spite of herself, but tried to shake it off.

"That's kind of you to say. But I must insist that we write

down a proper expenditure. Just like the ledger you have for Felton House. I intend to pay all of that back in full, just as soon as the farm can turn a profit. But I also wish to keep track of the cost of Katrina's dresses, as well as fans, gloves, and the likes for her—"

"And you."

Holly shook her head.

"No, and that's why I came to talk to you. I've no need for new dresses. I know your intentions are kind, but that money can go elsewhere. I have no need for frivolous things—"

"Clothing is hardly frivolous," he said with a frown.

"Shopping on Bond Street can be."

"Well, I'm sorry London doesn't meet your modest expectations, but as you and your sister will be representing this barony, I can't very well have you both looking like paupers. Can I?"

"Well... no." Holly had to admit, she hadn't thought of that.

"And I know you don't wish to offend the memory of my uncle."

"Of course not."

"Then might you do me this small favor of making yourself presentable for the ton, particularly because you will be representing Bairnsdale, and thus your old friend?"

Holly bit the inside of her cheek. Yes, she supposed she could do that.

"Yes," she said softly, annoyed at how deftly he had gotten around her defenses.

"Thank you," he said. "I've made several appointments for you and your sister in London this coming week. I hope you don't mind traveling to town a little earlier than what would be considered fashionable, but I've some business that requires my presence."

"What business do you have in London?" she asked, curiously, before realizing how forward she was being in asking such a personal question. "Oh, um, forgive me..."

He waved his hand in the air, as if it were completely normal for her to inquire about his private affairs.

"I've several dealings that need to be settled before I commit to this new baron role."

Holly tilted her head.

"Do you mean to retire? From your banking career, I mean."

"Ha," he said, glancing around. "I prefer to think of it as trading one job for another. Managing all the Bairnsdale properties and businesses will be a job in and of itself. Besides, the bank effectively runs itself now. For the past few years, I've really only been maintaining an office there as I'm on the board of trustees, but I'll likely retire fully now."

"Oh," she said, somewhat perplexed. "Your uncle once said that you enjoyed numbers. That's why you went into banking."

A short silence followed. Holly was unsure for a moment, but when he next spoke, she thought he sounded somewhat distant.

"Indeed," he said, somewhat stiffly, before reverting back to their previous conversation. "But I assure you, you will not bankrupt this estate by buying a few dresses."

"I'm eager not to empty the estate's coffers."

He let out a laugh that startled her, sending a warm wave of comfort down her back.

"You could buy a new dress every day for the rest of your life, and it wouldn't put a dent in the monies here."

"Yes, but what I mean is—"

"Do you know what I think?" he said, stepping forward. "I think you've forgotten what it's like to be taken care of."

Holly stared at Gavin, unsure of what to do. An uncomfortable laugh bubbled in her throat, but she stifled it, taking a step back. She didn't want to sound like a fool, yet what a ridiculous thing to say.

"I assure you, I do not need to be taken care of—Ah!"

In her attempt to avoid him, Holly hadn't been watching where she was going, and she tripped over a dirt-covered piece of wood. Her hands came up to brace herself against a fall when she was suddenly wrapped in the strong embrace of Gavin.

Kneeling in one swinging motion as he cradled her to his chest, he sat her on the ground as light as a butterfly dropping on a daisy's petals. Her breathing was erratic, but then so was the pounding of Gavin's heart. She felt it beating wildly against her shoulder.

He gazed down at her.

"Are you alright?" he asked, his tone concerned.

"I… uh, yes," she stuttered. "Yes, quite."

He didn't appear convinced.

"Is your ankle twisted?" he asked, his hand dropping to the hem of her skirt as if he were going to inspect it. Holly nearly shrieked as she pushed her hands to his shoulders to dissuade him from proceeding.

"There's no need for that."

"If it's swollen, you shouldn't walk on it."

"It's not. It's perfectly fine. I just need some help up," she said, stretching her hands towards him in an effort to distract him from examining her.

He frowned at her.

"I won't touch it, I promise," he said, lifting the edge of her dress. "But can you press the sole of your foot against my palm? Just to placate me?"

"But my boots are filthy. You'll dirty your hands."

"I'll survive," he said with a smirk.

Holly stared at him, curious about why he should be so worried, but nodded. He held his large hand up close to her foot and waited. Feeling foolish, Holly lifted her foot slightly and pressed the sole of her foot into his palm. Though she wore leather boots, she was uncomfortably aware of the feel of resistance against his hand. What would it be like if he did wrap his thick fingers around her ankle? If he pulled her towards him?

Holly tried hard not to think of such things as Gavin pressed his fingers against her toes, testing her reflexes. When satisfied, he sat back and stood, dropping his clean hand towards her, and helping her stand swiftly.

She fell slightly forward toward him, somewhat dizzied by the movement, but pulled away almost instantly, ashamed of her thoughts. Something on her face must have made it evident because his easy smile faltered as he stared at her. His dazzling warm stare turned heated and she found herself holding her breath when he finally spoke.

"You know," he said softly, "you could let yourself enjoy it. At least, for a little while."

"Enjoy what?"

"Our marriage. Well, for as long as we have one."

Holly stared at him.

"What would I possibly find enjoyable about our situation?"

His shoulder hitched up.

"Well, if not the money or the company," he said with a wink which somehow both annoyed her and aroused her, "you might learn to enjoy being taken care of for a bit."

"I don't need anyone to take care of me."

"No. No, I don't suppose you do," he said, and her shoulders dropped, whether from relief or discontentment, she did not know. "But I think you would like it."

"And you believe you're the person to do so?" she spoke, hating the breathlessness in her tone. He nodded. "Why on earth would you want such a burden?"

"I don't think of it as a burden," he said, crowding her. "Only my pleasure. As your husband."

Holly's heart seemed to skip a beat at the word "pleasure." Some carnal part of her wanted to lean into him and learn just what sort of pleasure they might find together, but she shook her head slowly. She needed to remind him that theirs was not a real marriage.

"Must I remind you, that we aren't really—"

But Gavin's hand brushed her cheek before she could finish, stifling her words.

"You keep saying that, but it isn't true, is it? We are married." She inhaled as his fingers trailed to the side of her neck. "Let me take care of you, Holly. If only a little bit."

A battle began to volley within her. Playing this game was ridiculous and preposterous, but she wanted to do so. The smile that always seemed to sit on his lips, the scent of lemon and mint, the weight of his hand. A nameless need coursed through her at his words, and she found herself fighting off the urge to lean toward him and press her body against his.

What was wrong with her? She had never wanted so badly to be held by someone before. It all set her world on edge; even now, she was trying desperately to hold on to reality.

"It's such a little request," he said softly, his head dipping close to hers. "Grant it to me."

Holly exhaled slowly. She let herself close her eyes and then softly nodded her head.

What a poor example she was for her sex. To melt at a few choice words. But then, those words had come from a man who had done little else but try and help her since his arrival—and he seemed just as genuine in his wish to please her.

"Very well," she said so meekly that her cheeks burned with embarrassment.

Gavin's fingers came up beneath her chin.

"Good girl," he whispered against her mouth.

Holly inhaled sharply at his words and before she knew it, she leaned forward and kissed him.

She fell against him as his arms came around her back, pulling her closer to his body, her eyes closing as his tongue swept into her mouth. He kissed her as if he were trying to consume every bit of her soul.

Holly's arms unwittily wrapped around his strong shoulders, her fingers digging into his back as though she were afraid he might disappear. What was the matter with her? Sparks seemed to alight every inch of her skin, and she felt desperate and devoted all at once, writhing uncontrollably as his hands moved down her back, gripping her buttocks in a firm grasp.

A gasp may have dropped from her lips as he continued kissing her, nipping at her bottom lip in a way that made her shake, when suddenly he pulled away, throwing her off balance.

Holly was breathing heavily as he watched her with a hard, confused stare. He appeared perplexed, and though Holly wanted to lean into him and continue, he set her back, his hands unsteady on her shoulders.

The look in his eyes seemed apologetic yet hungry. What was the matter?

"I... Excuse me," he said, shaking his head as he dropped his hands from her and quickly turned, leaving the room without another word.

Holly stared wide-eyed at the barn door as he exited, unable to move for a long time as her beating heart began to settle.

What had that all been about?

Chapter Eight

A S THE CARRIAGE swayed back and forth over the uneven dirt road that led to London, Gavin couldn't help but steal another glance at Holly, sitting straight back against the carriage wall opposite him. After several hours of travel, he found it challenging to feign much interest in the landscape rolling by. Still, he couldn't just openly gawk at her, not with Lady Violet and Katrina in the carriage. Besides which, he found it difficult to meet her eye. Gavin knew Holly was less than pleased with him.

He had acted like an idiot, kissing her in the brewery and leaving afterward, but he had been dumbfounded by his reaction to her. Getting out of her presence had been the only thing he could do to stop himself from taking her right there on the dirty floor of an empty building.

What had possibly possessed him to do something so rash? It wasn't as though he were some inexperienced, young lad. He had a string of former lovers who could attest to his patience regarding lovemaking, and yet all reason and sensibility had vanished the moment he held her in his arms.

It had come over Gavin suddenly, the burning need to have her, but if he was being honest, those feelings of desire had started the first moment he saw her. Her voice had plagued his dreams since coming to Kingston House. Whenever she spoke, her lyrical vocals reverberated in his very soul. Her blue eyes and walnut hair were a striking combination, in his opinion, and he couldn't quite recall a more attractive woman, but the tone of her voice seemed to hypnotize him every time.

Moreover, there had been a growing desire to care for her, especially when it became clear that she had little faith that he would or could. Was it because she was his wife? Or was it something else that drove him?

Questions that need to be answered, he thought as a substantial rain began to fall once again, the droplets slamming against the carriage roof and walls as they drove on. He supposed he could break the silence by mentioning that Mr. Mannion had written him a letter, offering to buy Felton Manor for more than whatever the imaginary buyer had offered Holly. It seemed the old man had finally realized his shortchanging would get him nowhere, especially when he was desperate for the property. But Gavin doubted that his new, higher offer would change anything. When it came to her home, he knew no money could persuade her to sell. On the other hand, Jasper would likely be thrilled to learn about Mr. Mannion's offer, but Gavin wasn't going to tell him about it just yet. The siblings still had things to discuss, and he wouldn't betray Holly's confidence.

The carriage was tight between him and the three ladies, but he did not complain. He had tried for a while to facilitate some small talk, but his mind seemed solely focused on Holly and she had done little but ignore him since their meeting in the brewery. He guessed it was because she was angry that he had left without explanation, but he wondered if it was better this way. The further she kept herself away from him, the better off he was. Less contact meant fewer mistakes.

Still, he couldn't help but steal a glance at her from time to time. The trip to London would take two days, and they had plans to stay the night at an inn, the Carriage and Crown, that sat nearly halfway between Kingston House and London.

At first, the silence seemed welcome, but as the hours passed, Katrina also became restless, and she began asking questions during the second leg of their journey.

"Are we to stay in Mayfair? I've heard that's the most fashionable neighborhood, but that there are many fine houses in other districts as well. I believe Marylebone is also nice, though I certainly have no reference for judgement."

"My own house is in Marylebone, but we'll be staying at the Berkeley Square residence. Bairnsdale Terrace."

"How exciting," Katrina said, turning to her left to see her sister. "Isn't that exciting, Holly?"

"Yes, very," she said, sounding anything but excited.

Katrina frowned at her before turning back to Gavin.

"I remember you saying that you'd only just arrived in London a few weeks ago, after your tour of the continent," she pressed. "I've never left England before."

"I highly suggest it," Gavin said, stretching out his legs as best he could. "The world is vast and beautiful."

"We haven't had the funds to travel to London, let alone the continent," Holly said quietly.

Katrina's shoulders slumped at her sister's practical talk, but Gavin wouldn't let her have the last say. Leaning forward, he spoke directly to Katrina.

"Traveling is a wonderous thing and I for one appreciate it. If only to get a different perspective on the world, it would be worth it, but then there is so much one can get out of it."

Katrina opened her mouth to speak, but Holly's voice hit his ears first.

"It's a wonder you came back to England at all then."

Was that annoyance in her tone? Wanting to tease her, he spoke.

"Well, I couldn't very well let my wife miss out on all the adventures."

The word "wife" seemed to catch everyone by surprise. Holly glared at him but refused to speak. Katrina, who had appeared hopeful that a conversation might evolve, looked defeated as Gavin sat back. She settled back in her seat and stared out the window as the skies turned darker. Two hours later, the driver was calling out, and Gavin peered out the window.

"We're here," he said, glancing up at the building. Fat droplets rained down, distorting the warm, cheerful glow of the inn. The number of carriages and horses Gavin saw outside the building made him wonder if they weren't the only ones wishing to reach London early. "And the storm hasn't let up." He turned to Holly. "Best cover your heads with your shawls."

Holly nodded tightly and turned to her sister and Violet, who were rearranging their coverings. As quickly as they could, Gavin hopped out of the carriage, helped all three ladies down, and hurried them across the courtyard to the safety of the overhanging roof. Gavin followed but slipped and fell flat onto his front on the muddy ground.

"Oh dear!" he heard Holly say as he cursed silently. Standing back up, he tried to wipe his muddy hands onto his jacket, but it proved a poor idea as the entire front of his body was covered in mud.

Holly gave him a sorrowful grimace, but she turned back towards the door, and they all stepped into the cozy tavern room.

The interior was abuzz with the lively conversation and noises of any well-run inn. Silverware clanged together, and plates and glassware rattled and clanked against rough wood tabletops as patrons were served their meals. The soft yellow hues of the oil lamps set the room in a cheerful glow. The scent of roast chicken, potatoes, and herbs filled the air as they walked along the edge of the room. Several travelers stopped mid-conversation to watch them walk by. Two men, in particular, watched the ladies far too intently for Gavin's liking.

Glaring at the men, Gavin escorted Holly, Katrina, and Violet to the barman.

"Rooms, sir?" the white-haired man asked cheerfully. "I'm sorry, but I cannot fit another tonight."

"I've reservations," Gavin said, earning him a surprised glance from Holly. "Bairnsdale. And I'll require a bath brought up to my room, obviously."

"Hmm, of course, sir," the short man said, staring at the mess that was Gavin's outfit before leafing through the pages of his leather-bound ledger. "Aye, here we are. Two rooms, one night." He cupped his hand around his mouth. "Molly! Show these guests to rooms one and two." He faced Gavin once more. "My wife will show you upstairs."

"Thank you," Gavin nodded as he raised his hands, effectively herding Holly, her sister, and Violet through the busy tavern again.

Their driver had come in from the rain, carrying two valises under his arms and another two in each hand. He met them at the bottom of the steps leading up to the second floor, where the innkeeper's short, plump wife stood, waiting for them with a wide smile.

"This way, my lord," she said, gripping her skirts as she climbed the wooden staircase.

Upon reaching the top landing, the woman reached for the first door on her left.

"Here's the lord and lady's room," she said before taking another step to open the next door. The driver placed Gavin and Holly's bags in their room. "And one for the young ladies."

Gavin noticed that Holly's back went rigid as Katrina and Violet moved toward the second room. He had intended for Holly and her sister to share. They had kept separate rooms in Kingston House, and it hadn't even occurred to Gavin that they would require more than two rooms since Violet had joined their company. If possible, he would have secured another room at that moment. But the innkeeper had just explained that no more rooms were available.

His jaw clenched. They would just have to push through it. It was only one night, after all.

"Thank you," Gavin said stiffly to the innkeeper's wife. "Might we have some trays of food brought up?"

"Of course, my lord," the woman said before turning and

rushing off.

Holly looked at Katrina. "You will be alright?"

"Yes. Good night," she said, with an exaggerated yawn, just as their driver came out of the room and followed the innkeeper's wife down the staircase.

"Yes, good night," Holly said, entering the first room.

Gavin followed, closing the door behind him.

At first, neither moved, seeming unsure how to go on, but after a moment of breathing to steady his erratic pulse, Gavin walked towards the fireplace, taking off his jacket as he did.

"What are you doing?" Holly asked suddenly.

He paused and turned to face her.

"Undressing."

"Why?"

"I don't suppose you think I should be dressed for my bath."

"You're planning to bathe? In here?"

The corner of his mouth pulled up at her questions.

"Well, I'm considering it. I *am* covered in mud."

"Oh, well, yes," she said, her eyes dropping over his body. "I suppose you are."

Her discomfort was evident, and for a moment, Gavin considered waiting until London to bathe, but then that would be ridiculous. He reached for his travel bag and pulled out a small bar of Pear's soap. If he had learned anything in his travels, it was that one should always have a bar of soap and a decent pair of boots.

He glanced at Holly as he did so and noticed a faint pink shade creeping over her cheekbones and the bridge of her nose. The added color to her cheeks made her look lovely, and Gavin's heart thudded loudly in his chest. Why he always found himself suddenly aroused by that blush, he did not know, but he tried his best to ignore it. Instead, he decided to focus on making amends for walking out on her in the brewery.

Still holding the soap in his hands, he took a step towards her.

"I want to apologize for abandoning you in the brewery the

other day," he began eyes on her. "I assure you, you did nothing wrong."

Her eyes squinted.

"Yes, I am aware."

His mouth quirked up again. He hadn't expected that.

"What I meant to say is, I shouldn't have put you in a position where you might have thought I was taking advantage of you."

Holly stared at him and then dropped her gaze.

"That is considerate of you, I suppose." Silence. And then, "But I did not think you were taking advantage of me."

"No?" he asked softly, stepping towards her.

"No," she said, her hands raised slightly at his advance. "But I am glad you stopped it. We should refrain from participating in any… physical sports."

He stopped his steps, his brow lifted. He hadn't expected such frankness from Holly on a subject most ladies would be uncomfortable discussing. It made him curious.

"Have you, well, participated in such sports before?"

Holly's eyes widened as the pink of her cheeks deepened.

"Absolutely not," she said quickly, shaking her head.

Gavin swallowed his pleasure at her answer. He nodded, though.

"You've a rather easy way of speaking about it, is all."

"Well, I'm not a child. I'm aware of the world and how it works, even if I've never…" She shook her head, looking briefly uncertain. "All I'm saying is, that I believe we should refrain from kissing one another. I fear it will only complicate matters when our annulment comes to fruition. Don't you agree?"

Not in the slightest.

"Yes, of course," he said as a knock sounded on the door.

Turning, he opened it as two maids entered with a pair of food trays, setting them down on the small square table in the corner of the room. A round, steady-handed man entered behind them, carrying a Parisian sponge bath, which he placed on the floor in front of the fireplace as Holly moved to take her seat at the table.

"Apologies, my lord," the man said. "But all our hip baths are occupied at the moment."

Gavin pursed his lips in displeasure but nodded, eyeing the steam rising from the water. He would have to use a cloth to clean himself as it was more the size of a bucket than a bath. The servants exited the room, and he began to tug at his dirty cravat.

"Well, you are in luck, Holly. You don't need to fight the urge to watch me bathe completely naked," he said, walking towards the sponge bath.

The very next moment, though, he heard her laughing. Turning, he saw that she was holding her hand to her chest, laughing as she gazed at him. The sound of it undid him, and at that moment, he would have pledged allegiance to any god that would give him the ability to make her laugh for the rest of his life.

Why was the ability to make her laugh so intoxicating? He didn't understand this yearning to make her smile, but her laughter curled around him so that it confused him. Frowning as he tried to comprehend, his train of thought came to an abrupt halt when her hands came up to distract him.

"No, no, you misunderstand," she said, swallowing her laughter. "It's just…You're completely covered in mud and they…" She tried to stifle her laughter. "And they barely gave you enough water to clean your face."

As soon as the words had left her lips, she fell into a fit of giggles again.

"Yes, terribly amusing, that," he said dryly, trying to sound annoyed even though her laughter made his chest swell with feeling. He would have to make do with what he had.

Undoing the ties at his wrists, he pulled the mud-covered shirt over his head, then took up one of the folded cloths the maids had carried in and began scrubbing his face, ears, and neck. He moved the warm, wet cloth through his hair, scratching his skull as he did so. The repetitive sloshing of water became the single noise in the room as he scrubbed the soap into the cloth, lathering it into a bubbly wash before moving it all over his neck and chest. Halfway through his cleaning, he turned his head over his shoulder to see if Holly was eating, but she was perfectly still, watching him.

She sat on one of the tiny stools around the table, eyes on him as he continued his task, if slightly slower now than when he had begun. He was intrigued when she didn't turn away as he cleaned his chest and torso with the wet rag.

"Eat something, before it gets cold," he said, causing her to jump slightly.

She cleared her throat.

"Yes, of course," she said.

She refocused on the dinner tray before her as Gavin finished cleaning his upper body. Now, he was presented with a problem.

Usually, he would strip completely. If he had been alone, he probably would have eaten his food naked before falling asleep. But with Holly a handful of feet away from him, he couldn't. As mature as she was, he was sure she had never seen a man completely naked, and while that pleased him, he had to keep in mind that she had led a sheltered life. He had no wish to shock or upset her.

Still, he couldn't go to bed with his lower body still covered in mud.

Undoing the front buttons of his mud-cover pantaloons, he was quick to remove them and his short under breeches. With a speed he hadn't known he possessed, he wiped the rest of himself down and pulled open his valise, removing a pair of long trousers.

To save Holly some embarrassment, he pulled them on as well as a clean shirt before turning towards her. He came around the table and took a seat, noting that she had barely eaten.

"Is the food bad?"

"Oh no," she said, not meeting his eyes as she tore a piece of bread in half.

Curious, he tore his own bread and dipped it into the medium-warm beef stew. The scent of sweet carrots, peas, onions, and potatoes wafted up, and he ate it, only then realizing how famished he had been. He ate heartedly and was nearly finished when he noticed that Holly had finally eaten, at least, a portion of her meal, though far from all of it.

"Are you not hungry?"

"Not terribly, no," she said, tugging at the damp collar of her dress.

Gavin's full attention focused on her fingers. When she noticed where he was looking, her hand dropped. He had been so focused on his undressing that he hadn't stopped thinking that Holly would have to undress as well.

"I suppose it getting late," Holly said, her eyes not rising to meet his.

"I suppose," he said, watching her.

After another minute of silence, she nodded and stood, as did he. She paused when she saw him stand.

"Um…I'm not sure… Well…"

"If you need me," he said, moving around his chair to stand before her. He lifted his finger and gestured to the corner. "I'll be over here."

A wave of relief came over Holly's face.

"Thank you, Gavin," she said as she moved past him, and Gavin froze.

It was the first time she had called him by his name, and the way her voice wrapped around the letters made him hard and soft simultaneously and in different places. He couldn't understand how a voice could make him rigid, but he knew he would give her the world if only he thought she'd accept it.

What a dangerous situation to be in.

He reached into his mudded coat pocket and pulled out one of the last lemony mint candies that he had devoured these past few weeks. Unfolding the tiny confection and popping into his mouth, he wondered if he would be able to discover the mystery sender, or if not, if he would at least be able to find the store that produced them.

The rustle of her undressing behind him, only a few short feet away, may have also contributed to his growing discomfort. Out of the corner of his eye, he saw her scurry onto the mattress, and by the time she said, "You may turn around," she was already beneath the covers, tucked into the corner of the bed, sheets pulled up to her chin.

He smirked, unable to stop as he moved around the room to turn down the oil lamps. He knew she was nervous, and as difficult as it was going to be sleeping next to her all night without touching her, he didn't have designs to ruin her.

"You know, there's no reason to be worried. I've no intentions of ravishing you tonight."

Holly's fingers curled around the top edge of the sheets and pulled them down an inch.

"You don't?" she asked, and his brow lifted. "I mean, good."

"Good," he answered.

Crossing the room, he lifted the sheets and climbed into bed. Gavin thought the space between them was impressively vast for such a small bed, and he wondered if it might decrease through the night.

Holly made a throaty noise, and he paused.

"Yes?" he asked after a moment.

"It's just... May I ask why?"

"Why what?"

"Why you don't have designs on... well, that?"

Gavin was glad it was too dark to see her face because he doubted she would have been able to bring herself to ask him if she could see his eyes. He laid his head back on the pillow, staring into the darkness above him.

"Do you wish me to?"

"N-no!"

Low laughter rumbled in his chest.

"No, I suppose you wouldn't. Which is precisely the reason I don't have plans to do so." After silence, he added, "You didn't think I would force myself on you. Did you?"

He felt the slight lift of her shoulder against the blanket that covered both of them.

"I wasn't sure."

He frowned.

"Because we kissed?"

"Oh no," she said, sitting up slightly. "Not because of that. I just… I don't know. I thought that since we're technically married, you'd want to, well, do that. Regardless of my feelings."

He turned to face her, the light from the fire illuminating only part of her face.

"Your feelings are at the forefront of my mind, and I hope you are aware that anyone who would disregard them would not be worthy of you." She was quiet, and so he continued. "The truth is, Holly, I would very much like to take you." Her sharp intake of breath only emboldened him. "But seeing as we're seeking an annulment, I'm afraid I have to agree with your previous statement. It isn't wise to touch one another."

"Oh," she whispered softly in the darkness, and Gavin had to bite his bottom lip to ignore the pain in his groin.

"Good night, Holly."

"Good night," she said before adding, "Gavin."

Chapter Nine

THE MILD SCENT of grass and rain filled Holly's senses as she was gently pulled out of the darkness of her sleep. The soft, well-worn sheets of the bed she lay in smelled like the outside, and she curled into a ball, rubbing her cheeks against the fabric as she drifted between reality and her dreams.

She inhaled deeply and noted other scents drifting by as well. Lemon and mint. She hadn't realized how sweetly those scents mingled, and in an attempt to be immersed in them, she moved closer, breathing deeply as her body met another person's warm, solid frame. A body.

A *man's* body.

Gavin.

Holly's eyes flew open, and she fought the urge to bolt away from him, knowing the jerky movement would surely wake him. Instead, she inhaled a careful breath and held it as she stared at her husband's sleeping face.

Exhaling shakily, she watched as his chest rose and fell gently. Really, there was no reason to be startled. She remembered falling asleep, her body pinned straight, as close to her side of the bed as possible without falling off the edge. But her heart was racing. She had never woken up next to a man before, and to see him so close and unaware of her made her pulse flutter.

The longer she watched him, the more relaxed her tense

muscles became. He was really quite handsome, with an upturned, full mouth. It almost looked as though he was smirking in his sleep, and Holly wondered if his facial muscles were stuck like that. He was always grinning at everyone, and she was curious why he should do so. He was certainly friendly, but there seemed something intentional about it.

Her eyes drifted upward, landing on the locks of his auburn hair hanging over his forehead. They covered his eyes, and her fingers twitched and rubbed together at the sudden desire to push his hair back.

The heat emanating from him was remarkable, and she vaguely wondered if she would ever need a fire again with him sleeping beside her. Not that they would be sleeping next to one another again. This was a simple mistake; indeed, they would resume keeping their rooms separate once in London of course. But still, he radiated *such* a heat. The fire had burned out during the night, and she was tempted to get closer to him, but she remained still.

The strong line of his nose, the high planes of his cheeks, and the soft, slightly parted mouth enchanted her. Something about this sleeping man reminded Holly of stories from her childhood about knights falling asleep in fairy rings and being held captive by fae queens. Holly always thought it was rather awful that those knights should be kidnapped, but staring at Gavin at this moment, she found herself somewhat sympathetic to the fairy queens. Unable to look away, she noted his steady breathing and wondered if he was dreaming.

His eyelids flickered and twitched beneath the edge of his hair. Not wanting him disturbed, Holly brought her hand up. Hesitating a moment, she gently tucked the tips of her fingers between his hair and his eyes, pushing it back softly. He inhaled deeply, turning his face in her direction as she quickly removed her hand, only to see his eyes open slightly.

She had wakened him, and she froze beneath his hazy glance. He smiled momentarily, closing his eyes once more before they opened wide again as if just realizing that she was there. She felt her heart flip, and his eyes focused on her.

His mouth parted, as if he were to speak but then he slowly raised one of his hands and brought it to her cheek. Embarrassingly, her eyes closed automatically, enjoying the heat from his fingers, and she was suddenly transported back to the brewery.

His fingers moved to the back of her head, curling into her hair. She thought wildly that he was going to kiss her, and it frightened her to realize just how much she wanted him to.

With painstaking slowness, Gavin pulled her towards him but hesitated for a fraction of a second. Holly sensed his reluctance but wanted him to continue. Bending forward slowly, she stopped just as her lips grazed his, and without any rhyme or reason, she gently nipped at his bottom lip, causing him to inhale sharply. Gavin's grip tightened suddenly in her hair, and he lifted her body, pressing his mouth to hers.

Holly felt her insides melt the moment their lips met. She kissed him back, the gentleness quickly replaced by a desperate eagerness. He tasted vaguely of mint, and Holly pressed against him as his arms moved to her sides. In a single, impressive motion, he hoisted her body up as if she weighed nothing and settled her onto his hard chest. Holly might have gasped if she wasn't so keen on keeping her mouth on his as his tongue swept into her mouth.

All reasonable thought had drifted from her mind like the cold of winter swept away by a spring breeze as Gavin's hands flexed into her back. The softness of her body seemed wholly opposite to the solidness of his. A moan escaped her lips as he held her, her breasts straining against him. Shockingly, she found herself wanting his hands to move down her body, to places she would never speak about out loud, but her mind could hardly focus, for in the next moment, Gavin's entire body moved upwards, pressing the firm length of his manhood into the inside of her thigh.

Holly had never been with a man, let alone held by one like

this, but the desperate ache in her seemed to call out in a way that made it clear exactly how it would go. She wanted to rid them of their clothes, sheets, and coverings and feel his skin against hers. Her fingers gripped at his shirt as desire swept over her. She might have ripped it if not for the faint knocking sound that echoed around her.

Gavin's hands came up to her arms, stopping Holly's unschooled ravishment just as her senses returned.

"Holly!" She could hear the muffled voice of her sister sounding through the wooden door. "Are you almost ready?"

Lost for words, Holly's mouth hung open as she stared into Gavin's dizzyingly heated eyes. He nodded, urging her to answer.

"Y-yes!" she called out, turning her head. "Only another moment."

The distinct sound of girlish giggles faded as the two lay perfectly still. For a moment, Holly wondered if they would continue their interrupted activity but then Gavin lifted her up and rolled her to the side. Swinging his legs over the edge of the bed, Holly watched his back rise and fall, his ragged breath slowly steadying. Without thinking, she reached out and touched his shoulder, but he flinched and stood up, seemingly unable to bear her touch.

"Oh. I'm sorry," she said quickly, but he held out his arm.

"No. No, love, you didn't do anything to be sorry for," he insisted, his tone husky and laced with something that set her heart ablaze. He peered over his shoulder. "But we should get dressed."

"Yes," Holly said, stunned for a moment.

That was twice that she had kissed him, and he had stopped it. Even though she wasn't the type of woman to doubt herself, Holly felt a sudden surge of humiliation. There was obviously something about her that Gavin found appealing, and yet it seemed not appealing enough to fully lose control. Was he just being considerate of the situation? Perhaps he had more self-restraint than she did.

Well, that was a humbling thing to consider.

Aware that he was still watching her, Holly whipped the sheets off her as she launched herself out of bed as quickly as she could. Going to her valise, she pulled out a carriage gown, a simple one that tied in the front, and began dressing.

Holly outfitted herself faster than she ever had, with her back towards Gavin as he did the same. A stilted tension hovered between them, and she feared they might carry it with them all the way to London. Just as they were about to exit the room, Gavin reached for her wrist, stopping her mad dash.

"Before we go, I think we should talk, Holly," he said, more to himself than to her, as her eyes remained low. "I know you want an annulment—"

"We both do," she said firmly. "Don't we?"

He hesitated, and Holly wasn't sure why she was so glad until he nodded, and her hopes dropped again.

"Yes, of course. But with our marriage likely to be reported on by the *Times* upon our arrival, as well as me already informing the Paynes, and well...I don't see how we can go on, pretending that we're not married."

Holly nodded, unsure what to do.

"I suppose we could call on Mr. Armstrong when we arrive. To see how it's progressing," she said tentatively.

Gavin didn't speak for a moment, but when his fingers dropped from her wrist, Holly's heart sank as well.

"As you wish," he said, turning to open the door.

Holly nodded and left the room, descending the stairs to take breakfast below in the tavern, which was decidedly less crowded than the night before. Why had she suggested a meeting with Mr. Armstrong? But no, why *shouldn't* she have suggested it? They were set on an annulment, weren't they? Or should she just accept that they were married, properly, and move on with her life?

Yet it hadn't been her choice, she argued in her head as they climbed into their carriage, taking off only moments after exiting the inn. John had deceived her, marrying her off to a relative he barely had contact with. It was deeply unfair to her—and equally unfair to Gavin. He was left without a say in his own choice of spouse too and besides the outrageous indignity of it all, what about their compatibility? John had barely known his nephew—how could he be certain that they'd suit? It could have easily been a nightmare.

But then again, they *did* suit—remarkably well. Gavin was unwaveringly generous, protective, kind, and patient, with a streak of diplomacy that Holly had rarely ever witnessed in society, particularly in men with titles. How could John have been so sure that their union would be so harmonious?

Puzzled, Holly mainly remained quiet for the duration of their trip. Only upon entering city limits did she let herself be distracted enough to join in on her sister's conversation.

"The buildings are so tall! And there are so many so close together," Katrina said, her nose practically pressed against the carriage windowpane. "How many people must live here?"

"Over a million and a half," Violet said, her head resting against the plush back of the carriage seat. "Or so my brother says."

"My goodness!"

Holly smiled at her sister's eagerness as she, too, peered out onto the busy boulevards. Dozens of pedestrians lined the cobblestone street, seemingly pleased with the sunny weather. The rain had stopped some hours back, revealing a dazzling blue sky just as they reached London. Carriages and carts drove up and down the streets, along with wooden hackneys and men on horseback, all bustling to get to their destination.

"Remember, you lot have an appointment at the modiste later this week," Gavin said, looking at Silas's sister. "I believe Lady Violet here has a standing relationship, Miss Piedmont?"

"That I do."

"Not *the* Miss Piedmont?" Katrina said, her smile growing.

"Ah, I thought we had decided on Mrs. Bean?" Holly said

worriedly.

"Well, we didn't actually agree on anything," Katrina said, looking nervous, as though she had been caught misbehaving. "But when I mentioned Miss Piedmont to Violet, well…"

"She's a fantastic seamstress, I promise," Lady Violet said.

Holly didn't doubt it, but the cost would certainly reflect it.

"Very well," Holly said, conceding that she had lost this battle.

Soon, the carriage turned down a quieter, if not posher, street. The houses here were tall and they all were made from some sort of off-white stone. When their vehicle finally came to a stop, Holly was surprised to find that her gloved hands were tightly laced together. When Katrina and Violet exited the vehicle, her shaking hands braced the carriage door. Then, before she could step down, Gavin's arm appeared.

Having avoided eye contact with him since leaving the inn, Holly let herself peer back at him. Her breath hitched at seeing his kind eyes, seemingly happy to have her looking at him again. It truly was unfair how attractive he was, particularly when he smiled.

She came out of the carriage, and Gavin was beside her in a moment, tucking her hand into the crook of his arm as a pair of passer-byers looked on, greeting them with a smile. Gavin only nodded at them before stepping forward.

The front of their London home was an impressive sight. It was four stories tall, with five windows stacked across each level except the ground floor, with a tall, blackwood door that rounded at the top. The exterior was cream colored, as was every terrace home on the block, making Holly suddenly nervous that she might mistakenly enter the wrong house one day.

Taking a deep breath, she let Gavin escort her toward the door. It was opened by some unseen servant, and Holly's mouth dropped upon entering.

The walls were tall and covered in maroon and gold damask wallpaper. Extravagant artwork, some very close to being risqué, hung from every available inch of wall space. The black and white marble checkered floors stood out against the dozens of exotic potted plants stuck in nearly every corner of the foyer. At least three different décor styles seemed to be battling against one another. Egyptian Revival, Ancient Greek, and French Rococo styles clashed around them, from furniture to vases to artwork. Busts of people Holly had never known lined the hallway, and every spare inch of crown molding was painted gold.

It was garish, to say the least.

"Oh John, whatever possessed you?" she whispered, still rather amazed that someone could have such outlandish tastes in décor. as Gavin pulled her further into the home.

"Having visited him once here, you can imagine my surprise when I saw Kingston House," he said to her as they met a line of servants. "I didn't know he had any taste."

Holly's head swiveled.

"You like the décor at Kingston House?"

"Yes, of course. It's subtle and rather comforting," he said, glancing around. "Quite the opposite of this place. It reminds me of a villa I stayed in once, while travelling through Italy." Holly's cheeks warmed, and he gave her a pointed gaze. "What is it?"

"Huh? Oh, nothing," she said, unwilling to explain that she had decorated Kingston House herself.

A stout man in his forties with salt and pepper hair stepped forward. Dressed in a butler's uniform, he quickly bowed, though he seemed rushed.

"Lord Bairnsdale, Lady Bairnsdale, may I introduce myself. I'm Mr. Spieth."

"Yes, I remember you," Gavin said with a frown as he noted the man's hurried appearance. "Are you all right?"

"Yes, my lord, I—"

"Gavin!"

A high-pitched screech echoed throughout the hallway. Holly faced her husband, whose warm, welcoming manner instantly vanished. His mouth became hard, his hazel eyes grew serious, and his entire body seemed to tense.

"Aunt Marnie," he growled under his breath as the butler hemmed apologetically.

"She arrived this morning and refused to leave, my lord."

A short woman with what looked like a permanent scowl came bustling out of the room to their left. She wore a high-neck lace collar that covered a high-neck gown the color of charcoal. A lace cape that covered her whitish red hair sat atop her head. Her pale eyes seemed both angry and frightened as she stared at the pair of them, arm in arm.

"Is this her? John's final mistake?" she sneered, coming forward as she glared Holly up and down. "Pretty, I suppose, if you were a weak man."

"I beg your pardon?" Holly asked when Gavin stepped forward, effectively blocking her from the old woman.

"I didn't know you were in London, Aunt Marnie. What are you doing here?"

"I only just arrived this morning. You know this was my home before that wretched brother of mine kicked me out and turned it into a house of vulgarity." She squinted around the foyer before her gaze landed back on Holly. "And I came because of a rumor I heard that I pray is not true."

"What rumor?" Gavin asked, moving passed her into an extravagantly decorated sitting room.

Holly struggled to keep her mouth closed as she gawked at the room. Three massive, floor-to-ceiling windows lined the front wall, framed by royal purple drapes hanging from the gold curtain rods. As her eyes scanned the brashly decorated walls, they rose to the ceiling where a shocking mural had been painted. Holly immediately adverted her eyes, making a mental note to avoid this room at all costs.

"Don't you feign innocence, my boy. I received a letter from my dear old friend Mrs. Shoemaker, who has lived these past seventy years a stone's throw from Kingston House. She said she heard it from Mrs. Crompton, who heard it from the elder Mrs.

Payne that there was a story in town going about how my brother hadn't married this woman," she said the last word with disdain. "But that he had stood in for you. A proxy marriage!"

"Is that so?" Gavin said, seemingly calm as he went to pour himself a drink, though Holly noted the tension in his shoulders.

"Well? Is it true?" she asked, her scornful gaze landing on Holly again. "Did my brother manage to ruin your life by shackling you to this... this *woman*?"

"'Ruin' is a rather harsh word, Aunt Marnie," Gavin said, his tone practiced as he brought the drink to his lips, his eyes catching Holly's. "I prefer to see it as 'gifted.'"

The old woman's eyes threatened to bulge out of her head.

"That wicked man! I knew it! I knew he would have his revenge on me!"

Holly was rapidly concluding that her presence was no longer needed. Backing away slowly, she tried to disappear into the hallway when the old aunt pointed a bony finger at her, stopping Holly in her tracks.

"I'm sure you're culpable! What did he offer you? A fortune, no doubt, to try and swindle my nephew—"

"Aunt Marnie," Gavin said, his tone one of warning.

"I didn't know about the proxy marriage, actually," Holly said, lifting her hands as if to deflect the old woman's accusations. "John didn't explain—"

"Didn't explain what? His evil lifestyle? His devious plot to steal Gavin away from me?"

"Aunt Marnie, I'm thirty-one years old," he said, the edge of frustration tinging his voice. "Stop acting like I'm ten and you just won custody."

She turned on her nephew.

"Won? Won? John didn't want you, remember? He practically laughed in my face when I asked for an allowance to bring you up."

"Yes, I am aware," Gavin answered, exasperated. "You've mentioned it."

Holly's frown increased at the old woman's words. John wasn't the type to cast out anyone, and she doubted that he would have refused this woman money to bring up his only nephew and heir. His own flesh and blood.

"Ungrateful boy! And now, when you've finally succeeded in inheriting the title, he's got you shackled to some local wench who is undoubtedly aware of his depraved sexual—"

"That is enough," Gavin said loudly, shocking everyone into silence.

Holly had never heard Gavin speak so forcefully, and apparently, neither had his aunt, who did a very good job at cowering. Just then, a long, irritated meow sounded from the corner of the room, catching everyone's attention.

"That blasted animal," Marnie mumbled, stepping back. "It attacks everyone. I've only been here since this morning, and it nearly mauled me alive when I arrived."

Holly stood on her tiptoes, peering around Gavin's shoulder as she saw a swish of grey in the corner. There, sitting on a green velvet pillow, was the cat Holly had been told she'd inherited. Pauline Musgrove.

"Supposedly it doesn't like raised voices," Holly said, remembering what Mr. Armstrong said, earning her a raised eyebrow from Gavin. Holly gave him a partial smile. "Or so I'm told."

"Gavin, you must listen to me," Marnie tried to interject, but he held up his hand to silence her.

"Aunt Marnie, it's been a long journey and I'd rather discuss this all another time. Now, I'm aware how you feel about Uncle John, but the fact of the matter is Holly and I are married." His aunt huffed indignantly. "And as upset as you are about it, I assure you we're taking all the necessary actions to dissolve it."

"Well, thank goodness—"

"But I will not accept anyone disparaging her," he said, his eyes meeting Holly's. "Do I make myself clear?"

Holly couldn't tear her gaze away from his, a bubbling of hot and cold coursing through her. He would defend her for as long as they were together, but what if they really were to be separated by an annulment? Would Gavin still try to protect her?

"That's because you are a gentleman, no thanks to that wicked brother of mine," Marnie said sourly after a moment. She turned. "And by the sounds of it, you've already begun to handle this farce. Which is good. We don't want John to win."

Gavin rolled his eyes as the old woman turned toward the door.

"Yes, heaven forbid a dead man get the best of *you* by marrying *me* off."

The sarcasm of his words seemed to land directly at his aunt's feet.

"I'll be retiring then, since you've gone into one of your fits," she said. "I'll be taking my old room. I hope John didn't turn it into a brothel."

"You're staying here?" Gavin asked, his tone annoyed.

"Yes, to make sure this one," she nodded at Holly, "doesn't keep her claws in you. Good evening," she said, and with a dramatic twirl, she left.

Holly, woozy from all she had heard, faced Gavin.

"John's sister, I assume?"

"Yes. Aunt Marnie. She brought me up when my father died. After John refused to do so," Gavin said, swallowing the last of his drink.

Holly's brow knitted together.

"Forgive me, but that doesn't sound like John," she said, approaching him. "Why would he refuse to raise you?"

Gavin shrugged, pouring himself another as the tension faded from his shoulders.

"Aunt Marnie always said it was because he was too busy, philandering with his vices or consorting with derelicts. It doesn't matter. I've not cared about it for some time."

"And Marnie was all you had?"

"Yes, though I often wonder if letting me to the elements would have been more beneficial," he said with a half-smile, coming around to an overstuffed chair. He sank into it, focusing on the fire as if lost in a memory. "She was so happy the first week that I came to live with her. She seemed to think that God had granted her a great gift, getting to raise me. It was flattering, I suppose, but I always thought it was curious that her greatest gift was my greatest loss."

Holly held her breath, unsure what to say. Gavin had never told her about his past, nor had John.

"Did you two get on well?" Holly asked after a moment.

Gavin shook his head.

"No. Not after that first week. She had turned bitter not long after my arrival, and for three years all she did was complain and harp on about things that either didn't matter, like the laundress's hair color, or things she had no power over, like not being able to afford things. It made me bitter. I was quite an angry lad myself until I went to Eton at thirteen."

"What happened then?" Holly asked, taking a seat opposite of him. The soft meow of Pauline caused Holly to turn, and she saw the large grey cat stand up.

Stretching her long front legs, the cat arched its back and approached them. Holly thought she might jump in her lap for a moment, but the animal only eyed them with mildly disinterest before leaving the room.

"Strange little thing," Gavin said before peering back at Holly. "To answer your question, I was a bit of a problem. I fought most anyone who rubbed me the wrong way. I was small, due to the scarlet fever that took my father three years prior."

"Oh, goodness. I'm so sorry."

Gavin waved his hand.

"The doctors believed it stunted my growth, but I believe this is the height I was always meant to be. My father was shorter than me. But many of the boys at school thought I was an easy target. They quickly found out I wasn't."

"Why were you so angry?"

He shrugged.

"I thought I had a right to it. I felt I was owed something by the world for having my parents taken from me. Not to mention I had three years of living with a woman who did nothing but complain. That sort of living will seep into your bones, rot you from the inside. There didn't seem to be anything that could make me happy," Gavin said with a smirk, twirling his glass in hand. "Until I happened to find myself in a brawl with Silas Winters and Derek Tremblay."

Holly cocked her head.

"Really? Clara's husband? And the earl?" she asked. Gavin nodded. "And fighting them made you happy?"

"Oh yes. Or at least, it led me to becoming un-angry, if you will. They made me see that my lack of family connections was really more of a blessing than a burden. I had no one to impress but myself, no one to care for. There wasn't anyone to depend on me or to worry about. I was essentially free to do whatever I wished." Though his tone was even, Holly noted a touch of sadness, and she wondered if he actually believed his own words. "Derek told me that if I went around fighting the world, I'd only catch fists. And while Silas had everything in the world, it became clear to me that it couldn't give him peace of mind. Of course, it took me five years to fully grasp these lessons, but by the time I founded the First Merchant Bank of London, I was quite possibly the happiest man in all of England."

Holly smiled.

"What a thing to say."

"It was true. At least, for a while. I was too distracted with work to notice anything else, but then... my old companion came back. I was unsatisfied, angry, and annoyed."

Holly's brow creased.

"Why?"

Gavin shook his head.

"I'm not certain, actually. I thought it was stagnation. I was simply bored with my life, with my work. So, once the bank began turning a profit and I wasn't needed on the floor, I decided to start traveling. A bit of wanderlust cured me, and for the last five years, I've gone all around the world." He sighed, and though he didn't say it, Holly could sense he was unsure. "But even that has lost its luster over time. Strange, as I never thought it would."

Perhaps that was why he seemed so unbothered by their current circumstances. He had needed a change and life had presented him with one.

She wanted to ask him more about that but wasn't sure if she should, so she changed the direction of their conversation.

"And your relationship with Marnie? Has that improved since your childhood?"

He shrugged.

"She loves me, though she's a misguided, miserable old bat. I suppose I love her too on some level. But isn't that the way of it sometimes with family? You can love them, but not like them." Holly could certainly attest to that. "Still, I've never wasted any time trying to make Aunt Marnie happy. The woman is perpetually upset, and I stopped trying to rectify that a long time ago." He stared at Holly, and she shivered. "You can't force people to change."

"No, you can't."

He smirked.

"But I'm a sight more pleasant than her, aren't I?"

Holly smiled back at him and let out a soft laugh.

"Yes, you are."

The pair stared at each other for a moment longer, and Gavin opened his mouth just as Katrina and Violet entered the room, followed by a young woman with bright red hair dressed in a grey gown with a white apron tied around her waist.

"Oh Holly, have you seen this place? It's marvelous!" Katrina said, before turning to the woman behind her. "This is Anne. She said she'll be seeing to us while we're here."

The maid stepped forward and curtsied.

"My lady."

"Hello," Holly replied.

"This house is rather strangely styled, isn't it?" Violet asked as her eyes drifted up. Her head tilted to the side. "My word…"

"Ah yes, it's certainly something," Holly said, standing up. Arms outstretched; she herded the girls out. "Why don't we go have Anne show us to our rooms, shall we?"

"Did you hear all that howling?" Katrina asked over her shoulder to Gavin. "I wonder if it was the cat making all that noise."

"Ah, yes. I forgot about her bad back," Gavin said to himself before speaking up. "Her name is Miss Marnie Winscombe. She is my aunt and unfortunately she's invited herself to stay here for an undisclosed amount of time."

"Really?" Katrina said, looking at Holly. "I thought John's sister had died."

"She is very much alive," Holly said, shooing the girls towards the door. "Now, let's go find our rooms," she said as they reached the doorway. She turned. "Goodnight."

"Good night, Holly," he said, raising his glass as if to toast her as she left.

Chapter Ten

T HAT NIGHT GAVIN suffered one of the most restless periods of sleep he had ever experienced. Nothing could make him relax, and as the night wore on, the only thing he could think about was waking the previous morning in bed next to Holly.

It had been a titillating experience, waking up next to her. Her inquisitive, yet still drowsy blue eyes had shined with curiosity. Her soft, walnut-colored hair fell around her shoulders, with pieces framing her face like a picture. He had considered her a beauty since the first time he saw her, but the way she had looked in the privacy of their room, in the early morning light, had made him feel like he was witnessing some sacred thing. He had reached for her on instinct, wanted to kiss and command her, but he had hesitated.

When she had brushed her mouth against his, nipping at his lip, all senses left his body. He was a man possessed, desperate to touch, taste, and learn every inch of her body with his own. He had nearly spent himself when he pulled her soft body against his—and he likely would have if not for being interrupted.

Gad, it was almost embarrassing how affected by her he was. Gavin had experienced waking up naked to a fair number of women before. He had even been somewhat experimental in his younger years. The wide range of sexual activities he had done would make most men blush, but waking up next to a nightgown-covered Holly had been infinitely more erotic than anything else he had ever experienced. It was utterly foreign to him, waking up next to someone he cared for.

The realization that he cared about Holly had become the singular thought in his mind. When and where it had happened was a mystery, but it *had* happened. He cared for her, and he wasn't quite sure how to handle it.

He had managed his whole life without the care or concern of another person. Of course, there were his friends and the like, but he had never once entertained the idea of having someone rely on him. He had always been too busy with work or his travels. Whenever his old, bitter feelings about life would surface, Gavin would throw himself into something new to drown it out. If he was being honest with himself, he had felt that way about his last trip. Was that why he was so charmed by Holly? Because she was a distraction?

He needed time to consider that.

Unable to remain in bed, Gavin got up and began dressing, glancing at a stack of black leather ledgers that were stacked against the far wall in several towering piles. These were undoubtedly his uncle's journals that had been left to him, though Gavin didn't understand why the former baron had wanted him to read them. He hoped they weren't the stories that had been rumored to be written by his uncle—erotic stories involving all sorts of members of the ton. Gavin wasn't terribly interested in reading something he would later regret. He ignored them as he moved about the room.

Dressed in grey trousers, a matching waistcoat, and a black wool jacket, Gavin exited the lavish bedchambers into the hallway and headed down the opulent, gold-inlay wooden staircase. It was almost painful for the eyes to behold such a garish living space. The dining room wasn't decorated much better, with royal blue walls, forest green curtains, and three crystal chandeliers hovering above a dark wood table ladened with hundreds of pieces of brass and crystal dinnerware.

Three large vases sat directly beneath the chandeliers and were filled with dozens of purple tulips, each petal striped delicately with a faded slash of green as if they had just barely finished blooming. The entire room had seemingly been prepared as though they were expecting royalty to visit, a vast difference from the simple breakfast that Gavin had expected.

Turning, he saw two footmen stationed at the entryway. He needed to speak to someone about all this.

"Where's Mr. Spieth?" Gavin asked the footmen.

Neither moved, other than to let their eyes drift over Gavin's shoulder.

"Yes, my lord?" a voice sounded behind him.

Gavin turned around, his brow lifting as he saw Mr. Spieth beside the dining table. He hadn't been there a moment ago.

"Ah, yes, Mr. Spieth, what is all this?"

The butler didn't move.

"Breakfast, my lord."

"Yes, I gathered. But it's a bit opulent. We aren't having guests this morning, are we?"

"One never knows, my lord. The previous baron was very much devoted to the idea that the people who should follow social directives, rarely do, and thus always wished to be prepared to host. Particularly his friends, my lord."

"Ah, so he was prepared for the prince regent to drop in at any moment?"

The butler didn't flinch at the sarcasm.

"His majesty often did, my lord."

Gavin stared at the man before letting out a laugh.

"Very well, Mr. Spieth, but going forward I don't think we will need such extravagance."

"I understand perfectly, my lord," the butler said with a deep bow. The soft shuffling of slippered feet sounded in the hallway, drawing Gavin's attention, and when he turned back, the butler was gone. Violet and Katrina entered the dining room a moment later, arm in arm and whispering. They seemed to be thick as thieves.

"Good morning," Violet said with a charming smile, eyeing their surroundings. "My, it's as if each room is more opulent than the last."

"Kingston House was like this, before Holly was asked to redecorate it last spring," Katrina said, untwining her arm from Violet's as she went to the sideboard table. "Poor old John was admittedly awful with design."

Gavin turned to face her.

"Holly decorated Kingston House?" he asked.

"Yes," Katrina said, pointing to a serving tray of sausages as a footman helped make her plate. "John practically begged her to do so. Poor Holly had conniptions spending such money on furnishings, but John insisted. He wanted her to do it just as she liked."

"How intuitive of him," Gavin murmured.

Gavin wondered just how long his uncle had considered his plan to marry them by proxy. It must have been at least a year in the making, as he had undoubtedly decided on it when Gavin last visited him. He couldn't help but wonder why. John seemed to have cared deeply for Holly and her family's wellbeing. Perhaps he hadn't been as selfish as Gavin had always assumed in his youth.

A sudden spark of unwanted jealousy simmered deep in his heart. Why had his uncle been so generous to Holly when he had refused his nephew the same amount of generosity? Echoes from his past rang throughout his brain. Aunt Marnie's complaints about not being able to afford food, let allow clothes, seemed engraved in his memory. They were exaggerations, of course—they had never actually starved, nor had they dressed in rags—but the quality and selection of both food and clothes had certainly not been what one might expect in the home of a future baron. John's allowance had given them enough to survive on, but it certainly could not have been very generous, considering how meagerly they lived.

Shaking his head, not wishing to dwell on such blistering thoughts, he turned back to the ladies as they sat at the table. He went towards the sideboard table and brushed off a servant as he fixed himself a plate of poached eggs and toast.

"You both are up rather early," Gavin said, coming around the table to sit as he tried to focus on portraying a good mood. "What activity do you two planned for today that you would need to rise with the sun?"

"Well, Holly has promised that we can go shopping with Violet," Katrina said, facing her friend. "Since she knows all the best shops on Bond Street. Her sister-in-law will be accompanying us."

"The duchess?"

"The duchess to you," Katrina said warmly. "But to Holly and me, she'll always be Clara."

Gavin was aware that Holly and the Duchess of Combe, Clara, had been good friends most of their lives, and having met the duchess before, it wasn't hard to see how Holly and Clara could be close. The duchess had a sweet, if relaxed sense about her and was one of the most patient and gentle women Gavin had ever met.

"I didn't think she or Combe were in town."

"We weren't," a deep, male voice sounded from the doorway, surprising everyone. "We've only just arrived."

"Silas!" Violet called out, jumping up from her chair and hurrying around the table.

Gavin turned to see his tall, black-haired friend greeting his sister. Silas, the Duke of Combe, had once been the gloomiest man in England. A divorced duke, he had a black mark against his name until winning his wife in a shady card game that had scandalized the ton. But something had happened between the broken Silas and the ever-gentle Clara. A friendship had formed, and before anyone knew it, the two were married, and Silas had slowly become one of the more satisfied people in London. Happier than Gavin himself, even.

"Silas," he said with a grin, standing up as the duke hugged his sister. "It's been ages."

"You've been away. Again," he said as he patted Gavin on the back. "I swear, I'm beginning to doubt your nationality. You're out of the country more than you're in it."

"Who wants to be in England during the winter? It's dreadful."

"Not when you have the proper company," Silas said, smirking as he turned to face his wife.

Clara's cheeks turned crimson at her husband's comment.

"Silas," she said with a warning tone. "Hello, Gavin. How are you?"

"Very well," he said with a nod.

"Thank you for seeing Violet to London," Silas said, turning about the room. "We weren't sure how long we were going to be detained, but as it were, our business wrapped up faster than we expected."

"Good news, I hope?"

"Very," Silas said.

"Where is Holly?" Clara asked, stepping forward. "I've been quite anxious to speak with her in person."

"She'll be down any moment," Katrina said. "I just left her room, and she was nearly dressed."

Gavin had hoped to be out of the house before she arose.

"Oh, I'm glad. I wanted to go straight to her after the letter where she told me she had married John, but we couldn't manage it," Clara said, looking at her husband. "We were rather stunned to discover that she had finally accepted one of his proposals. I'm sure she only agreed to appease a dying man, but knowing Holly as I do, I can't imagine it's been easy, especially considering how dear he was to her."

Gavin stood perfectly still as Katrina came forward.

"Oh dear. You do not know."

"Know what?" Clara asked, worried.

Gavin took a deep breath.

"Holly did not marry my uncle," he said.

"She didn't?" Clara asked, her brow scrunching slightly, looking between Gavin and Katrina. "But her letter said otherwise."

"The old baron was only standing in. Holly is married to *this* baron," Katrina said, nodding toward Gavin. "It was a proxy marriage."

Both Clara and Silas stared slack jawed at Gavin.

"What?" Clara asked, confused.

Gavin opened his mouth to explain but was once again interrupted.

"Gavin?" the high-pitched echo of Aunt Marnie's voice carried through the hallway.

Silas's face became drawn as Gavin gave him a pained smile.

"Oh no," the duke said.

"Oh yes," Gavin said under his breath. "Listen, might you care to meet me at White's later? I've a meeting this morning, but I would like to speak with you later."

"Um, yes, of course," Silas said, turning to protect his wife from the coming onslaught that was Aunt Marnie. But the old woman appeared too quickly, dressed more conservatively than a governess in full mourning.

"What is this? Why are there so many people in this house at this hour?" she snapped, no more chipper after a whole night's rest. She squinted at Silas, her eyes widening as she recognized him. A thin smile curved her wrinkled lips. "Well, if it isn't the Duke of Combe."

"My apologies, my lady, but we really must be going," Silas said, eager to be out of the old woman's vicinity. She had always seemed fond of Silas, though no one understood why. Gavin suspected that the duke must remind his aunt of an old beau she had known in her youth, but envisioning her as a young, loving lady always seemed out of his ability to imagine. "Come, Violet."

"Oh, but we were all going to go the shops today. Holly, Clara, Katrina, and I."

"Is that so?" Aunt Marnie said, moving towards the sideboard.

"Off to spend the house's purse on frivolous fabrics and unseemly gowns? It's tragic the way young people fashion themselves these days. Why, when I was a girl, full court dress required at least two petticoats!"

Silas turned to his wife, unwilling to leave her. A calm, sweet smile crossed Clara's face.

"I'll be fine, Silas," she said softly. "Promise."

Gavin was sure his friend wasn't comfortable leaving his wife near the sharp-tongued banshee that was his aunt, but then Clara seemed determined to see her friend. Just then, Holly appeared, seeming slightly startled by how many people met her in the dining room. Gavin ignored the urgent desire to go to her but was silently emboldened when her eyes landed on him and didn't waver.

"Goodness, so much company at this hour," her velvety voice carried throughout the room. She noted Gavin's dress, and her brow pinched. "Are you leaving?"

"Yes," he said, his tone even. "To see Mr. Armstrong."

"Oh," she said with a tight nod. "That is a very good idea, indeed. Hopefully he will be able to help us out of this situation."

Gavin nodded, his mood souring. Clara interrupted Gavin's line of sight as she approached her friend with outstretched arms.

"Holly!"

"Clara!"

The duchess hugged Holly as multiple conversations seemed to break out at once. Silas edged towards the doorway, and with a last, longing look at his wife, he left, prompting Gavin to follow him.

Silas had trouble being in crowds. While his discomfort had diminished somewhat since his marriage to Clara, he still disliked being around too many people. Gavin was quick to catch him before he reached the front door, though, as a footman brought him his hat and overcoat. Silas gave Gavin a strained smile as he pulled on his coat.

"I wasn't aware Marnie was in residence."

"Neither was I. We only arrived last night and she was already here."

"And I didn't know you were married." Gavin shrugged, unsure what to say. "A marriage by proxy? That was a right devil thing your uncle did."

"Yes, well, that is why I'm hoping to catch the estate lawyer at his offices this morning."

"Do you have plans to dissolve it?"

Gavin let a moment of silence pass before answering as his gaze dropped to the floor.

"It would be best to do so."

When Silas didn't respond, Gavin glanced up to see the duke staring at him with a curious expression.

"Well, it would be, wouldn't it?" Silas finally said. "I mean, without either of your consent, the license shouldn't hold up in court."

"Correct."

Another moment of silence passed, and Gavin was sure his friend was thinking something. But in the next instance, he finished putting on his hat and nodded.

"White's then? Noon? I'll send word to Trembley."

"Yes, that should be fine."

Without anything more as a goodbye, Silas left, and Gavin, uninterested in returning to the dining room, decided to send for his horse to be saddled.

He traveled across town to Mr. Armstrong's offices to find out about their pending annulment. It was all he could do to keep himself busy before his bank's offices opened, although he would have preferred doing anything else. When he finally reached the opposite end of town where the offices of Armstrong and Leach stood, he found that only Mr. Leach was there. Evidently, Mr. Armstrong was tending to a matter in court and wouldn't be available until that evening, at which point Mr. Leach promised to inform Mr. Armstrong that he needed to come to Bairnsdale Terrace at once.

Thanking him for help, Gavin left and rode to the First Merchant's Bank of London, on Cornhill Street, near the city's center. It was a neoclassical-style building that sat just behind the Royal Exchange—five stories tall, with an entrance on the corner of the building. It was an impressive sight, but Gavin did not pause to admire it as he entered his place of business.

A long row of wooden desks lined the right-hand side of the building in front of a two-story paneled wall. Mr. Leman, a tall, redheaded fellow and the acting floor manager, was passing behind one of the tellers when Gavin caught his eye. He nearly threw up the papers he was carrying when he saw his boss and hurried down the line of desks at the end of the room, where a set of stone steps led up to the offices.

"Mr. Winscombe! I er, I mean, Lord Bairnsdale," Mr. Leman said, shaking his head at his mistake. "My apologies. I was not aware that you were coming in today."

"Have no fear, Leman. I'm only coming to have a few things collected from the office and sign whatever papers I have left to formally end my tenure with the bank."

Gavin reached the staircase and hurried up them, followed by Leman. Why he was walking at breakneck speed, he didn't know. Perhaps he was trying to outrun the poor mood he had been in since leaving Bairnsdale Terrace that morning.

"Are you certain this is the best thing to do, sir? You and the other partners have only just begun to compete with the Bank of England—"

"I'm already richer than Midas, Leman, and I've just inherited an estate that makes its own fortune. There's nothing left for me to do here, except sell my portion and live happily ever after."

Leman sighed loudly, unhappy with his boss's words, as he followed Gavin into the office. It was an impressive room, with four rectangular windows, looking out over Finch Lane, a little street cut between their building and the Royal Exchange. A handsome, dark wood desk sat at the center of the room, lined with a neat pile of papers, all requiring his signature.

Sitting in the leather chair behind his desk, Gavin got to work. Leman brought him a cup of tea and a plate of mint hard candies as Gavin signed page after page, effectively removing himself from any claim to the bank he had founded.

It might drive someone like Leman mad that he could so easily give up his life's work, but Gavin hadn't ever planned on working his entire life. He had only wanted to make a sufficient amount to carry himself comfortably throughout the rest of his life, and he had managed that tenfold. Now that he had a barony to run, he was too busy to focus on work here.

During the hour it took for him to sign all the papers, several people, from managers to clerks, came in to say goodbye and to wish Gavin luck on his new life as a baron. After finishing his task, Gavin stood up and stretched. Leman hadn't left, instead busying himself with his paperwork in the corner at a desk once used by Gavin's secretary. Leman came over to Gavin's desk and looked sadly at the pile of papers that effectively removed Gavin from the company.

"Will that be all then, sir?" he asked sadly.

Gavin smirked. He plucked one of the mint candies off the dish and tossed it into his mouth.

"I've petitioned the board to hire you as my replacement," he said, ignoring the shock that came over the floor manager. "It will double your work load, but you'll make far more than a floor manager."

"B-but, sir, why?" Leman stuttered.

"Leman, you know more about this bank than most people know about their own mothers. If there was a more capable person, I've never met them."

The floor manager began to shake his head, seemingly unsure how to accept such a thing.

"Thank you, sir."

Gavin nodded, and with a firm pat on the back, he left.

It was a strange feeling, leaving one life behind as another was beginning, but then Gavin was used to the unsteady ground.

There was a comfort in knowing that he had managed before and would do so again. At least Leman would have a better day than Gavin.

He was trying his hardest to find a good disposition, but he could not do it. There seemed to be a familiar dark cloud hanging over his head, and he didn't know how to shake it.

After reaching his horse, he rode back towards White's for luncheon. Riding all over London on an empty stomach, with little sleep and the sexual frustration that had plagued him for days, was doing little to better his mood.

Upon arriving at the five-story, Portland stone building, Gavin felt at home. White's had been a common thread in his life since graduating from Eton. Of course, some thought Gavin was mucking about when he decided to have a career like a working man. There had been a gentleman or two at White's who had suggested he seek membership down the street at the Clemet Club, or one of the other establishments that had no requirements to join aside from a sizeable bank balance. But Gavin was always destined to inherit a title and had ignored those who had turned up their noses when he worked.

Coming around the carpeted corner of the foyer into a vast open room, Gavin saw his friends waiting for him, sitting before a spread of cold pheasant, jellies, jams, and puddings. He picked up a biscuit and bit into it, nodding at Trembley.

"Good to see you, Gavin," the tawny-haired earl said, eyeing his friend with speculation. "It's been a few months."

"Six actually," Gavin said around a mouth full of food.

"Yes," Trembley answered. "Silas here was just informing me that there was a call for congratulations. I had no idea you were planning to marry."

"Neither did I," Gavin said, taking a seat on the plush leather club chair, his back facing the window. "But Uncle John apparently thought it was imperative."

Trembley shook his head.

"What an idiotic thing to do," he said. "Surely he would have guessed that you would have the entire thing annulled." Gavin shrugged. "You are having it expunged, aren't you?"

"If I could find my lawyer," Gavin mumbled, his gaze lifting across the club's main floor.

"It's rather interesting, isn't it?" Silas said. "Inheriting a wife. I never knew it was possible."

"Yes, well, that and a prosperous estate and a dozen or so journals. I don't suppose I have much room to complain."

"Journals?" Derek repeated. "What journals?"

"I don't know. Some ledgers the old man kept for a hundred years."

Derek's brow cinched together.

"Wasn't there a bit of a rumor about the baron being some sort of writer of the erotica?" Derek leaned back. "Supposedly, it was a well-known secret amongst the ton."

Gavin rolled his eyes. So he wasn't the only one to know about it.

"Every peer with a journal thinks he's a modern-day Marquis de Sade," Silas spoke absently. "But I'm sure it's nothing more than a few personal experiences."

"Oh, and I should want to read that," Gavin said sarcastically as he gazed off around the room.

Dozens of gaming tables stood in a wide-open space. The club was quiet for an afternoon, but there were still a handful of men here and there, playing cards or reading the paper. Gavin knew one or two gentlemen personally, while another young man seemed familiar, though his face kept disappearing behind the shoulder of another.

But that wasn't what he was focusing on.

Against the back wall were two sets of doors. The left set followed a hallway that led to the billiards and private card-playing rooms. The ones on the right led to several dozen apartments where members could sleep off their drunken stupor or be entertained by one of the nightingale ladies who frequented the club each night.

Though he had entertained the idea, the moment Gavin's eyes landed on the doors that would lead him to a wench, he frowned. He could go over there and meet his needs, but he knew already that his appetite wouldn't be stated.

He took another bite of his roll and returned his attention to his friends. Both were staring at him in the most agitating way.

"What?"

"Nothing," Silas said, his gaze falling on Trembley.

"You seem not yourself, Gavin," Trembley said. "There's a weight about your shoulders such as I haven't seen in some time."

"There'd be a weight on you as well if you suddenly found yourself married with two dependents, one of which is trying to send my wife into an early grave."

The term *my wife* seemed to vibrate in the air, and Gavin inwardly groaned, preparing himself for one of Trembley's lectures. Only, as he waited, no one spoke.

"It can be burdensome," Trembley said slowly. "But there is a satisfaction that comes with being responsible for those who depend on you."

Gavin glanced at his oldest friend with astonishment.

"Good god, you sound like your father," he said as Silas let out a chuckle, while Trembley only appeared slightly annoyed. "I've no need to find satisfaction in any of it. My peace will be restored once the season is over. As soon as Holly's sister is married, the farm that forms her brother's inherence is restored to functionality, and our marriage is annulled, I should be squarely back where I was before my uncle's meddling."

"And where was that?"

"Alone."

Gavin was sure Silas and Trembley were exchanging expressions. He had tried to make his tone light, but it had come out rather miserable. Though he had tried to make the best of his day, it seemed his dark mood would not release him.

After a moment, Silas spoke.

"An annulment might not be as clear cut as you assume, unfortunately. Speaking from experience, the public can be wildly invasive. Take it from someone who's lived that life."

"You were divorced though. An annulment is completely different."

"Not in the eyes of the ton."

"And I should care because?"

"Well, not you. But Holly might suffer. She won't be accepted. Of course, she'll always have our support, but two people in a city of nearly two million is hardly fair."

Gavin disliked the idea of Holly being snubbed by society, but he knew she would rather have their connection severed. She simply did not wish to marry him, and he wouldn't try to hold on, even if he found the entire thing rather convenient.

He was about to explain as much when raised voices suddenly sounded from one of the gaming tables. All three men turned to see what the commotion was about when a man, whose back was facing them, pushed another, sending him to the floor.

"Gates!" The wide-shouldered man yelled for the factotum, an employee who did several jobs at White's. "Toss this swine out!"

Jeremy Gates, an even-tempered man Gavin had known for several years, appeared, coming down the rounded staircase.

"What's this about?" he asked as several men picked up the youth who had been pushed.

Gavin squinted, unsure if he saw correctly. The partial profile of the young man looked vaguely familiar.

"He's cheating! I saw him move a card up his sleeve."

"That's a serious allegation, Lord Sundale," Gates said, coming around. "Oi! What's your name?"

But before the factotum could get an answer, the accused simultaneously stomped on the foot of the man holding him and knocked his head backward, hitting the other man in the mouth. With a grisly roar, the man stumbled back, releasing the youth, who darted between others as he escaped. Gavin, Silas, and Derek stood as he ran out, but not before his eyes caught Gavin's.

Bloody hell. Was that Jasper? What in the world was he doing in London?

Without thinking, Gavin pushed passed his friends and ran after the young man.

"Where are you going?" Silas called after him.

"Let the house take care of him!" Derek shouted.

But Gavin was out the front doors and down the front steps in moments, staring into the crowded street. Had that been Jasper? Why wasn't he in Eton? And how the devil had he been allowed into White's? He couldn't find the familiar face and, after several more minutes of searching, was caught on the shoulder by Silas's hand.

"What is it?" he asked, concerned. "Did you know him?"

"I don't know. I thought I might."

"He was a young lad," Trembley said, coming down the steps. "Not someone I recognize as friends with either of my brothers. I don't believe I've ever seen him before."

"No, it wouldn't be through them that I know him. I thought it was Holly's brother, Jasper."

Silas tilted his head.

"One of the twins? Clara mentioned that they aren't even eighteen."

"Yes, and he should be in school," Gavin said, peering around. He shook his head, giving up. "Perhaps he was only a lookalike." He sighed. "Well, I'm afraid I must be going. I've got to visit my old apartments and sort out what should be done with them."

"Very good," Derek said.

"Oh, Clara wanted to host a dinner party tomorrow night. Just for us and the families. A pre-season feast, she says. You both will attend, yes?" Silas asked. Gavin nodded. "Trembley? Your mother and brothers are invited of course."

"You'll only have Fredrick's company, I'm afraid. Alfred is still in the Americas."

"Still?" Gavin asked.

"Yes. Although he is set to return in about two months' time. I expect my mother will want to throw a welcome home party for him."

"And maybe you'll host one of your infamous card games?"

Derek smirked but shook his head.

"I'm afraid I've put those days behind me. Besides, hardly anyone would show after all that to-do last year," Derek said, eyeing Silas.

"Yes, well…" the duke said with a shrug as he donned his hat. "Tomorrow night then?"

They all agreed and nodded their goodbyes, disappearing in three directions as they left. Though Gavin tried to focus on what needed to be packed away and what should stay once he arrived at his apartments in Marylebone, he couldn't shake the sense that he had seen Jasper. He would need to inform Holly immediately when he returned to Bairnsdale Terrace.

Having settled on a list of things that needed to be packed away, including his wardrobe, ledgers, and the like, Gavin made his way home. By the time he reached Berkeley Square, the sun was setting.

Upon his arrival, he was informed that dinner was just being served. *Perfect*, he thought as he shrugged out of his coat. He was starving. But it wasn't just Aunt Marnie, Holly, and Katrina at the table. To his surprise, he found Mr. Armstrong was there as well when he entered the dining room. Gavin's gaze immediately settled on Holly, whose pursed lips made him curious.

"Mr. Armstrong," Gavin said, walking down the length of the table. "I didn't know you were coming for supper."

"I only just arrived, and the baroness insisted," the lawyer said, appearing somewhat uncomfortable.

"Yes, I thought it would be nice to have the company," she said stiffly as Aunt Marnie spoke.

"My brother made a fine match for you, he has," she said sarcastically, staring daggers at Holly. "Never in my life have I ever met someone so argumentative."

Gavin sat, suddenly aware of what the tension was about.

"Is that so?" he said mildly, giving his aunt a disbelieving look.

"It is! She doesn't like the fact that I knew my brother far better than she did—"

"I never said that," Holly said, her shoulders straight back as she refused to be cowed by the old woman. "I simply said John and I were good friends."

"He was a fornicator."

"He was a kind person," Holly said, her tone slightly louder as she turned to face Gavin. "But we are at an impasse, it seems."

"Aunt Marnie, I think you should accept the fact that there are plenty of people who quite liked your brother," Gavin said. "As much as you disapproved of him, there were plenty who didn't."

"Animals, the lot of them," she hissed.

He half expected her to continue with a lecturing tirade, as she had done so many times in the past, but to his surprise, she held her tongue. Curious, he wondered if his newly inherited position held her in place. She would not give Holly the respect she deserved as Gavin's wife, but she had been conditioned her entire life not to cross the head of the household. Of course, that had never stopped her from disparaging her brother behind his back, but Gavin suspected that she likely kept her mouth shut whenever she was in his presence.

Gavin took a sip of wine as the first course was served. Onion and beef broth soup was ladled into the delicate, floral pattern bowls before each guest. Gavin inhaled deeply, enjoying the scents of fresh rosemary bread, steamed asparagus, and carrots before turning to the lawyer.

"I'm assuming you've brought good news with you, Mr. Armstrong?"

Shifting uncomfortably as the top of his brow began to glisten with sweat, the lawyer gave Gavin a pained look.

"Actually," Holly said, catching his attention. "Mr. Armstrong has come barring... *interesting* news."

"Interesting news?" Gavin repeated. "What sort of interesting news?"

"Well, my lord, as you know, annulments can only be permitted in the following three cases. Fraud, incompetence, and..." he coughed, "...impotence."

Holly's cheeks turned a gentle shade of pink, and at first, Gavin thought she was embarrassed by the word. But when her hand came up to cover a smile, he had the peculiar sensation that he wouldn't enjoy what came out of the lawyer's mouth. He remained perfectly still.

"It has been a long day, Mr. Armstrong and I'm afraid my patience is not long. Please say what it is you've come to say."

"Of course, my lord. Well, you see, fraud is only described as using fictitious names. If either of you had used a nickname, for example, or if either one of you had signed only part of your name, that might have been enough to lay claim to fraud, but unfortunately it isn't the case. And as neither of you stand to lose any inheritance—"

"This *woman* is using the barony's money to finance her family's lifestyle—"

"And she's bloody well allowed to do so," Gavin snapped. "I will not hear one more word about your misguided worry for this title's spending habits." He turned back, focusing back on Mr. Armstrong. It seemed this day would not end without getting the better of his temper. "Go on, then. What about the fact that neither one of us was consenting? Would that not fall beneath fraud?"

"Yes, and I've tried my hardest to explain that, but... well, it's become more complicated, I'm afraid. Since neither of you appears to be incompetent, we couldn't claim that. So, the only option left would be to claim... well..."

The lawyer scanned between Gavin and Holly, unwilling to speak, but Gavin had lost all patience from the day, and this was undoubtedly the last thing he wanted to entertain. Mr. Armstrong was out of his bloody mind if he thought Gavin would claim impotence.

Standing up, he took the napkin draped over his lap and tossed it on the table.

"I'll take the rest of my supper in my room," he announced, motioning to one of the footmen. He turned to Holly, who was trying to keep her face blank. "We'll discuss our other options later."

The lawyer's eyes bulged as Gavin walked down the table.

"But my lord, what will you have me do?" he asked, turning in his seat.

"I'll have you finish your meal and see yourself out."

"About the marriage, my lord."

"Find another way."

"But if you only claimed impotency—"

"Mr. Armstrong, I've had a trying day and the last thing I wish to discuss, with you or anyone else, is my potency. And as I refuse to claim it anyway, you will simply have to find another way."

"But, sir—"

Gavin flung his hand over his shoulder as he left the dining room, irritation bubbling throughout his body.

Chapter Eleven

HOLLY WATCHED GAVIN leave the dining room without a look back and frowned. She hadn't expected him to be so out of sorts over Mr. Armstrong's information. In fact, she had thought it somewhat humorous, if unfortunate, and had expected Gavin's good humor to make light of the situation. She had even looked forward to seeing his amusement, in hopes to salvage some joy out of this day. Aunt Marnie had been nothing short of a headache all day, insisting on accompanying Holly and her sister. Holly had been amazed at how much she missed Gavin since his departure that morning. When Mr. Armstrong had informed her about the routes to applying for the annulment, she had laughed, though it had been more out of shock than amusement. It was ridiculous and a part of her thought to tease Gavin a bit, but seeing the tension in his gait that evening gave her pause. He was not his usual self, and she was surprised how much that affected her. She wanted to help him but wasn't sure how to do so.

The rest of dinner was uneventful, and Mr. Armstrong left before the last course, apparently uncomfortable with being the reason Gavin retired early. Marnie didn't help either, with her snide comments about how Mr. Armstrong had to be one of the worst lawyers England had ever seen. Katrina quickly removed herself from everyone's presence, retiring once the last plate was cleared. Since Marnie insisted on tending to her sewing in the parlor, Holly decided to retire too.

Only she wasn't tired, and her concern for Gavin continued to grow. Though he left the dining room without much of an argument, Holly had sensed that he had barely kept his composure.

Reaching her room, she debated checking on him as Anne helped her undress and change into her night clothes. He certainly didn't need to be worried about, and she was hardly a confidant of his, but something prompted her to do so.

Dressed in a lace-trimmed nightgown, Holly took the heavy velvet robe on the inside hook of her wardrobe, one of the comforts that John had supplied for his guests. It was peridot green with a tropical bird pattern and far heavier than any of her gowns. Though technically undressed, she tied the gold rope belt around her waist and felt confident that there was more than enough fabric wrapped around her so it wouldn't be indecent.

Knocking gently at the door that separated her rooms from his, she waited to be called in, but the call never came. Concerned, she rapped again, and when he didn't answer, she nearly lost her nerve.

Turning to lean her back against the door, her gaze rose to the ceiling, and she sighed. What was she doing? Obviously, he didn't wish to be bothered... yet they had much to discuss. He even said before leaving the dining room that they would speak later. Well, was it not later?

Convinced that her thin argument was strong enough to be forgiven for her intrusion, she inhaled deeply, turned back to face the door, and gripped the brass handle. Pushing forward, she opened the door and peered into the room.

The bedchamber was dark, save the fireplace before which rested a set of chairs, one occupied by Gavin, who had one leg slung over the armrest while his hand held an empty glass as he gazed into the flames. Holly frowned slightly as she came into the room and realized that he was in a state of half-dress. He wore his shirtsleeves and grey trousers but nothing else. His bare feet gave her the oddest sensation of intimacy. She had never seen a grown man's bare feet before.

Gavin turned slightly, showing only his profile as her attention snapped to his face. He appeared neither angry nor upset, but the room atmosphere felt heavy and sad.

"Gavin?" she said cautiously, stopping as she reached the foot of the large bed.

"Holly," he answered, his tone odd.

She tilted his head. Was he drunk?

"Are you well?"

He turned his wrist, glass still grasped in his fingers.

"As well as possible, I suppose."

The vagueness of his answer concerned Holly. He was being ambiguous, and she didn't like it. He was usually very open when she spoke to him, and she wanted him to be honest.

Coming forward, she sat opposite him just as a giant ball of gray fur emerged from underneath the chair. She pulled her legs up, temporarily startled as it brushed against the hem of her robe, before escaping through the opened door between their chambers.

"Blasted thing won't leave me alone," Gavin said, his attention returning to the fire.

"You know, John left her to me in his will."

"Did he? Good. You may take it with you when you leave."

"I think she may fancy you."

Gavin watched her with evident curiosity as she leaned back against the plush chair. The corner of his mouth was pulled up slightly, and her heart pounded loudly. He seemed more himself, and she wondered why he was always so amused by her.

Taking a deep breath, she brought her hands together in her lap.

"I know Mr. Armstrong's suggestion wasn't exactly what you wanted to hear, but he is trying." Gavin's smirk faltered as his gaze drifted back to the fireplace. Perhaps he didn't want to talk about it? She swallowed and changed the subject. "How was your visit with Combe and Trembley?"

"Fine."

He obviously wasn't in the mood to speak, yet she wasn't willing to leave. He leaned over the arm of the chair, placing his empty glass on the floor. She sighed loudly and his attention lifted back to her.

"Is there something the matter?" he asked.

"You're being purposely obtuse and it's frustrating," she said quickly, peering down at her interlocked hands.

A long moment passed before either of them spoke.

"I'm sorry," Gavin said eventually. "I'm usually better at keeping my dark moods at bay."

Holly tilted her head.

"Dark moods?"

"Yes. If I'm not busy or distracting myself, I can become... well, peevish. And when that happens, I can become outright miserable." He glanced at her. "It's not pleasant. I don't mean to bother you with it."

"You're not bothering me," Holly said earnestly. "Everyone gets into bad moods."

"I don't."

"But you can, if you want."

"I choose not to."

"But why—"

"Because I don't—" he said quickly, but then stopped himself. He took a deep breath and closed his eyes before speaking again. "I have a theory that the difference between a good life and a bad life is outlook. Now, I'm aware that outlook isn't the only factor, but I mean to say that I've known poor men who've led great lives and rich men who do nothing but complain. I never wanted to be the latter and so I decided, a long time ago, not to let myself get in the way of being content." He opened his eyes then and looked back at her. "I don't like being miserable and I chose not to be."

Holly stared at him for a moment.

"I don't think anyone enjoys being miserable."

"I disagree. I think there are plenty of people who like it, who marinate it and surround themselves with others like themselves. But it's not for me."

"I don't think anyone can be happy all the time though," Holly argued. "It would be impossible."

"As I'm finding out," he said, almost under his breath as he turned his focus back to the fire.

Holly frowned.

"What do you mean?"

"Only that I'm realizing that some things don't have a bright side, no matter how much I look for one."

Holly wasn't quite sure she knew what he was talking about, but something about it made her uneasy. She swallowed, suddenly eager to change the subject.

"I'm sorry you were upset about Mr. Armstrong. It's why I came to check on you."

"You needn't check on me."

"But when you left the dining room you seemed irritated."

"Even so, there's no need to worry."

She gave him a strained expression.

"Of course I worry."

"You don't have to."

Holly shook her head, not understanding.

"What do you mean I don't have to?"

Gavin seemed to hesitate for a moment before taking a deep breath.

"No one has ever much worried about me, and I'm afraid it's a wasteful prospect."

Holly stared at Gavin, their eyes not quite meeting as his words sank in. It was an odd thing to think about. Even on her worst day, she was confident that people cared enough about her to worry about her. After her mother passed away, Holly at least had her siblings, and her friends had been great supports to her.

Leaning forward, her curiosity piqued.

"What about your friends? And your family? I know your aunt can be… a lot." Gavin snorted, but Holly continued. "But she's still your family."

Gavin shrugged.

"Is she? We haven't spoken in nearly five years. I hadn't seen her in half a decade until last night."

"Really? Why?"

"We don't get on." Almost automatically, Gavin reached into his pants pocket and pulled out a small piece of wrapped parchment. Holly had become accustomed to his candy habit and waited for him to continue after dropping the small confectionary between his teeth. "I'll always be grateful to Aunt Marnie for taking me in when John didn't, though."

Holly was unsure if she had a right to say anything, but it was the third time she had heard him speak about John refusing to house him, which simply did not make sense. From everything she had learned through her interactions with John, she would have expected his behavior to be the exact opposite.

"Gavin, did your aunt tell you that John didn't want you?"

"Yes, of course," he said. "Why do you ask?"

"Well, it just doesn't make much sense. John was always so eager to help his friends and during our more private conversations, he always made it seem as though he regretted not marrying earlier in life, if only to have a child."

Gavin didn't speak as the information sank in, but the crease in his brow made Holly unsure. She was about to press the issue when he leaned back.

"It doesn't matter, does it? I'm better suited to being alone."

"But you aren't alone," Holly said softly. "Not anymore."

He glanced at her; his hazel eyes steady on her face.

"I will be though. Soon enough."

Holly felt a slight jab of guilt. It was true. She and her siblings would leave as soon as their annulment went through.

She shook her head slowly, her gaze dropping.

"Even still. I should think we would remain friends, after all this is figured out." Gavin didn't answer and so she continued. "I don't know why John thought this was a good idea. I wish I had known about it. I could have talked some sense into him."

Gavin's hand suddenly reached for hers, and to her surprise, she let him as she stared into his eyes.

"You know, I've tried to be indignant about it. But all I can muster up is that, I'm not sorry it happened."

"You're not?" she breathed.

"No."

Holly's heart began to thud hard against her chest as their hands interlocked. The excitement that had filled her body the morning at the inn came flooding back, and she sensed something on the horizon, but she didn't know what.

Nervously, she slowly pulled her hand back and stood up.

"Well, I suppose I should return to my rooms."

Gavin nodded. He exhaled loudly as he stood up himself, coming terribly close to her. Holly's breath hitched as she stared at her for a long moment, and she was sure she was turning all shades of red.

"Good night then," he said quietly, and to Holly's surprise, he leaned forward and kissed her gently on the cheek.

The barely-there stubble of his jawline grazed hers, and her eyelids fluttered shut. The scent of lemon and mint filled her senses, and when he didn't pull back immediately, she felt herself begin to sway.

The slight, slow burn she felt whenever they were near one another seemed to ignite once more. Her eyes flickered open as the heat between them grew, and she saw his hands lifting, hesitating to touch her arms. There always seemed to be some resistance within him, as if touching her would pain him somehow.

Leaning closer toward him, she tried to let him know that she wasn't afraid of his touch. Prompted, his fingers lightly gripped her upper arms as his head lowered toward hers. Their mouths nearly touched when he suddenly stepped back, holding her at a distance.

Holly nearly stumbled, so lost in the moment was she, and when he spoke, she barely registered what he was saying.

"I'm sorry," he said, the faintest hint of self-deprecating humor in his tone.

"Why do you do that?" she whispered, unable to stop herself.

"Do what?"

"Pull away."

She looked down after a moment, aware that she was asking an obvious question. He clearly stopped them each time because it was the correct thing to do, because he was a gentleman. She, on the other hand, couldn't help herself. He was merely doing what she couldn't.

"Because I'm sure I can't keep you," he said, derailing her thoughts. "And if I knew what it was like to truly have you then I don't think I should react very well if I couldn't have you always."

Holly's mouth fell open, stunned at his confession. He wanted to keep her? Why, what a strange, wonderful thing to say. She didn't know why such a response should make her feel so giddy and heartbroken at the same time, but in the next instant, she stepped forward and kissed him.

Something had broken within her. *He wanted to keep her.* Her fingers curled into the front of his shirt as she held on to him, afraid that he might stop her, but his arms came up around her, to her delight and fright.

Glee rolled through her bones as Gavin kissed her. But as soon as he started, he pulled away again.

"Wait. Wait," he said, his tone husky. "What are we doing?"

Holly stared at him, half confused, half mortified. Didn't he know?

"Um, well, I'm actually not quite sure. I've never—"

"No, no," he said quickly, cutting her off, the faintest tone of humor on his breath. "What are *we* doing?"

The meaning of his question dawned on her.

"I… I don't know," she whispered, more to herself than to him.

What *were* they doing? It was a precarious situation they found themselves in and an increasingly difficult one to navigate. On the one hand, Holly had very much wished for an annulment and believed it was the correct thing to do, considering that neither of them had asked for this marriage. But on the other hand, she found it difficult to stop herself from caring about him. Gavin had been more accepting and accommodating than she ever expected. Not only had he proven himself to be good-natured, but her attraction to him only seemed to grow each day.

But it hadn't been her choice. Nor had it been his, and that made her tentative. Could two people, pushed together by circumstance, really be happy with one another? Wouldn't one eventually come to resent the other?

She shook her head, unable to answer her question, but then Gavin spoke.

"I want you, Holly. I do," he said softly. His words sent a shiver down her spine. "But if we continue with this, any talk of an annulment will be off the table." Holly nodded. "Do you understand what that means?"

She did. They would be properly married and bound to one another for the rest of their lives. Although a warm, comforting feeling settled over her at the thought, the practical part of her resisted.

"It's ridiculous," she whispered, her eyes drifting down his face. "We were essentially tricked into this. But I just don't want…"

He nodded, understanding that she was apprehensive. She wanted him, very much so, but the idea of giving up her entire life seemed too great a sacrifice. And she didn't like the idea of Gavin giving up his choice in life just to provide for her, particularly if there was a chance he could find true happiness and love with someone else. It was the same reason she had rejected Mr. Payne's marriage proposal. It didn't sit well with her that someone should have to sacrifice so much for her.

Letting her head drop, she tried hard to ignore the wave of humility she felt. It wasn't his fault, nor even hers, but it washed over her like a wave on the shore, and she pulled away from him.

"I suppose I should go."

But Gavin's hand caught her wrist, and she froze. For a long moment, she heard his breathing as she stared at the ground. He moved closer and, leaning forward, spoke in her ear.

"Not yet."

Confused, Holly noted the sudden display of mischief in his hazel eyes, highlighted by the light from the fire. Leading her away from the fireplace, he walked her to the foot of the bed. Unsure, Holly followed. Leading her to turn, Gavin crowded against her, causing the back of her legs to press against the edge of the bed. He leaned forward, his mouth beneath the hollow of her ear. Shivering, Holly spoke.

"What are you doing?"

"Nothing that will have a lasting effect, I promise," he said, leaning forward. "Now, stay still."

Holly did as she was told, just as Gavin continued kissing and nipping at the column of her neck. Heat bubbled within her core as his hands moved freely over her body, caressing the underneath of her breast as she felt her equilibrium slip.

He leaned her backward and, sensing her uneasiness, he reached for her hand and pressed it against his chest as he stilled. Then he spoke.

"Do you wish me to stop?"

The words seemed to catch in her throat. Holly shook her head.

"Do you want me to continue?" She gave him a hesitant nod. "Relax, love."

Was he asking or commanding her? She couldn't differentiate. She didn't understand what was happening. Never in her life had a man commanded her things while simultaneously ensuring she was in control. It was a heady experience, and she had no doubt that whatever they did would have a lasting effect on her.

Gavin's hands moved down her torso, and he untied her robe. She heard the slight intake of breath as he caught sight of the thin night rail she wore beneath it. A wild part of her was satisfied by his reaction even as his hands moved, touching every aspect of her. Breathing deeply, she tried to ignore her nerves as she shook beneath his fingers, but she froze utterly when he began to pull the hem of her nightgown up.

Detecting her apprehension, Gavin lowered himself and kissed the inside of her knee.

"Don't tense," he said softly, kissing her legs. "Not yet."

"I… I don't know…"

"Shh, I know," he said, continuing his exploration of her.

"But—"

"Trust me, Holly."

"I don't know if I can," she said softly, her eyes shut tightly for fear that he might stop.

But thankfully, he didn't, and she heard the softest of smiles in his voice.

"Then let me prove that you can," he said.

How this particular event would lead to her trusting him was beyond her comprehension as the slow, simmering heat began to roll within her. Before she knew it, his mouth was on her, inside her, his tongue tasting her deepest center as his fingers gripped her hips with bruising tightness, as if he were afraid to let her go.

She bucked at the invasion, equally mortified and ecstatic as he feasted upon her. She knew she should want to push him away, but jolts of pleasure began to spread all over her body and instinctively her hands went to his head. She hesitantly ran her fingers through his hair and the sound he made when she touched him encouraged her. She tangled her fingers into his hair and held him against her as he growled, the vibrations of his voice reverberating into her very soul.

Gavin's hands held her tighter and Holly knew there would be black and blue spots from his fingertips, but she had never felt more willing to be marked. The edges of a storm began to brew within her. Something she had never experienced before. Her heart began racing as sparks ignited all over her skin. It felt as though a cord had been pulled tightly from her head to her toes through the center of her body and Gavin was slowly strumming her into oblivion. She tried to fight off the rising urgency in her body, but he wouldn't relent. One hand reached up to find the peak of her breast and rolled it between his fingers as her world began crashing into her.

A moan escaped her lips as her body convulsed beneath Gavin's expert touch, and she felt suspended out of her body as an outrageous series of thoughts and feelings washed over her. It was cataclysmic. His hands had become firmer still, as if he were trying to hold her very spirit as he came up over her. Strong arms wrapped around her prone, shaking body and he held her against him, his own breath nearly as unsteady as hers.

Holly curled her own arms around Gavin's back as she slowly returned to herself. For several moments, neither of them moved. The only sound was the ragged pants of their breaths and the pounding of their own hearts. Holly wanted nothing more but to hold him indefinitely as she inhaled the faint scent of his skin. How she would ever be able to look him in the eye again, she did not know, but she was desperate to stay there in his arms, on his bed, for as long as possible.

All too soon, Gavin pulled away, standing above her as his wild eyes searched hers. There was something else, she thought vaguely. Something else that could be done, though she knew not what. But just as quickly as she realized it, a shadow passed over his face. His chest rising and falling, he watched her with what she assumed was satisfaction and need. Holly stared at him, wanting to feel his arms around her again, to be pulled against him. Instead, after several moments, he held his hand out to her and she took it. He drew her up to her shaky feet and pressed his mouth to her temple. Holly didn't understand why, but she felt as though he was going to let her go.

"Goodnight, Holly," he said, his tone rougher than she had ever heard it.

Goodnight?

After all that, after the way he had touched her, kissed her, made her experience... well, whatever that had been called, he was sending her away? She wanted to ask him why. She wanted to tell him that she wished to stay, but apparently she had been robbed of speech because all she did was nod and move away from him when his hands dropped from hers.

What was going on? She did not wish to regret that they had done something wildly intimate, but to be so flippant or even cold afterward left her feeling rather shameful.

Holly entered her bedroom without a backward glance, locking the door behind her for her sense of peace. Why on earth had she even gone to his room? She certainly hadn't expected that interaction, yet it was what she had wanted since that morning in the inn. To be held by him, kissed by him. Gavin's mere presence made her warm and giddy. To be handled so gently and so expertly made her feel cherished, yet the way he had let her go made her feel somehow cheap. As if he had been capable of doing that with anyone.

Holly's hand came up and wrapped around the edges of her robe under her neck. Had it meant anything to Gavin? Or had he simply been trying to placate her?

Confused by all the contradictions, Holly crawled into her bed, huddling beneath the covers. It was embarrassing, to say the least, and she was sure she would simply melt beneath his knowing glance tomorrow, but for now, she was in a state of mortifying bliss.

Chapter Twelve

GAVIN WATCHED AS the door shut behind Holly, the definitive noise of the latch locking him out conveying a world of words that needn't be explained. He had surprised her, pleasured her, and discarded her in mere minutes and he knew she would likely be confused for days on end.

But it was all he could do to keep her away from him.

Leaning his forehead against the bed post, a deep groan escaped him. Why in the world had he permitted himself to do that? Surely he could have just pushed her out of his room before things went that far. Hell, he should have locked his door the moment he arrived to his bedchamber, but it had never occurred to him to lock her out. More to the point, he probably should have considered locking himself *in*.

The all-consuming need to touch her, taste her, had seized him the moment she reached for his arm. She cared about him and had confessed it without any issue, which both alarmed him and made him suspicious. Never in his life had anyone admitted out loud to caring about him, and it unnerved him.

Trust me.

He had asked her, commanded her, and pleaded for her to do so all at once and she had complied without any question. He had wanted to sate the ever-growing desire between them, but it had the opposite effect. The desire to give her a release she had never known had been too powerful to ignore and when she had the satisfaction that had rolled through his chest, knowing that he had caused it was the most powerful thing he had ever felt.

Perhaps it was better to leave a man to starve then to give him a morsel. For now, he was aware of what he couldn't have.

Of course, he could have her, again and again, if only their annulment situation was obliterated. Yes, they had been tricked into their marriage, but with every passing day it seemed more and more like he had actually won some sort of prize as opposed to having his choice snatched away.

Yet his feelings on the matter were moot. Regardless of how he felt, Holly would have her choice and nothing else mattered.

A part of him considered trying to convince her that their marriage was a good thing. She was a baroness now, with money and a certain amount of social power. She was as free as she could be, except that she would have to remain married to him. But did she want that?

Was he good enough?

A long-forgotten pain seized his heart at the question. How many times in his youth had he asked that very question? For years, he'd doubted himself. John hadn't wanted him, hadn't even supplied him with enough money for him and his aunt to survive with comfort, and Gavin had longed for things out of his reach. A family, financial independence, the genuine love of another human being instead of being viewed as something to be dealt with. He had trained himself to be a man who did not need any of those things and had thus far enjoyed his solitary life.

But the question he had fought so long to forget resounded in his mind. Was he good enough for someone like Holly?

The deepest parts of him doubted it, but then something about her made him equally confident, which only confused him more. He was strangely self-assured yet doubtful when it came to her. She made him want to beg her for things, while possessing her at the same time. It made little sense, and Gavin wasn't as desperate now as he had once been. He was a different man than the one he had started out as, and he was simply too reluctant to trust anyone. Even Holly.

It was outrageously unfair to ask her to trust him when he didn't even trust himself, but she had and his heart had swelled like never before. Holly's pleasure was his to give and it had physically pained him to stop himself from taking her fully, having wanted to provide her with soul shattering releases over and over again. But they couldn't. Not without her accepting what it would mean if they did so.

When had he become so desperate for her? Surely his uncle hadn't known that a woman of her quality would be nearly everything he had ever privately desired? She was thoughtful and bright, kind and caring. Beautiful and gentle, but with a spine of steel that didn't even cower to Aunt Marnie.

Gavin smirked as he removed his shirt and climbed into bed. He had a wife who was fearless and cared for him and who was just as desperate to go to bed with him as he was to keep her there. But he wouldn't have her forever.

Perhaps she might only need to be persuaded to seeing how well they suit. Their evident physical attraction to one another was palpable and even that was secondary to how easily they interacted with one another. It was as if every part of him responded to every part of her, from intellectual, to practical, to sexual. They were two halves of the same coin.

Now he only needed to explain it to her. But how?

It was a question that plagued him all night and well into the following morning. Sleep had once again evaded him through the night and he was eager to be awake and out of the house before Holly woke. He needed time to consider his argument.

He spent the majority of his day out, only returning to Bairnsdale Terrace that evening to change into his formal wear to attend the dinner party Combe was hosting.

Unfortunately, upon entering, he ran into Aunt Marnie.

"We're to be late!" she squawked the moment he entered the foyer. "What the devil kept you all day?"

"I didn't think you were attending," he said mildly, ignoring her questioning as he handed his coat to the footman.

"Of course I'm coming. Combe said family, didn't he?"

Gavin sighed as he walked past her. Climbing the steps two at a time as he reached the stairs, he called over his shoulder to reassure her.

"I'll be ready in just a few moments."

Hurrying towards his room, he heard the muffled voices of Holly and her sister in the baroness's room as he passed. He wondered bitterly if she would insist on wearing one of her mourning gowns as he entered his room, finding his formal wear all ready for him.

Dressing quickly, he tried to focus on the fact that he would be amongst friends tonight. Perhaps Combe and Trembley could offer him some advice on how to handle the situation he was in with Holly, even though he doubted he'd be able to explain it. Still, once his cravat was tied, he left his room, hurried down the stairs and found all three women, wrapped in formal fur lined coats, waiting for him.

"Shall we?" he said with a nod, stretching out his arm for Holly.

She took it, albeit gently, as they led the way to the carriage. Blessingly, no one seemed much in the mood to speak during the ride to Combes, which was really only a few short minutes away.

By the time they arrived to the four-story white stone house, a strange atmosphere had settled over their company. It seemed everyone was emanating a sort of excitement. Even Aunt Marnie's usual scowl seemed lessened, most like because the Duke of Combe's London residence was one of the finest in all the city. Though Gavin had been there a number of times, it still held a wild fascination for most of the ton, including the ladies. But while Holly, Katrina and Marnie stared out of the carriage window, a pit seemed to grow in Gavin's stomach. Somehow he sensed that this night would not be the easy gathering of friends that he expected.

The carriage door opened and they filtered out one by one. Holly took Gavin's arm again, and he escorted her in through the glossy black door of the manse. They were greeted by a butler, who took each of their coats and wraps before leading the way to the parlor.

When Holly pulled back her hood and turned her back to the butler so that he might take her heavy coat, Gavin expected to see her usual black frock, but to his surprise, she was wearing the most brilliant emerald-green gown that made him lose all concentration.

Gold leaves had been embroidered under the bust and up around the short, slightly puffed sleeves. The neckline was low, edged with some gauzy gold trim that barely hid the roundness of the top of her breasts, making it appear as if she were showing more than she was. Tiny, shimmering beads were scattered across the fabric, making her appear as though she were some garden queen. Emerald and pearl pins adorned her walnut hair that had been styled with the majority pulled back into a chignon, with several curled pieces framing her face.

His absorption in his wife must have been noted, for Holly appeared uncomfortable after a moment or so. Clearing her throat, she came forward and spoke, unsurely.

"Is it… is it not to your liking?" she asked quietly, so that Aunt Marnie and Katrina did not hear.

"Excuse me?" he asked, his voice husky.

"The dress, I mean."

"No, it's… it's very much to my liking." He paused as his eyes roamed over her. "I didn't not think you could have a dress made so quickly."

She smiled.

"It wasn't made for me, actually. Miss Piedmont had a number of gowns finished for another lady who left London rather unexpectedly. So, she had a number of dresses, just my size, as it were." Holly's cheeks turned slightly pink. "They were cheaper, since they were already made and I confess, that is why I bought them as the colors are darker than what I prefer, but I quite liked this one." Her hands moved down to her hips and she gently gripped her skirts, as if to display them.

"It's stunning. You're stunning," he said softly. "But I told you, you needn't worry about spending money on clothes."

"And you needn't worry about going to the poor house because of my spending," she countered with a grin.

She took his arm and Gavin's mind slowly began to work again. He turned to follow the butler as the heat of Holly's fingers coursed down his forearm.

Was she always so considerate? And since when had the style of gowns become so daring? He could barely concentrate on his own footsteps, knowing that she was dressed so alluringly.

Consumed in his own thoughts, the butler reached the doorway to the parlor and bowed before announcing their arrival as they entered a room full of familiar faces.

"The Baron and Baroness of Bairnsdale," he said with a nod. "As well as Miss Margaret Winscombe and Miss Katrina Smyth."

The Duchess of Combe, Clara, nearly skipped across the room as she came forward to embrace Holly, who had pulled away from Gavin. He was sorry to release her, but reassured to see how unencumbered the two women were in their embrace. No amount of fortune could take away their gentle country charm and Gavin was quite taken with it.

"I'm so glad you came," Clara said, her chin tucked over Holly's shoulder. "And Katrina! My, you look just the perfect young lady. You will be the pride of Lincolnshire at your debut."

"Thank you, Clara," Katrina said with a deep curtsy just as Violet entered the room, her smile genuine at the sight of her friend.

"Oh good! You've arrived," Violet said, taking Katrina's arm. "Fredrick and Lord Trembley should be along any minute. I can't wait to introduce you to Fredrick," she said with a loving sigh. "He's quite brilliant."

"When you aren't sparring with him over literature," Silas

said from behind a small pink chaise lounge sat in the center of the room.

Violet gave her brother a teasing glare, just as Derek and his brother Fredrick arrived. Once the butler announced them, Violet was quick to introduce her fiancé to Katrina and Holly.

"A pleasure," Fredrick said to Katrina, his tone light as his gaze fell on Holly. "And Lady Bairnsdale, it's wonderful to see you again. We met last summer at Kingston House."

"We did," Holly said, recalling the house party. "How do you do?"

"Very well," he said, turning to the man next to him. "May I introduce my brother, the Earl of Trembley."

She curtsied before the earl, whose appearance was similar to his brother's, though the earl was taller.

"Gavin has told me so much about you," the earl said. He reached for her hand and pressed his lips to her knuckles. "But I'm afraid his description hardly did you justice."

"That's very kind of you to say," Holly said, blushing.

Though it was a simple gesture, a custom of long standing between gentlemen and gently bred women, Gavin felt the oddest twist in his gut as he stared, unimpressed with his wife and his friend's introduction. Instinctively he moved between them, effectively separating Holly from Derek, who gave his friend an odd gaze.

"Gavin, you didn't tell me that you married one of the loveliest creatures this country has seen," he said, oozing charm while Gavin felt the prickling of irritation grow. "She is a vision."

Holly's blush deepened and Gavin felt suddenly murderous.

"You are too kind, my lord," Holly said.

"Yes, Trembley," Gavin said, his tone gruff. "Stop."

The simple command caught the earl's attention as a single brow lifted. Holly's smile fell away and she looked as though she was about to speak when Aunt Marnie's voice sounded behind them.

"Ah, Trembley, still flattering everything with a pulse I see," she said, holding out her hand. "Very well. Do you worst."

"Miss Winscombe, what a pleasure," Derek said through his teeth as he took her hand and bent over it. "I wasn't aware that you would grace us with your presence."

"Of course. The weather has been fair and isn't attacking my poor bones. Now tell me, Combe," she said as she turned around the room. "Who decorated this parlor? It is just the understated, tasteful style that is needed at Bairnsdale Terrace."

"I believe my wife would be better suited to answer that question."

"Nonsense. I wish to hear it from you."

As Aunt Marnie crowded Silas, effectively forcing him to escort her about the room as she rambled on about paint colors, Clara smiled. She was obviously very entertained by the brash old woman.

"I should rescue him shortly," she said softly to Holly, though loud enough for Gavin and Derek to hear. "But I think he should entertain her for a moment. I've heard she is fond of him."

"She always has been, for some reason. Supposedly Silas reminds her of someone from her youth. Maybe Sir Walter Raleigh," Derek said, causing Clara to hide a sudden peal of laughter. He turned to Gavin. "I didn't think she would still be staying with you."

"What am I to do with her? I can't very well throw her out," Gavin said under his breath. "Once I figure out how to get her to leave and go back to her house on Park Lane, I'll be a happy man. But she refuses to leave Bairnsdale Terrace for some reason."

"You're a good nephew, Gavin. Far more patient than I would be."

"Yes well," Gavin said, feeling annoyed when Holly's hand touched his elbow.

"It is kind of you to care for her."

The tight, prickly tension in his stomach released suddenly and a ridiculous feeling of pride filled his chest. *Good god*, he thought. It was unfair how much her words could govern his mood.

"Come, Fredrick," Violet said to her fiancé. "I wish to know your opinion about the flowers…"

Violet, Holly, and Katrina fell into a conversation about floral arrangements, while Fredrick tried to appear similarly interested. As charming as the Trembley brothers were, Frederick was wholly smitten with Violet which allowed Gavin a break in the ridiculous feeling of jealousy that had consumed him.

Why should he feel jealous? It made no sense. Derek was hardly the sort of man to betray his friends and Holly was already married, wasn't she? Yet the flattery had been almost too much for Gavin to bear, and he found that he was equal parts prideful and jealous for the remainder of their time in the parlor.

When dinner was announced, the guests followed Silas and Clara into a brightly lit, peach-painted dining room, adorned with wall sconces made of amethyst and brass. Only one portrait hung in the room, above a large marble fireplace behind the head of the table. It was a painting of the duchess, wearing a white silk gown, standing in front of a stone baluster set before a wooded country estate. It had been done to perfection and Gavin noticed Silas gaze up at it in fond admiration before turning around to take his seat.

It was obvious that the duke was besotted with his wife and Gavin wondered if he had found it difficult to allow himself to love so deeply after the disaster that was his first marriage. Gavin was sure he wouldn't be able to trust anyone after what the duke had gone through.

Conversation flowed freely between the guests and though Gavin was unusually quiet, he did enjoy how readily accepted Holly and her sister were by his friends. Of course, Clara and Holly had been dear friends for years. Trembley, who had initially been leery about Combe's bride, had come to recognize that Clara was rather perfect for Combe and the two had developed a friendly banter that often put the duke in a bemused state. Meanwhile, it did Gavin's heart good to witness the others' kindness towards Holly.

Except, of course, for the quips they all endured from Aunt Marnie.

For a woman so focused on female propriety, she certainly didn't adhere to her own stifling rules. For instance, it was custom that ladies drink their wine watered down and never ask for more than one glass during a ball or soiree. A dinner party might be different, but Aunt Marnie had already consumed three glasses of wine and did not seem to be slowing down. Instead, she simply kept interrupting conversations that were happening around her, as if her opinion was wanted by all of them.

"When does your brother arrive home from the Americas, Trembley?" Silas asked between the soup course and the main course. "He's been gone for nearly seven months, hasn't he?"

"He has, and the fool won't stop sending mementos home from every new place he visits," Derek said, turning to Gavin. "Speaking of which, how do you like those lemon candy things?"

Gavin's brow raised.

"Were they from you?"

"Well, my brother. I tried one and despised it, but I remember you always had a penchant for sweets."

Gavin grinned.

"I've enjoyed them immensely. Send my thanks."

"I will—"

"Tell me, Lord Trembley, have you held any of your famous card games recently?" Aunt Marnie interrupted loudly as she took another sip of her claret.

"Ah, no, madam, I have not. Not since... well..."

"Since the duke here won himself a wife?" she asked, glancing at Clara. "Such high stakes. It's no wonder you've canceled your tournament."

Gavin turned towards her.

"Aunt Marnie," he said with a warning.

"Yes, well, it was a foolish pursuit. And considering what occurred at the last game," Trembley said, giving a sympathetic look to Clara, "I decided it was best to conclude my involvement in gambling."

"Is that so? I should let you know that I find it highly insulting that you never considered hosting a card game for the ladies of your social circle." Aunt Marnie hiccupped, evidently relaxed by the wine. "It wasn't very sporting of you."

"My mother actually used to host one for her and her friends."

"Really?" Aunt Marnie said with interest.

"Yes, but she hasn't done so since my father passed away."

"Oh. Hmm, what a pity."

It was clear that Aunt Marnie's dismay was over the absence of the card game, not the death of Trembley's father. Gavin cleared his throat, hoping to deter his aunt from speaking again by changing the subject.

"This is a potent vintage, isn't it?" he asked, holding up his own glass. "Is it French, Silas?"

"I'm afraid so," the duke said. "Although I've been more inclined to the Italian wines recently."

"Posh, this is a fine vintage," Marnie said with a hiccup, staring at Gavin.

"I always preferred French to Italian myself," Clara said, glancing at her husband with a smile. "I've tried to prove French superiority, but Silas refuses to concede."

The duke smirked back at his wife.

"Because you are wrong, my dear. Italian is better."

Missing the obvious playful tone between the two, Aunt Marnie leaned forward.

"You should not be so opinionated, my dear," she said to Clara. "It isn't becoming of a wife." She took a sip of wine before continuing. "And with all the annulment talk going around London these days, I would be worried if I were you."

Clara smiled tightly, though her eyes bounced back and forth between Aunt Marnie and the duke. Gavin groaned inwardly. His aunt was getting in her cups. He needed to get see her out of the dining room under some sort of false cover.

"Aunt Marnie, would you mind—"

"Did you know that these two," Aunt Marnie said, gesturing her glass at Gavin and Holly, "are getting an annulment? They have a lawyer and everything."

Everyone around the table froze. Though Gavin had confided in his friends and Holly no doubted had done so with hers, it was an inappropriate thing to bring up during a dinner party.

"Aunt Marnie—"

"We are not seeking an annulment," Holly said quietly but firmly, effectively silencing Gavin as everyone faced her.

Aunt Marnie hiccupped again, her brow scrunching.

"Yes you are."

"No, we are not."

"Yes, the lawyer said... um," Aunt Marnie said, waving her hand to her left. "Armstrong, was it? He said that, um…"

"The lawyer's suggestion was to claim fraud. We cannot. And as neither one of us is incompetent, we are unable to file." She looked at Gavin. "As it is, there is no way to proceed."

Everyone stared quietly at Holly while Gavin tried to settle his pounding heart. After a moment, Clara leaned forward.

"Obviously, we would all be very happy for you both if this was what you wanted." She paused, staring at the both of them. "*Is* this what you want?"

Gavin knew the question was directed at the both of them, but he waited for Holly to speak.

"Yes. Yes it is," she said softly and picked up her fork, signaling the end of the topic.

Apparently Gavin's grand plan of convincing her to stay married to him was not needed, for Holly had decided to do so on her own.

Chapter Thirteen

The remainder of the evening was spent in pleasant enough conversation without mentioning Holly and Gavin's marriage again. It was as if the scene had never happened, but Holly knew a significant shift had taken place. She witnessed the intensity of Gavin's stare once dinner finished and they readied for their departure. She gently pulled Derek away from the rest, as she was interested in learning the name of the American candy manufacturer he had mentioned so that she could order more lemony mints for Gavin as a surprise.

"Of course," Derek said with a friendly smile. He dipped his head close to her ear. "I shall send over the package and the letter my brother wrote so that you can send for them straight away."

"Thank you," she said as he straightened back up.

"My pleasure," he said, taking her hand to bow over it. "It was an interesting evening, my lady. I'm glad to have finally met you."

"You as well," she said with a dip of her chin.

Looking across the room, Holly saw Gavin's dark face, glaring at the earl's back as he moved away from her. Unease rattled throughout her body. Was he upset with her for declaring outright, in a room full of people, that they would indeed remain married?

But if he was upset, why hadn't he said something? Was it

just because he was too good a person to make her out to look like a fool in front of their friends? Oh, what a mess she made. Why had Marnie opened her mouth? And why had Holly risen to the bait?

Never in Holly's life had she met a more disagreeable person. She certainly had a high opinion of herself, which would have been bearable if that was her only flaw, but how she spoke about Gavin had bothered Holly greatly. She made it seem like she was somehow a presence in his life. She practically demanded compensation for raising him, but wasn't that what the family was supposed to do? Holly had done it, and never once had it ever crossed her mind to seek payment from either of her siblings for doing so. Family took care of family. That was it. But Marnie had seemingly done so out of spite.

Holly couldn't figure it out. Why hadn't John not fought harder for his nephew? Indeed, he had to know what sort of woman his sister was. Holly wondered if there wasn't some sort of letter stored somewhere detailing the situation regarding Gavin's guardianship when it suddenly hit her.

His diaries.

John had kept extensively detailed accounts of his activities for all his life. Perhaps something was written in those journals that could better explain why he had given up Gavin to his sister.

As the carriage arrived back at Bairnsdale Terrace, Holly, Katrina, and Gavin exited and entered. Holly was sure Gavin was following her and her sister, but when they reached the second landing on the staircase, she saw he wasn't behind them. Deflated somewhat, she tried to hide her worry and retired to her room where Anne was waiting to help undress her.

Reaching around her neck, Holly unclipped the pearl and emerald choker Anne had brought earlier that evening. It had been part of a small collection of jewelry that had been gifted to her upon her arrival. The pearl and emerald parure set also included a bracelet, ring, and a pair of earbobs, though Holly had only opted to wear the necklace, which she now placed into a small rosewood box.

The evening had been a success, particularly for Katrina, who had managed to impress and withstand the company of some of the most powerful men in the realm, and Holly couldn't have been more pleased.

Except for the tension that had grown between her and Gavin since dinner.

Holly sighed as she stared into the fireplace. She hadn't meant to make such a proclamation, but Marnie had been so sure that she and Gavin didn't suit that Holly's spite got the better of her, and she had spoken without thinking, simply to hush the woman up. But Gavin's eyes later that night when she spoke with Trembley told her he wasn't pleased with her. And he was well within his right to be upset. It wasn't fair for her to say such a thing without discussing it first. He likely wasn't too thrilled to be saddled with a wife he had hoped to be rid of by the end of the season.

Still, Holly was surprised when he came through the door that connected their rooms. She knew he would want to discuss her outburst, but she had assumed he would wait until the morning. Seeing the displeasure on his face made her stiffen her spine.

"Holly—"

"I know it wasn't my place to say that," she said quickly before he could start. She held up her hands to stop him from talking. "But I didn't know what else to do. I know she is your aunt, but I don't think that gives her the right to air our business the way she did. And while I spoke in haste, everything I said is the truth, isn't it?" She spoke quickly. "Without a notice from the Catholic church, our marriage cannot be annulled. And who knows how long that will take? Months? Years? Are we to live, married, for a decade before either of us are permitted to move on? So, while I should have discussed it with you first, before announcing it to everyone, I don't believe anything I said was technically wrong."

Gavin watched her, his brow creased.

"You've... Wait a moment. That's not what I wish to discuss."

Holly tilted her head.

"It's not?"

"No."

"Then what do you wish to discuss?"

"I want to know what you were talking about with Trembley."

Holly blinked. That was unexpected. What could her silly conversation with Trembley matter compared to the fact that she had effectively decided, without so much as a word from Gavin, to remain married?

"I beg your pardon?" she asked with a frown.

"After dinner, you were speaking with Trembley in the parlor. About something private, I assume. I would like to know what it was about."

"Oh," Holly said, her cheeks warming beneath his gaze. "Why do you wish to know?" She had hoped to be able to present the candies to him as a surprise.

To her surprise, Gavin's nostrils flared slightly as he began to pace, arms held behind his back.

"I should have guessed, although I must say, he's got some nerve."

"Who? Trembley?"

"Of course."

"What are you talking about? Wait, Gavin."

But before she could continue, he turned, stalking towards her, coming within inches of her.

"Just because our marriage was set up doesn't give him the right to bother you with his lecherous behavior."

"Lecherous?" Holly repeated, stunned. "He wasn't being lecherous."

"Wasn't he?"

He glared at her, and for the first time since meeting him,

Holly realized he was genuinely upset. And if she wasn't mistaken, it was because he was jealous. Jealous that she had been talking to his friend.

A strange, guilty pleasure unfolded within her. How silly it was to be both annoyed and pleased with his reaction. But she didn't want him to be jealous, especially towards a friend, so she smirked, lighting a fire in Gavin's eyes.

"What?" he asked heatedly.

"It's a secret."

That was the wrong thing to say, for in the next instant, Gavin's hands were on her arms, holding her firmly in place.

"I'll not have secrets between my wife and some bas—"

She couldn't help but let a small laugh escape, both amused and wildly worried. He was indeed infuriated now as he glared at her. "Bloody hell, Holly, what is so amusing?"

She brought her hands up to his face, and though he flinched away at first, she held him steady.

"I was asking Trembley for the name of the confectioner who makes your lemon and mint candies," she said softly. "That is all."

He stared at her for a long moment, evidently confused.

"Why?"

"Because I wanted to get you some more, though you've taken the surprise out of it." She shook her head. "You're not a very good sport about secrets, are you?"

Her playful words didn't seem to sink in. He was watching her with a perplexity that unnerved her, and suddenly she was very sorry for having teased him.

She was about to apologize when he suddenly pulled her against him and kissed her hard. Holly felt as if the air evaporated in her lungs. This wasn't like the other kisses they shared. This was something else. Something deeper, stronger. When an undetermined sound escaped her lips, she felt him pull away, kissing and nipping at her ear. His hand came up to her neck, holding her in a positively possessive way. Her eyes closed as he spoke.

"I don't know what you're doing to me, Holly. I don't like it."
She nodded, knowing exactly how he felt. "I'm rarely the type of
person to be out of sorts. I've worked very hard to maintain an
even temper and good nature for most of my life. I am not prone
to jealousy or fits of whatever this is," he said, looking down at
her. "But my god, if I am not tormented by this…"

Gavin's mouth found hers again, and she eagerly moved her
body against his, her hands exploring the large expanse of his
muscular back. It was a bizarre experience. Holly had never felt
so sure, so comfortable, while also terrified. She didn't know
what she was doing and only had the instinct to follow, but the
thoughts and desires running through her mind were far too
outrageous. And yet, being with Gavin made even her most
scandalous ideas seem perfectly reasonable.

She should say something, should explain that she didn't
know what she was doing, but Gavin seemed to read her mind.
He pulled back ever so slightly, his forehead resting against hers
as he spoke.

"I need you to tell me to stop, Holly," he said, his eyes closed
as a pained expression passed over his face. "If this isn't what you
want, you need to tell me, because I'm not going to be able to—"

"Don't stop," she whispered breathlessly against his mouth
before kissing him.

That was all Gavin needed to hear, apparently. He seemed
emboldened at her words and picked her up in a sweeping move,
which caused her to gasp. She clutched her arms tightly around
his neck as he continued peppering kisses across her face.

Holly was aware of what he was feeling. It was as if a dam
had broken. For weeks there had been a thread running through
them, an intangible thing that seemed to hold them together, and
it had finally been brought to light.

As he laid her on the bed, his mouth moved down her neck
and, to her mortified satisfaction, her breasts. Never in her life
had she experienced such a sensation, and she bucked her hips
upward at the feeling. He suckled and teased her until she was

panting by the time he pulled away.

The petulant part of her moaned with discontent as he removed himself from her, but in the next moment, he was undressing, and she closed her mouth to watch him. His eyes were locked on hers, but her gaze dropped to his chest. Some of the tenant farmers in the summer months had removed their shirts in the blazing heat, but they had been so far away, and as talented as the master painters were, none had ever captured the vigor that seemed to be radiating from Gavin.

Rolling his shoulders as he removed the clothing, he bent down over her, his eyes boring into her. His mouth dropped to hers, and with deliberate slowness, he kissed her, but only until she kissed back. Then he pulled away, causing her to groan once more. Then, that irritating smirk appeared, and she was exasperated and charmed.

"Easy," he whispered. "You'll rush it."

"Yes," she said, almost pleading. "Please."

But he shook his head.

"No. It's better when it's slow."

Holly was sure he was lying, and even though she had half a mind to argue, she really had no experience, except that time he... Her entire body suddenly warmed at the memory, and it must have been displayed on her face, for Gavin's grin widened though his eyes turned dark.

"Yes, love, you'll have that again."

Holly wanted to shrink into the bedsheets beneath her back, but instead, she simply closed her eyes and enjoyed the slow, torturous examination beneath Gavin's hands. He was pretty thorough, and as each piece of fabric was removed, he placed a dozen kisses on her exposed skin.

Soon, she was completely naked, and Gavin had successfully kissed every inch of her. But the unbearable heat that had built within her made her quiver at every gentle touch.

He came up over her then, teasing her mouth open as his hand snaked down her torso. His fingers moved between her legs, slowly moving inside her, and her mouth opened. He licked at her lips as he rhythmically pushed and pulled his finger inside her.

She felt the same extraordinary build she had experienced days ago begin to simmer in her belly as he touched her, and she was sure she would explode soon when he removed his hand, leaving her again deflated.

"Gavin," she said pleadingly.

"Yes. Say my name," he said into her ear. "Beg me for it."

"I can't."

"But you can. You already are."

"Please. Just do it."

"I'm getting there, love. But I had to make sure you could fit me."

Holly's brow furred when he suddenly moved, and she felt a significant invasion enter her. She gasped and wrapped her arms around his neck as his arms moved beneath her, holding her close.

"Easy, my love."

Holly nodded silently, and after several minutes, the sting subsided. She was sure her release had disappeared, but the moment he began to move, just as his fingers had, Holly felt a wash of giddy heat splash over her. Nothing in her life could compare to this moment, and she began to move with Gavin. He grabbed her hand and kissed her fingertips. He forced her hand to his chest and held it there as he kneeled between her thighs, pumping into her with a quickened pace.

Holly was concupiscent. No image had ever been produced that was more sensual than Gavin knelt before her, shirtless, moving inside her. Without warning, sparks began to light all over her body, and her back arched involuntarily as the same euphoric feeling crashed into her. Only this time, it didn't disappear as soon as it came. Instead, it rolled through her like waves, and she was vaguely aware of Gavin's body, coming back down over her, squeezing her against his chest as he convulsed.

The hazy aftermath of lovemaking was so heavy that Holly was barely awake when she felt Gavin's warmth leave her. Humiliatingly, she felt a warm, wet cloth being swiped between her legs, and she refused to open her tired eyes to witness it but was grateful when Gavin returned to her moments later. Slipping beneath the covers, Holly tucked herself against his chest and, huddled together in a gentle embrace, fell asleep.

Chapter Fourteen

G AVIN WAS IN a deep, blank state of blissful slumber when he became aware of the room around him. He frowned, fighting to go back to sleep and rubbed his face into the pillow to hold at bay the temptation to wake up when he recognized Holly's soft, silky hair beneath his cheek.

Opening his eyes, he saw the walnut-colored hair of his wife spread out all over the place. It covered her face, the pillows parting on either side of her bare shoulders. For a moment, he was stunned to find Holly sleeping next to him. Still, having immediately passed out after cleaning her after their lovemaking, he had fallen into the most profound, soundest sleep he had ever experienced.

Inhaling deeply, he found that there was never a more pleasant scent than that of her hair. It smelled faintly of lavender water. She must have sprayed it in the night before because all evening at Combe's, he had been distracted by it and wasn't quite sure where it had come from.

Last night had been an eye-opening experience. Holly was protective of him, and though she needn't be, he found he quite liked the sensation of it. Of course, he hadn't realized it until he had learned the truth of why she had sought out Derek to speak in private.

She wanted to get him a gift.

The realization had broken over him in a way he had never expected. He was instantly at her service. Gavin was eager to give her anything, provide anything to her. It was foolish to be so taken with a small act of kindness, but Gavin wondered if he hadn't been predisposed to his reaction all his life.

He had longed for this, a need to belong to someone—to have someone wish to claim him, look after him, cherish him. It had been something he had beaten down for years. But now, it seemed to flow within him. He wanted to be loved and not just by anyone. He wanted to be treasured by Holly.

Staring at the curve of her shoulder as she inhaled and exhaled slowly, he wondered if he had been given an ounce of genuine, untampered affection in his life if he might have been able to stop himself from falling at her feet. It unnerved him how much he was in her control, and he knew he needed to get a hand on the situation should she take it upon herself to become some sort of controlling wife, but even as he thought it, Gavin doubted Holly had it in her to be anything but genuine.

Lifting his hand up, he trailed his fingers against the smooth skin of her shoulder, and to his pleasure, she inhaled deeply. He wanted to roll her onto her back and kiss her, but he waited as her eyes slowly blinked open and met his.

Neither spoke momentarily, and Gavin's smirk melted away as he looked at her. Of all the words between them, it seemed the most was spoken in silence. Holly's shocked expression melted away as she slowly smiled at him, leaning forward slightly with her forehead, which he kissed.

"Good morning," she murmured against the sheets before pulling back.

God, her voice was like velvet.

"Indeed," he said, and to his own embarrassment, they both laughed.

What a bizarre way to start a day, but Gavin was sure he had never been as settled as he was at that moment. If he could spend all day in bed with her, he would and was very close to suggesting it when a knock sounded at the door.

"Holly?" the voice of Katrina sounded.

Panic shone in Holly's eyes as she sat up, the covers tightly tucked with her hands beneath her chin as she rolled over. The expanse of her naked back caused parts of Gavin to wake. His hand came up and drifted up the smooth straight dip of her spine.

Holly turned around and frowned at him, shaking her head.

"Yes?" Holly answered loudly, swatting Gavin's hand behind her.

"Um, I think you should come down to the parlor," Katrina's muffled voice sounded through the door, and something in her tone suggested urgency.

"Yes, dear, I'm nearly dressed."

Gavin sat up and, leaning forward, nipped at the shoulder that so tantalized him. Holly made a show of trying to push him off but sighed as her head tilted, allowing him access to her. Indeed, nothing was as essential to distract Gavin from feasting on Holly for the next hour or two.

"It's just that, well, I think you should know that Jasper's here."

Gavin froze as tension snapped through Holly's body. *Of course.* So, it *had* been Jasper who he saw the other day at White's. Gavin had meant to tell Holly about possibly seeing her brother, but he had become distracted.

"I'll…" Holly started, her voice breaking. "I'll be right out."

They heard Katrina walk away, and Gavin watched Holly with piqued interest as she pushed back the covers and began rushing about the room to dress. For his part, he was slow to get out of bed.

"He's probably been tossed out of Eton," Holly said, quickly pulling on her drawers and bringing her short stays over her head. She turned her back to Gavin, prompting him to tie them. He stepped forward to do so, quietly enjoying the somewhat domesticated task of helping his wife dress. "I hope he's all right." Gavin paused in his task, and noticing his hesitation, she turned her head. "Is something wrong?"

Gavin sighed, finished tying her stays, and turned her around.

"I thought I saw him the other day. At White's."

"Saw who?"

"Your brother."

Holly frowned.

"At White's? No, that's impossible. He doesn't have a membership and he doesn't know anyone who is a member there."

Gavin shook his head.

"I'm not so sure about that. I was sitting with Combe and Trembley around noon when a fight broke out—"

"A fight?"

"Yes, and the floor manager was about to toss him out when he broke free of his would-be captors and ran out."

"Why didn't you tell me?"

"I had intended to, but it must have slipped my mind."

Holly pulled a dress on over her undergarments. It was a striped blue and cream day gown Gavin had never seen before. One of her new gowns, he supposed.

"You forgot?"

"I was distracted," he said with a pointed stare, which made her blush.

"Oh. Well," she said, remembering the night she had gone to his room. She observed him up and down. "Might I suggest some clothes?"

Remembering that he was naked as the day he was born, Gavin gave her a tight nod and stalked back to their joining door. Back in his room, he dressed in grey trousers, white shirtsleeves, and a diamond-patterned vest as quickly as he could. Grabbing his coat, he pulled it on as he exited his bedchamber, half expecting to see Holly waiting for him, but she hadn't.

Frowning, he guessed the worry for her brother had been too much. Hurrying down the steps, he came around the railing and headed for the parlor. Upon entering the room, he found that Katrina, Holly, Jasper, and Aunt Marnie were all there, bickering with one another.

"What do you mean you left school—"

"—there's another one of you Smyths—"

"—I have every intention of paying him back—"

"—you're going to ruin my debut, Jasper!"

Gavin searched the room, wondering if most families argued like this. It was indeed a new phenomenon for him to be a part of, and while it was certainly noisy, he found it rather interesting to watch, despite his concern for Holly, who no doubt would blame herself for whatever problem Jasper currently found himself in. Leaning against the edge of a marble-topped credenza against the wall, he folded his arms and watched until Holly spotted him.

"Gavin, can you please come here and tell Jasper that he must return to Eton?"

"I don't need your faux husband acting as my keeper, Holly," Jasper said.

"You're going to ruin everything, Jasper!" Katrina whined. "Why must you cause such trouble?"

"My, what a colorful family you've married into Gavin," Aunt Marnie sneered. "A troupe of uneducated, bickering country fools."

Sighing, Gavin pushed off the credenza. Although Aunt Marnie's snarky remarks would usually earn her a sarcastic comment or two, Gavin was currently in far too good of a mood to let her bother him. He gave her a contemptuous smirk.

"Aunt Marnie, if you please." He made a gesture for the door.

She stomped her foot.

"I'm not going anywhere. This concerns me just as well as anyone. If you're emptying coffers to pay off this young derelict's gambling habit—"

"He's not a derelict," Holly argued. "Not yet anyway."

"What a dazzling recommendation, sister," Jasper said sarcastically.

"She's not wrong," Katrina said, earning her a scowl from Jasper.

"That's it," Gavin said, holding his hands up, trying to stop the squabble before it could go any further. "Jasper, can your sister and I please speak to you, in private?"

Appearing apprehensive, he gave Gavin a long glare before shrugging.

"Very well," he said, dropping to a chair as Holly nodded.

"Good. Now, Aunt Marnie—"

"I'll not be tossed aside, Gavin!"

"You'll be tossed out forever if you don't do as I say. Now, go on and show Katrina the portrait gallery or the gardens or something."

The old woman made a *Humph* sound and stalked out of the room. Though Katrina seemed to want to do anything but go towards the picture gallery with the old woman, she knew she was being dismissed. They left without another word, and Gavin turned back to focus on Jasper.

The young man was a tall fellow if not completely filled out, as he was still young. He was a handsome lad with hair the same color as Holly, though the resemblance ended there. Jasper had dark eyes, a square face, and an angry air about him that Gavin couldn't quite understand. There was something bitter in the boy's face that seemed vaguely familiar to Gavin.

Seating across from him, Gavin leaned forward.

"What is it then? Why have you left Eton?"

Jasper rolled his eyes like any insolent youth.

"Why? What are you going to do? Send me back?" Jasper asked sarcastically, not answering Gavin. "Just because you married my sister doesn't mean you can tell me what to do."

"Jasper Francis Smyth," Holly said through clenched teeth. "What is the matter with you? Where are your manners?"

"Manners? Why should I show anyone any manners? Especially him? You didn't even know you'd married this man," he spat out. "Until Mr. Armstrong informed you that that old fool managed to trick you into it."

Holly inhaled sharply, ready to break out into an argument

again. But Gavin put his hand on her knee. Though it was a small enough gesture, she stopped. Gavin faced Jasper.

"Are you finished puffing out your plumage?"

Jasper glared at him.

"Listen—"

"No. Not until you tell me what you were doing at White's the other day."

Recognition flared in Jasper's eyes. Folding his arms against his chest, his gaze dropped to the floor.

"So, you were there," the youth said, sitting back. "I wasn't sure."

"What were you doing there?" Holly asked. "You're too young to enter that place."

"I'm not too young. I'm perfectly capable of holding my own at a hazard tables. And figuring out what to do about Felton Manor," he added. "We don't need any charity."

And there it was. Gavin saw what Holly couldn't.

Jasper was on the cusp of manhood, and yet he had no idea how to behave like a man. It was a confusing time in a boy's life, especially when he didn't have anyone to look up to model some of his behaviors. Some men fared well alone without any examples, but most people needed, or at least benefited from, having someone to emulate.

"Our marriage wasn't charity, Jasper," Gavin said slowly, careful not to upset the young man further. "It was a surprise, I'll give you that." He glanced at Holly. "My uncle was Holly's friend and genuinely wished to care for her after he died."

"Well, we don't need it," Jasper bit out. "If Holly would have just let me handle it, she wouldn't be in this mess."

"Handle what?" she asked, exasperated. "You're in school, Jasper. You don't have any resources or skills—"

"I have ideas! I could have made sure neither you nor Katrina would have to be forced to marry someone you don't know," Jasper argued, giving Gavin a distasteful glare.

"You're a boy—"

"I'm a man!"

"Easy, easy, the both of you," Gavin said, standing up. It was obvious that neither sibling would be able to get a handle on their emotions when both were firmly fixed on the notion that they were correct. Just then, an idea began to form in Gavin's mind, and he turned, facing his brother-in-law. "Jasper, is there a reason you left Eton?"

A cloud came over the young man's face.

"No."

It was obviously a lie, but not one Gavin cared to dissect at the moment. He wished to speak privately with Jasper, if only because Gavin believed he would be more forthcoming if his sister wasn't around.

"Will you be going back?"

"He certainly will," Holly interjected, but Gavin held up his hand to let her brother speak.

For a moment, he didn't answer but stared at Gavin with questioning eyes. It seemed he didn't believe he was being asked a serious question, but after another moment, he relented and answered.

"No."

Holly sighed, but Gavin continued.

"Well, if that's the case, I don't think you should stay here."

Both Jasper and Holly shot up.

"What?"

"Excuse me?"

"But we wouldn't have you wandering the streets. I'd like it very much if you would do me the favor of taking over my former residence in Marylebone for the time being."

Holly and Jasper stared at him. For a moment, Gavin wondered if either of them had heard him.

"Are you serious?"

"Absolutely not," Holly said.

Gavin knew Holly wouldn't appreciate what he had to say, but as she had never been on the verge of becoming a man, he hoped she'd at least try to understand. Jasper was likely to sell Felton Manor and live off the funds until he ran through them all, and then who knows where he would end up. But if Gavin could delay that for a while, give him some time to learn how to care for his inheritance while allotting him a certain amount of freedom, he might be able to negotiate something both Holly and Jasper could come to terms with. Gavin continued.

"I obviously cannot live at two residences at the same time. Please don't expect luxury. It's a bit spartan. More a gentleman's house, if you will."

Jasper's eyes lit with eagerness, but he let out a stunned sort of noise before turning to his sister.

"Is he having a laugh?"

"I hope so," she said, turning to face him. "You cannot be seriously considering letting a seventeen-year-old boy live alone."

Gavin let out a breath, knowing that she would likely argue with him later over what he was about to say, but Holly had been mothering her siblings for far too long.

"He isn't a boy, Holly. He's a young man, and a young man requires space."

It hurt him to see the betrayal that flashed in her eyes, but Gavin knew what it was to be angry and young. Stifling Jasper would only lead to a combustible situation. Although he was in much need of guidance, he wouldn't accept any unless he wanted it.

Holly's mouth set in a hard line as she turned and left the room. Gavin wondered if he had crossed the line. After all, Jasper wasn't his brother. And yet they were all his family to protect now, and as much as Gavin adored Holly, he wasn't willing to blindly accept all her opinions as indisputable facts.

The low laugh of Jasper caught Gavin's attention.

"I don't know what you're playing at, but I think you've just made a mistake," Jasper said, staring at the door his sister stormed out of. "Holly doesn't like being proven wrong."

"Well, she hasn't been. I'm just giving you the benefit of the doubt." Jasper frowned, not quite sure what he meant. Gavin brought his hand up, brushing his fingers through his hair in concentration. "Holly thinks you are a boy and boys need to be watched after. Prove to her you don't have to be coddled anymore and she'll see you as you are. A young man, capable of handling his own affairs."

Jasper's smirk faltered as a shadow of doubt crossed his face.

"Do you think she'll let me sell Felton Manor?" He asked.

Gavin tilted his head.

"Now, why would you wish to sell Felton Manor? As we speak, it's being properly restored and all the livestock is being handled by Mr. Granger, who has graciously allowed us to hire one of his hands to watch over the cows until we can secure some tenants, which shouldn't take too long. And Mr. Lemon has nearly completed the repairs to the roof and the third story. It will be a right working property in a few seasons, one that will provide a comfortable income for you. Why sell it?"

"Well," Jasper began, his gaze dropping to the floor, "I may own some debts."

"School is already paid for."

"No, not that," he said. "Gambling debts."

"Ah, I see. I remember tossing some dice at Eton. What do you own? Fifty? A hundred pounds?"

"Twelve thousand."

Gavin blinked once. And then he blinked again.

"I beg your pardon?"

"It's not anything I can't handle. I just need the deed to Felton Manor, and then I'll be able to start clean and fresh without this debt hanging over my head."

"Yes, you'll be able to start over with nothing," Gavin said, suddenly irritated that he had granted him to stay at his Marylebone home. "How the devil have you managed a debt that large?"

"It wasn't my fault," Jasper said defensively. "I was sure to win. It was set up that way."

Gavin's brow creased.

"It was a marked game?" he asked, incredulously. "Jasper, I don't have to tell you what cheaters are thought of in this world—"

"No. It wasn't like that," he said exasperatedly. "I was just trying to earn some coin, so that I might be able to get that stupid tree off our house. I'm a fair hand at faro, but none of the lads at Eton had the amount I needed. So, I went to try my luck with horses. Only I wasn't so lucky." He looked up. "I couldn't tell Holly. She'd never let me hear the end of it."

Gavin stared at him. He had been trying to help his family, but in the most foolish way possible. He shook his head.

"It's commendable, wanting to help your family, Jasper. But gambling is never the way to go about it. And there's never a sure thing." The boy dropped his head. "Go to my house in Portman Square and don't go out. I can fix this, I'm sure of it, but I'll need a few days."

Jasper nodded.

"Can you talk to her about letting me sell Felton Manor?"

"I thought you were going to sell it once you turned eighteen, regardless?"

Jasper shrugged.

"Yes, I would like to, but I know Holly and Katrina would never forgive me," he said, but Gavin frowned, noting the tightness of the lad's voice. "I just need to pay back my debts. As soon as possible."

There seemed to be an urgency about him that made Gavin uncomfortable, and he lowered his voice.

"You're not in trouble with the wrong people, are you?"

For a moment, it seemed like he might admit it, but then he shook his head nervously and smiled, though it didn't reach his eyes.

"Of course not," he said, moving quickly around the room. "It's sporting of you to lend me your residence, Bairnsdale. I shan't forget it."

With a quick nod, Jasper left the parlor. Gavin couldn't help but suspect that his brother-in-law was in more trouble than any of them realized. He would need to discuss it will Holly just as soon as he discovered who Jasper was indebted to.

Chapter Fifteen

G AVIN TOOK JASPER to his apartments in Marylebone, on a street where each red brick terrace home looked identical to the next. It was far too modest a place for someone who had partnered with a bank, but it suited Gavin well enough. He wasn't the sort to host parties, and he rarely had visitors, making the quiet home on Portman Square perfect for someone like Gavin.

As he watched the look on Jasper's face, however, when the carriage stopped in front of the unassuming building, Gavin wondered what the youth was thinking.

They exited the vehicle and walked the white limestone walkway to the front door. An old butler with white hair and faded brown eyes answered, hunched over slightly. At the sight of Gavin, however, he tried to straight up.

"Lord Bairnsdale!"

"Hello, Everton," Gavin said, handing over his hat to the butler. "This is Mr. Jasper Smyth. He'll be staying here for a few months."

Gavin looked over his shoulder at Jasper, inspecting the white chair rail that lined the narrow foyer. The wallpaper was a royal blue with a white filigree design, and for a moment he wondered if Holly would like his home.

"Very good sir," Everton said. "Shall I ring for tea?"

"I don't see why not," Gavin said as he led the way to the large office on his right.

It had once been the former residence's library, but Gavin had found that it had best suited his needs as an office. Its tall mahogany bookshelves held more records and bank notes than books and a large oak desk sat in the center of the room.

"This is all yours?" Jasper asked, turning around the room. "And you are not indebted to anyone?"

"I am not," Gavin said, watching the boy with a curious gaze. He folded his arms across his chest and, coming up to his desk, leaned against it as he watched his brother-in-law. "You know, your sister is near furious with me for letting you stay here. I hope I shouldn't have to worry about her anxieties."

Jasper turned to face him and shook his head.

"Holly is dramatic. She assumes I'm going to burn down every place I enter."

"Why is that?"

He shrugged.

"Who knows? I mean, it could be that I once started a fire at the barn at Felton Manor, but I put it out," he said quickly, giving Gavin pause.

"You almost burned down the barn?"

Perhaps Holly was right about her brother. But there was something familiar in him, something Gavin could understand, and he wanted to know more if only to appease his own curiosity about him.

"Almost. And really, it was all Katrina's idea. But I was blamed, as always," he said, unable to keep the bitterness out of his tone as he looked down. "Holly always thinks I'm the one messing things up and while I have, it doesn't mean I'm always *going* to mess up. Does that make sense?"

"It does," Gavin said with a nod. "Which is why I'm trusting that you'll take your time here seriously. I'm aware that Eton is not for everyone and if you don't wish to return, I don't see why you must. If you can earn a viable living without learning Latin, I think you should." The drop in Jasper's shoulders told Gavin something he already knew. "But you don't want to earn a living, do you?"

"It's not that I'm opposed to work," the youth said. "But why work when there's so many other things to do?"

"You have no way to support yourself. If Felton Manor isn't where you intend to make your fortune, what else do you have planned?"

Jasper was quiet momentarily, and Gavin thought he saw something flash across his face. Some sort of yearning, but he didn't press. Instead, he simply waited for Jasper to respond.

"I'm not lazy," he said suddenly, looking up. "I know that's what she thinks. But it's not true. It's just that I don't want to be a farmer." Gavin nodded, encouraging him to continue. "I know it's what I was born for. I'm a gentleman's only son and my lot in life was to maintain that farm, but it isn't what I want and the longer I stayed there, the more I grew to hate it. Particularly because Holly was so sure that it was what I was meant to do, what I should be striving for."

"And what is it that you want to do?"

"I want to travel. I want to leave England and go overseas and discover things and whatnot," he said, his tone earnest as his gaze dropped to the plush, ornate carpet beneath their feet. "It's ridiculous, I know, but it's another reason why I've been trying to earn money gambling. I'm good with numbers and it's easy for me. I just don't want to worry about wheat and cows and if the Mannions were going to show up every week and talk about the same old things."

Gavin observed him. He could understand the desire to leave, to go out into the wide world and discover a part of himself that was on the other side of the world and in his heart simultaneously. Yes, Gavin could understand that, and it was somewhat jarring to hear it from someone other than himself.

After a moment longer, he pushed himself up off the desk.

"Then I think you should."

Jasper's head whipped up; shock displayed on his face. He seemed suspicious of Gavin's words.

"You do?"

"Yes, I do."

"But Holly will never agree."

"Agree to what? It's your home, to do with as you wish. In a few short weeks, she won't be able to stop you. Speaking from experience, I know what it means, to want to leave everything behind. That said, I obviously wouldn't want to break your sisters' hearts by having you disappear."

Jasper frowned.

"What do you want me to do then?"

"I want you to come up with a plan. I have some connections that can get you on a dozen or so merchant ships. I know you'd rather just tarry about, but travel across the seas can become tedious and it's always good to keep busy. Not to mention that without your farm, you'll need funds. The sale of Felton Manor won't line your pockets forever. Sooner or later, you'll be required to work."

"But I don't know how to do anything."

"Nonsense. You may not be graduating from Eton but you just said you were good with numbers. In the meantime, figure out how long you wish to be away for, but plan for a short return in at least six months. It'll be easier on Holly to know you intend to come home, at least to visit."

"Are you serious?"

"Very much so. And I hope your penmanship is up to snuff. You'll be writing both Holly and Katrina daily."

Jasper's mouth tightened, and he looked like he was considering something.

"I would still like to sell Felton Manor. I have my debts, you understand."

"Yes, I'm aware."

"As well as a membership that wants paying."

That caught Gavin's attention.

"What membership?"

"To Clemet Club."

"Clemet Club?" Gavin repeated, his brow rising. "Why on earth are you muddling around with that place?"

"After I was kicked out of White's, I went to one of the taverns around that way. I saw a card game going on and managed to get myself into play. It turned out, one of the players was the proprietor to the Clemet Club, Mr. Kilmann himself." Jasper puffed out his chest proudly. "He offered me a year membership, due to how well I was playing."

Gavin stared at the young man. Was he so unaware of those who would take advantage of him?

"Kilmann isn't the sort of man to be trifled with, Jasper. He's dangerous and will likely end you if you aren't able to pay your debts. Why he's offered you a membership to his club when you're already in debt is beyond me—"

"Well, that's it. I told him Felton Manor was as good as sold. I was just waiting on the money to be delivered."

Gavin's mouth nearly dropped.

"Have you gone mad? Lying to a man like Kilmann will get you murdered."

"But you just said I should sell Felton Manor," Jasper said defiantly.

"I did, but I didn't tell a lie about it. Especially not to one of London's most notorious gamblers." Gavin shook his head, increasingly unsure if his original intent to help his brother-in-law was correct. "Listen, I want you to stay here. Don't go out and certainly don't go to the Clemet Club until the sale of Felton Manor is complete. Do you understand?"

"But who's going to buy it?"

"Leave that to me," Gavin said. "In the meantime, just stay put and don't go making waves." Jasper looked like he might want to argue, but then he smartly nodded. "Now all I have to do is somehow convince your sister that this is the best option."

"Good luck. She'll never willingly give up the manor. She's so damn sure that if she can hold onto it, she might be able to turn back time and be happy. But there's no use."

His words caught Gavin off balance.

"What do you mean, be happy?"

"Don't you see it? She's miserable."

"Surely not."

"Well, not since you've been around, I suppose. But before, she was always worried and miserable. I know your uncle set up this whole, proxy marriage thing, but if I were you I'd be furious to be linked to someone who's so tightly wound."

"Your sister isn't tightly wound," Gavin said more annoyed than he intended. "She's strained and working against to wind when it comes to her family," he said pointedly. "But she's smart and resilient and far stronger than you give her credit for."

For a long moment Jasper remained silent. Gavin turned, wondering if he should leave soon when his brother-in-law spoke. "Do you really care about her?"

Gavin turned back to face him.

"I do."

A moment of silence, then.

"Well, I'll be. I guess old John knew what he was doing." Jasper shook his head. "You know, he said something to me once last summer. Something about how Holly would do well to meet you, but I didn't think he was serious. He was always coming up with ideas and writing them in those daft journals of his."

"Journals?"

"Yes, the ones he left you, I gather. He always was so sure that whatever he wrote down in those books was brilliant, but I never believed him." Jasper shrugged, looking around the room. "So, which room is mine?"

Gavin was temporarily distracted, thinking about the journals. But the next moment, he called for Everton and instructed his butler to show Jasper the rest of the house as he left. He needed to return to Bairnsdale Terrace.

So, Uncle John had written about them? Gavin was suddenly

consumed with a need to read through all his uncle's journals immediately. He wondered what else his uncle had managed to write down. Maybe he could understand Holly a little better if he could read about her from a friend's point of view.

He also now needed to figure out how he would facilitate the sale of Felton Manor so that Jasper could follow his dream while simultaneously crushing Holly's hope of keeping her family home in her brother's possession.

Ah, the joys of dealing with in-laws.

Chapter Sixteen

Holly could barely contain her aggravation as she prepared to travel to Bond Street that morning after breakfast. Gavin had taken his leave with Jasper to settle her brother at his old Marylebone residence without so much as a goodbye. Well, that was just as well. She didn't wish to speak to either of them, particularly if they were busy congratulating themselves for making such a careless mistake.

The nerve of Gavin! Jasper was still a child, completely unfit to govern his own life, let alone anyone else's. And it didn't have anything to do with his age. Katrina was born the same day and was vastly more competent than her twin brother. Jasper simply didn't have the maturity to be given an entire residence without supervision.

It bothered Holly to no end that Jasper had somehow gotten his way once more. Not because she didn't wish the world for him but because he had never learned to handle disappointment properly. He was always bitter and sarcastic as if the world had done a great injustice to him and only him. It was infuriating, to say the least.

Still, some of her hoped Gavin knew what he was doing. Holly truly wanted Jasper to become a successful, happy man. She knew a time would come when she would have to let him stumble as he undoubtedly would, but at this point, he was more likely to fall flat on his face. She lacked the ability or the money to pull him back from the brink of failure, and she hoped she wouldn't need to.

Thankfully Katrina didn't give her such issues. Never had a set of twins been more different than Jasper and Katrina. Waiting for her sister in the foyer, she was surprised to see Katrina come down the stairs, accompanied by Marnie. Holly tried not to grimace. Surely she wouldn't be coming with them again, would she?

"Holly, Aunt Marnie has decided that she is in the market for new gloves," Katrina said without a hint of aversion. "She doesn't have any for the St. James Palace."

Holly kept her face blank though her insides shook.

"I didn't realize Miss Winscombe would be accompanying us to St. James."

"Yes, I'm sure you would rather I stay locked up here," Marnie said, brushing past her. "But at least one of you Smyths has learned some manners. Miss Katrina here has invited me."

Holly's eyes widened as she looked at her sister, who silently shook her head as they followed Marnie out the door.

"Did she?" Holly asked.

"Yes, and it was with a dutiful heart that I accepted. Surely there isn't anyone better than I to instruct this young lady on court life. I've been attending Queen's ball since the very first. Now, of course, since our King no longer has his queen, the ball is being hosted by Princess Elizabeth, but she is quite dedicated to maintaining the old traditions in her mother's memory. So, it is a good choice of your sister to call on me for my services."

"A blessing we were not aware of, I'm sure," Holly said as she climbed into the carriage.

For the entire ride to Bond Street, Marnie delighted in telling the two about all the times she had attended the annual debutante event. She spoke of her favorites which somehow always coincided with the most successful lady of the season, and named several choices marked with favor by others who had not lived up to their names. She also mentioned several disappointments and famous errors she had witnessed over the years and how each person had fared afterward.

Holly tried to catch Katrina's eye but she seemed entirely engrossed in everything Marnie said. She continued talking as they entered Miss Piedmont's establishment to pick up their ballgowns. Once finished there they went next door to the glove and fan shop. Marnie's recitation continued unabated, but to Holly's surprise, Katrina seemed genuinely interested, leaving Holly wandering about the shop idly as the two chatted.

Lifting a silk kerchief laid out on a dark-grain wood display table. Holly traced the fine cloth through her fingers as she watched the two pick out gloves. Perhaps Katrina had found something amiable about the old woman, though Holly wasn't sure how that was possible. Still, she might try to befriend the old woman, if only to minimize Marnie's hostility towards her, mainly when she brought up John.

Holly sighed at the thought of her friend. She had so many questions. Ever since his death, it seemed she was bombarded with mysteries, and every day, she seemed to get further from the truth. Holly wanted to ask him about his sister and why she was so hellbent on keeping the coffers full. Was it because he really hadn't provided an adequate allowance to support Marnie and Gavin? That didn't sound like him at all—but she knew the relationship between the siblings had been strained, and perhaps anger had driven John to behave uncharacteristically. John had even mentioned once that he didn't enjoy the London season much and rarely visited the town during the spring and summer for fear of running into his sister. Holly thought avoiding an entire city for one person was silly, but then she'd supposed that John had his reasons.

And Marnie was a particular reason. Now that she'd had the chance to spend time with the woman, Holly could well understand how someone might go to great lengths to avoid her. Holly would do so herself if she had the opportunity. But instead, they had all been thrown together, and she supposed she should try and make the best of it, especially now that they would likely remain in each other's lives.

Coming around the display table, Holly heard Katrina asking which shade of orange she might use as a ribbon, holding two different trimmings on either side of her head.

"Which contrasts better with the shade of my hair?" Katrina asked.

"This one, I think," Marnie said, pointing to the thicker ribbon. "Always best to go with bolder accents as opposed to the bolder gown. It catches the eye without drowning out everything else. A tip shared with me by the Duchess of Wellington."

"How very interesting," Katrina said thoughtfully.

"Over there," Marnie pointed to a cupboard against the wall. "See if you can't find a pair of gloves with tangerine thread."

Katrina did as she was told, and Holly stepped gingerly into her spot. Lowering her voice, she leaned in.

"It's very kind of you to share your knowledge with my sister. To be sure, neither of us would have been very prepared for St. James Palace."

"No," Marnie said. "You wouldn't have been." Holly nodded, unsure what to say to break through to the old woman when she spoke suddenly. "It might have done you a bit of good, had you had a season."

Holly lifted one of her shoulders before dropping it.

"It was not meant to be, I'm afraid. There's little room in the ton for poor country gentry."

"No, and yet you've managed to catch yourself a baron."

Holly tried not to make a face but turned fully to face her.

"I am sorry, Miss Winscombe, that you have been disappointed in the great hopes you had for your nephew. I can't imagine it's been easy for you, raising him as you did on your own. And with so little help."

Holly was baiting the woman, but she was eager to learn all she could.

"It wasn't easy," Marnie said slowly. "But it was my duty."

"I know about that. It was my duty to raise my Jasper and Katrina when our mother passed away."

Evidently, it hadn't ever dawned on Marnie that she and Holly had both raised children that hadn't been their own. As if seeing her for the first time, Marnie's expression lightened as she looked at Holly with a new appreciation.

"Then you know the weight of it. You know, I was the eldest as well."

"Were you?"

Marnie nodded.

"Indeed, I was. John was two years younger than me, but Joseph, Gavin's father, was ten years my junior," she said, the faintest of smiles touching her wrinkled lips at the memory of her youngest brother. "We doted on him as a child, John and I. He was so even tempered. Such a darling boy."

Holly smiled, charmed to learn about Gavin's father as Marnie continued, her brow pinching together as her eyes went out of focus as if watching a long-forgotten memory play out before her.

"A darling boy, but he didn't have a strong constitution. He was often sick. I wanted to protect him from the world, but John insisted otherwise. He was so sure that Joseph could do anything, be anything, that he never accounted for the risks if he should be pushed too far."

Holly's smile faded as she tilted her head.

"Too far?"

Marnie nodded slowly as if in a daze.

"It was John who insisted that Joseph travel with him on some wicked, depraved holiday on the continent. Joseph fell ill and returned home a short time after. He never recovered. Gavin had caught whatever illness had taken his father and for a time we didn't think he would make it either. But then he did, and I promised the Lord that I would take care of him... but John had other ideas. He argued that as he wouldn't have any children of his own, Gavin was his heir and should be raised by him."

Holly frowned.

"John *wanted* Gavin to come live with him?"

"Yes, but I couldn't let him do to Gavin what he had done to Joseph. No. Joseph's death was a punishment for all the gambling and carousing under John's dissolute guidance." She shook her head as if trying to shake away the memory. Turning to face Holly, her brow puckered. "John was a wicked man."

Holly's brow pinched together. She doubted there had been a wicked bone in John's entire body, but Marnie seemed too deep in her beliefs to be convinced otherwise, and Holly couldn't see that there was anything to be gained by arguing. Taking a deep breath, she pressed on, trying to sympathize with a woman who had lost her brother.

"I suppose it would have been difficult for you to let Gavin go, to be raised by John."

"He tried to take Gavin from me once. Threatened me with legal action, but I told him that if he dared bring me to court, I would expose him," she said with a definitive nod.

Holly stared at the old woman, conflicted. She understood the desire to protect one's family, especially a child in one's care. Still, in doing so, Marnie had lost her relationship with her other brother. She had succeeded in retaining guardianship. But at what cost?

Gavin hadn't known a happy home with Marnie growing up; he said so himself. It seemed her bitterness had boiled over once she got the better of John, which also explained why the old baron hadn't had any contact with Gavin during his formidable years. Because Marnie had made sure that they wouldn't be close.

A tiny worry began to break over her as the comparisons between Marnie and herself became more apparent. While Holly had never meant to suffocate Jasper, she started worrying that her concern for him was overzealous. He was still foolish, but perhaps she shouldn't try to hold on to him as much as she did, lest they find themselves in a situation where she and Jasper never spoke again.

"It was John's own fault. Had he never stolen Gavin's father away from me—"

"No, no, I understand," Holly said, her hand coming up, even if she didn't quite agree. "I guess I'm just confused. Why would John refuse even to provide adequate financial support for you and Gavin?"

Marnie's eyes shifted downward, and though Holly couldn't be sure, it seemed she was hiding something.

"Yes, well, some people have a harder time with managing monies," she said, her tone strained, turning around. "Where has that sister of yours gone off to?"

She skirted away, leaving Holly to wonder what she meant by managing monies. Had she had trouble managing her accounts? Holly knew from experience with Felton Manor that mistakes could prove costly... but she still got the sense that there was more to it than that.

Holly had a suspicion that she hadn't learned everything she could from Marnie. At least, not yet.

The remainder of the morning was spent gathering the final touches needed for Katrina's debut at St. James Palace. Holly and Marnie didn't speak much for the rest of the trip but were sure to beam at Katrina whenever she asked a question or solicited one of their opinions. Her excitement for the season was palpable and contagious.

With their shopping excursion finished, the carriage was loaded with the final boxes of necessities. Marnie continued to school Katrina in everything she thought was important while Holly's mind turned thoughtful.

Upon arriving home, the grey cat Pauline stood on the bottom of the staircase, dutifully watching the women as they entered.

"Oof, that rotten animal," Marnie said, waving her hand at it. "Shoo. Begone."

"I quite like cats," Katrina said, handing boxes to one of the maids who had come up to help them. "But this one isn't terribly friendly, is it?"

As if the cat understood and wanted to prove her wrong, it stepped off the stair and slowly walked toward Holly. Marnie skirted away from it quickly, evidently still wary of the animal since it attacked her.

"Keep it away from me," she said, cowering behind Mr. Spieth, who shielded the old woman as if he were some gallant knight.

With the tip of her tail switching back and forth, the cat approached Holly's feet and sat down, looking up at her. She half expected the creature to rub against her leg, but it only sat there, watching her.

"Peculiar little thing, isn't it?" Holly said, bending down.

She stretched out her hand to pet the top of her head, but instantly it swatted at her, missing her by a hair as Holly jolted back up.

"It's a menace," Marnie hissed.

Holly could barely disagree, but that was hardly the poor cat's fault. It had been locked away alone for ages. It probably wasn't sure how to be around people. Supposedly the entire staff had learned to avoid the animal, which made Holly feel sorry for the little thing.

Walking around the cat, Holly, Katrina, and Marnie went to their rooms with their purchases. Holly set her gloves, stockings, and hairpins on her dresser before changing for dinner. After several moments, she heard Gavin's arrival. Staring at the wall that separated their rooms, she ignored the impatient yearning to see him.

They had decided to have a quiet dinner that evening since the debutante ball at St. James Palace was to take place the following evening. Her nervousness surprised Holly, especially considering she wasn't even being presented. Still, it was an extraordinary event, especially for a country miss.

Holly paused in dressing and started at the door connecting

her and Gavin's room. She was surprised to find she had been eager to be in his presence all day, even though she was still annoyed with him for inserting himself between her and Jasper.

Remembering that, she turned away from the connecting door and opened the door into the hallway. Except she didn't get very far. Standing in the hallway, leaning against the opposite wall, was Gavin.

A flutter went through her as she saw him, and he pressed himself off the wall, stepping toward her.

"Hello," he said, his voice a balm to her agitation.

"Hello," she said softly.

"May I have a word? In private?" He nodded towards her room.

"Of course," she said, gesturing him in.

Once he had entered, she closed the door behind them, ignoring the rising giddiness she felt in his company. It was silly, she knew, to be so infatuated with someone. Perhaps she was embarrassed to admit it, but her feelings for Gavin continued to grow. She could no longer choose to have or not have emotions for him. No, now her affection for him had taken on a life of its own.

Turning, she watched as his hand reached out of her vanity table, lightly touching a series of objects, such as a hand mirror and a pin she had decided not to wear that evening. His fingers landed on the wooden box that held the jewelry that John had left her and paused.

"You know, you never received a ring."

"Excuse me?"

He turned to gaze at her, his hazel eyes tinted with something she couldn't pinpoint.

"For our marriage."

"Oh," Holly said, shaking her head. "I did. Or rather, I was offered one."

Moving about the room, she headed towards a table at the edge of her bed. Opening the tiny drawer, she pulled out an old reticule. Fishing out the slim gold band John had given her, she brought it over to Gavin and held up her open hand. The small ring sat in the middle of her palm.

Gavin examined it, and to her surprise, he picked it up. After a moment, he stared at her.

"It's a tiny thing. I wonder why he didn't give you something grander."

"I don't think the timing allotted allowed him to be grandiose," Holly said, reaching for it. Gavin let her take it. "Besides, John was more than generous with what I was left here."

Gavin turned around, eyeing the jewelry box.

"Yes, John was generous to certain people."

Though he didn't sound bitter, Holly knew he harbored an old wound on that score. However, after discussing with Marnie that day, she wondered how much John's generosity had been bestowed on them when Gavin was growing up. Perhaps the shortages in their household accounts were more due to Marnie's mismanagement than John's lack of generosity?

She opened her mouth to inquire, but then Gavin spoke.

"Still, I should like to have a new one made. Not to detract from your friendship with my uncle, or anything. But..."

A minor, knowing ache pulled at Holly's heart.

"Yes," she said, vaguely aware of what he was trying to express.

Though they had started off as strangers, their relationship had developed, and he wanted to honor it by giving her a proper wedding band. She was rather pleased with that thought, and she smiled.

"As for what I wanted to talk to you in private about," he said after a moment. "I've set up your brother in Marylebone, in my old apartments."

Holly's smile faltered.

"Oh. Well. That's fine, I suppose."

He took a step towards her.

"Do you understand my decision though?"

"Yes," she said, dropping her gaze as she moved around him. "Yes, I do. You're giving him the chance to prove he can be responsible. Although I doubt giving him all the freedoms in the world will teach him anything except excessiveness. I can only imagine that he'll be mortgaging Felton Manor at the hazards table by the end of the week."

"I've not given him anything a young man cannot handle."

She gave him a knowing look.

"He's a boy."

"He's not though, Holly," Gavin said, walking towards her, effectively cornering her between a pair of chairs and her wardrobe in the corner of the room. "And trying to keep him so will only cause him to resent you."

She thought back on her conversation with Marnie from earlier. She certainly did not want to make the same mistakes, but it was still difficult to believe in her brother. She shook her head.

"His only idea to get out of his debts is to sell the one thing that, given a little time and care, could support him his entire life. He has no foresight."

"It's because he's young, but he can still learn."

"And you think you're able to teach him?" she asked, unable to keep the disbelief out of her voice.

Gavin's expression remained blank.

"Might you let me try, before concluding that I've failed?"

Holly swallowed. She didn't want to believe that Gavin would fail, but her brother had proven time and time again that he wasn't mature enough to conduct himself or his own affairs. But what could she do? Gavin seemed determined and she needed to trust him.

She dropped her head and shrugged.

"If you genuinely think this will help Jasper, then I don't suppose I can stop you."

Gavin's hand appeared beneath her chin, lifting her head up, and their eyes met.

"No. But I'd rather have your support."

She inhaled mint and lemon and sighed. It was unfair how that scent had become something she craved. His desire for her backing was touching.

"Very well."

He smirked, and without preamble, he leaned forward and kissed her. Holly was instantly separated from all her worries and cares as he wrapped his arms around her. Good Lord, he kissed her with such yearning that she was sure her toes were shaking when he pulled back.

Despite knowing dinner would be served momentarily, and she really should finish getting ready, Holly leaned into him instead. She curled her fingers beneath the lapels of his coat and pulled him towards her, leaning back until she felt the wardrobe door behind her.

Lifting her chin slightly as he kissed down her throat, she spoke.

"We're going to miss dinner."

"Good."

She rolled her eyes, smothering a smile.

"They'll know why."

Gavin pulled back and stared down at her.

"I should hope so."

Holly laughed as Gavin continued making easy work of her gown.

"Might we go to your room?" she asked softly, earning her a questioning look. "It's warmer there."

"As you wish," he said.

Holly had imagined she would walk to his room, but the next instant, Gavin bent over and hoisted her up into his arms.

"Gavin!" she gasped as he walked her across her bedchamber. "What on earth are you doing?"

"Fulfilling your request."

"I can walk."

He shrugged as he opened the door between their rooms.

"Can you? How interesting."

Holly had to stifle a laugh as he crossed the threshold. He was impossible to argue with sometimes, particularly when he was determined to do something his way. But Holly had to give him credit. She had never felt so secure as when she was with him, which was indeed a testament to the sort of person Gavin was. He did not brood, nor did he treat her or her family with a heavy hand. He was thoughtful and gentle, though he could be mischievous occasionally, just as he was at that moment.

Gavin walked around the edge of his bed and dropped her gently onto the counterpane. Holly's gaze fell on the stack of black books lining the wall beneath the window for a moment. John's journals.

Gavin followed Holly's line of sight and sighed when he realized what she was looking at.

"Have you started to read them yet?" Holly asked as Gavin began to undress.

"I flipped through a few, but the earlier ones are not very interesting," he said, shrugging off his coat and then vest. "I've actually been looking for some specific information."

"What information?"

"Something your brother mentioned."

"Oh?" Holly said. "What about?"

The corner of his mouth pulled up, though his gaze didn't meet hers.

"Something about how my uncle mentioned that we should meet. Jasper said John brought it up last summer."

"Really?"

"Yes, but so far I've only found something pertaining to last year's house party. The former Duchess of Combe showed up unannounced?" He shook his head as he began to crawl onto the bed. "It's not exactly exciting."

"That happened last summer," Holly said, scooching back. "You must read further back."

"Further back? Why?"

"Because," Holly said, suddenly unsure.

Should she tell him her theory?

"Because why?"

She shook her head. She wouldn't tell him what she had learned that day, about John wanting custody or her theory that he might have been more generous with his allowance than Gavin had been led to believe. Not when she still wasn't sure she had the whole story.

"I only knew John for a portion of his life and I must confess, I'm terribly curious about his early life," she said as Gavin advanced. "I think you should read them and tell me about it."

"You're welcome to read them yourself."

Holly shook her head, an idea forming. Hesitantly, she stepped back up and looked directly into his hazel eyes.

"I want you to read them," she said softly. "And tell me what's written."

Gavin tilted his head, watching her with a curious, sultry stare.

"Is this about those supposed wicked stories he wrote?" he asked, and Holly nodded. Whatever she could do to get him to read them. Gavin smirked. "Very well. Then I'll start them tonight."

Pleased, Holly leaned forward, kissing him. His hand came up and held her mouth to his, and Holly became breathless.

Chapter Seventeen

T HE EXCITEMENT AT the start of the social season was unlike any other, particularly the day of the debutante ball. It was as if all of London was teeming with enthusiasm and possibility. Holly had kept herself busy for most of the day, writing letters and whatnot, but Katrina had been skipping and dancing around the house. She reminded Holly of a bee, buzzing from room to room, counting the hours before it was time to get ready.

Gavin had decided to visit Mr. Armstrong that morning to rescind his and Holly's request for an annulment, but when he returned to Bairnsdale Terrace, he explained that the lawyer hadn't been in his offices.

By one o'clock, Katrina couldn't wait any longer and insisted that she begin to prepare herself. Even though the ball would not be being for several hours, they were to be presented in court before the soirée began. Holly assisted her sister in her preparations and made sure Katrina was meticulous before dressing herself.

While the debutantes being presented were restricted to white gowns and white plumage in their hair, Holly was permitted to wear any color she wished as a married woman. She debated wearing a lilac colored gown but was a devoted fan of green and chose a simple but exceedingly elegant pine green satin dress with a natural waist fitting. Holly felt rather beautiful.

Just as she finished donning her a la Grecque headdress, which was more of a thick band of fabric than a true headdress, Gavin came into her room without warning. Holly turned to see his attention entirely focused on his wrist as he tinkered with something.

"Bloody useless things," he mumbled as he entered her room, the maids scurrying off. "Holly, might I have some help from…"

He looked up then and stopped in his tracks. Holly stood in all her finery as her breath caught. He watched her with the most intent stare, and as he approached her with deliberate steps, she half expected him to say something when his arms suddenly wrapped around her, pulling her against his chest as he kissed her.

She let herself be embraced, but after half a moment, she drew back.

"Stop. You'll ruin my hair," she chided, her skin warm with appreciation.

"I can't help it," he said, kissing her chin. "You're a vision."

"That's very kind of you, but you needn't say such things."

Gavin paused in his handling of her and tilted his head.

"Why needn't I?"

"Well, because…" she fumbled. "It's not… It's overt."

A challenging smirk crossed his full lips as his hazel eyes gleamed.

"I think I shall call you a different version of beautiful every day, just to make you used to it."

Holly's cheeks warmed.

"I pray you do not."

"But it's so fun watching you change colors," he said, kissing the rim of her cheekbone. "Do you know what I first found most attractive about you?"

Holly shivered.

"No."

"Your voice," he whispered into her ear.

"My voice? Oh, dear, no. It's too deep."

"Mm, no. I think it's perfect." He kissed her earlobe, and a jolt went through her. "It's my favorite thing in the world when you say my name."

"Is it?"

"Hmm."

Holly smiled as his kisses trailed down her neck.

"Gavin," she said gently, and he groaned against the pulse in her throat.

"Say it again."

"Gavin," she said, slower this time.

His fingers dug into her backside, crushing her gown as his mouth opened, his tongue trailing down the hollow of her neck. Frantic, she pushed him away before she completely lost control.

"We've already dressed, Gavin, please."

He released her, breathing heavily. Evidently, his teasing had gone too far, and he now looked at her like she was prey.

"Stop saying my name then."

She nodded and headed for the door, but before she left, a teasing part of her took the reins and she looked over her shoulder and smirked.

"Come along. *Gavin*."

He strode towards her, and she let out a little yip as she dashed away from him, hurrying towards the stairs. They were halfway down the steps when they saw Katrina and Marnie waiting patiently by the door.

Straightening her shoulders as Gavin cleared his throat, they exited the house to make their way to the coming-out ball.

St. James Palace was one of the most impressive buildings Holly had ever seen in her entire life. The sheer size of it gave her something to awe at. They waited in the carriage queue for nearly a half hour before exiting. Though it was a medieval palace, Holly couldn't help but feel she was entering some magical stronghold. And once they were brought inside, her jaw actually dropped.

The floors were covered with red carpets with a gold diamond-shaped pattern. The two-story high windows were lined with matching curtains. The walls were all painted bright white, and gold-framed paintings, the size of carriages, hung from the walls.

"Impressive, isn't it?" Marnie whispered to Katrina as they walked ahead of Holly and Gavin.

"Yes," Katrina whispered as Holly felt Gavin's bicep flex beneath her fingers.

She looked at him, his eyes sparkling with amusement as he watched her. He leaned towards her as they continued to follow a line of people to the ballroom where Katrina would be presented.

"You aren't nervous, are you?"

"Of course not," Holly lied.

"You know, if you'd like, we could have Felton Manor decorated in this same style?"

Holly grimaced.

"Oh, goodness no. This is much too..." Holly caught the teasing grin on his lips and smirked. "You're jesting?"

"Not if you actually want it."

"No, thank you," she said as they reached the doorway into the ballroom.

It was a vast room with gold accents and crystal chandeliers. White flowers had been gathered and set in large assortments around the room. Hundreds of guests filled the chamber, and Holly, Gavin, and Marnie were soon introduced. At the same time, Katrina was sequestered in another room where the other debutantes were kept before the official meeting with the head of state.

Holly peered down at her gown, wondering if she had picked the proper attire. A sheer silver netting laid over the green satin, splitting down the skirt in an upside-down V. It was a new style she hadn't ever worn before, and her nervousness must have shown for the moment after they were announced, Gavin made sure to compliment her again as he led her to the refreshments table.

"You are beautiful, Holly. You know that, don't you?"

She felt her cheeks warm.

"Thank you."

Never in Holly's life had she felt more pleased. Although she never would have guessed that being here would have that effect on her. Large parties had never interested her, but for some reason, she felt a little taller than she ever had before, simply being on Gavin's arm.

He led her through a crowded side room, nodding and greeting people as they went. He seemed to know everyone. If Holly allowed herself to indulge, she might feel insecure about it, but then it would be evident on her face, and she wouldn't want to appear anything less than perfect. Not because Gavin wanted her to be perfect but because she wished to make a good impression, for the sake of Gavin's reputation as well as Katrina's. But even as she thought these things, she knew Gavin's opinion of her could never be altered by anything the ton said or did.

It was why she loved him.

She loved him. She loved him? When in the world had she decided that? Just now? Before they arrived?

Holly's face must have demonstrated her inner turmoil, for Gavin leaned in and whispered into her ear.

"Are you all right? Is something the matter?"

Holly shook her head, unable to speak. She couldn't tell him what she had just thought. He would think she was crazy. They had only known each other for a few months. But then, why did it feel so natural to believe it?

The memories of the night before caused a flood of feelings to course through her. Desire, shame, anticipation. She wanted this entire evening and the entire ball to be in the past, not only to quell her anxiety but because it meant she would be in Gavin's arms again.

Gavin gently squeezed the tips of her gloved fingers as they walked, causing Holly to glance back at him. Evidently, the sentiment about wishing they were home was shared, for the expression he gave her was warm and deliberate. She shivered slightly as they met Derek.

"I swear, these mamas grow bolder each year," he said lowly to Gavin. "One just nearly assaulted me into agreeing to dance with her daughters."

"It does seem a cutthroat business," Gavin said, glancing at Holly. "Thankfully I'm out of it."

"And not a sight too soon. The minute you inherited that title of yours, they would have been swarming."

"Then perhaps I owe a great deal of thanks to my uncle."

"Because a few mamas wish you to dance at a ball? Surely you both aren't afraid of a few devoted mothers, are you?" Holly asked, earning her a skeptical glare from Derek.

Holly knew very well that debutante mamas were some of the most ruthless people in the kingdom, but she did enjoy teasing Derek, and the tiny nod from Gavin encouraged her to do so.

"I see this is your first time at St. James," the earl said sardonically.

Holly smiled.

"The only balls I've attended are public ones in the country."

"Well, prepare yourself. For there's never been anything quite as dangerous as a coming out ball."

Just then, it was announced that the presentation was about to begin. For the next hour, lady after young lady was presented to Princess Elizabeth, the king's sister. In Holly's opinion, each lady was more lovely than the last, and she was surprised to find that she was holding her breath by the time Katrina made her way down the crowded corridor.

Her sister's gown was simple in design, unlike many of the overtly embroidered dresses chosen by other young ladies. Katrina had decided on it herself, and while Holly had been nervous that a lack of beads and crystal might make her sister appear provincial, the opposite effect happened. Katrina seemed fresh and beautiful, not needing any fringe or embellishment to distract the eye.

It was soon whispered that Miss Katrina Smyth was the loveliest of the debutantes, and Holly's heart nearly exploded with joy. Never in her life had she much cared for the approval of anyone, but to know that her sister would be a success was enough to give her a great deal of joy.

After the presentation, the guests were ushered into the ballroom, where a few dozen musicians began to play. It was tradition for the debutantes to dance first, and Holly was rather charmed when Gavin offered to dance with Katrina.

Holly smiled as she watched them twirl away as the music began, only to be met with Mr. Mannion. She tried to make her face impassive, so as to not let him see how surprised she was to see him. What was he doing here?

"Lady Bairnsdale," he said with a slight nod, gazing at the floor. "A pleasure seeing you again."

"Mr. Mannion. I didn't expect to see you here."

"Yes, well, you're not the only one lucky enough to be connected. I've a cousin who is a marquis. Well, a second cousin, but I was able to get the old goat to invite me and the missus so that we could present our daughter," he said, scanning the floor. "There she is! Dancing with the Earl of Trembley."

Holly glanced over the crowded room, and sure enough, she was able to spot Derek, stone-faced, dancing with a young blonde lady Holly recognized as Daphne. The girl seemed to be talking excessively, as was her wont. Holly had to bite her lip to stop herself from smirking.

"How lovely," she said eventually.

"Lovely nothing. My wife is certain the earl will propose to our girl in a week or so. She had to practically push him away when he first saw her, you know. Said he'd never met a prettier girl."

"Is that so?" Holly said. "Well, my felicitations to you."

"Thank you," the man said, facing her. "I hope there aren't any hard feelings between us. What with that business with your brother and all."

Holly's smile shrank slightly. She didn't wish to discuss her brother, but ignoring the topic would only encourage Mr. Mannion.

"Of course not. It is in the past."

"A kinder lady I know not. You're quite like your mother; god rest her soul. She was an exceedingly gracious woman."

"Thank you for saying so Mr. Mannion."

"I was never able to get her to sell me Felton Manor either, you know. She was dedicated to that house just as much as you were."

Holly's brow pinched together.

"I beg your pardon, Mr. Mannion?"

"Ah, I only mean your mother was absolutely against me purchasing Felton Manor off her, even though I offered her exactly what it was worth," he said as if he was being generous by being fair. "But she wouldn't have it. A stubborn lady, she was, but I am grateful that you've at least come to your senses."

Holly shook her head, unsure of what she was hearing.

"What are you speaking about, Mr. Mannion?"

"The sale of Felton Manor, of course," he said as if she should know. "I had papers drawn up at your brother's request. It was our whole reason for coming to London. Well, that and all this, of course." He nodded around the room.

Holly's stomach dropped as she stared.

"Excuse me?" she asked, feeling suddenly light-headed. "Jasper requested papers be drawn up?"

"Yes."

Jasper had threatened to sell Felton Manor for months, but she never believed he would actually do it. He wasn't even of legal age to do so. He couldn't have had the papers drawn up until the following week.

"Mr. Mannion, I'm not sure what my brother said to you, but he isn't the executor to the property yet."

"Well, I know that."

"Then you must forgive me, because it sounds as though

you're sure that someone has sold you Felton Manor."

"Well, yes, your husband has."

"My...husband," she said slowly as it dawned on her.

Gavin sold Felton Manor? But it hadn't even finished being renovated. And indeed, he wouldn't have done something so outrageous behind her back. Would he?

Suddenly desperate to speak with him, Holly made her excuses to Mr. Mannion and moved along the edge of the ballroom, following Gavin and Katrina as they moved effortlessly with the other dancers. A slight ringing filled Holly's ears as pain seized her heart.

How could she have been so foolish? Apparently, Gavin and Jasper had decided to get rid of her family home without mentioning it to her. She was furious at the betrayal, but even more surprisingly, her heart hurt. Why did she feel so heartbroken?

Unable to keep up with their dancing, Holly walked quickly, only to be stopped by Clara.

"Holly," her friend chirped until she saw her face. "Oh my, what's wrong?"

Holly opened her mouth to speak when a sudden commotion erupted behind them in the ballroom doorway. Confused, both women strained their necks to see over the crowd. The familiar, walnut-colored hair that bobbed back and forth in a devil-may-care way made Holly's insides twist.

Good god, *no*.

"—I've reason enough to challenge you, but I'd feel remorse for killing a child."

"Go on then!" Jasper's voice pierced her ear through the gasps and chatter. "Let us settle this like gentlemen!"

Holly was suddenly frantic. Jasper was going to kill himself, and she didn't know what to do. Thankfully, Clara gripped her wrist and pulled her down the way.

"We'll find Silas at once. He'll do something," Clara said as they moved. "What on earth is Jasper even doing here?"

"I don't know," Holly said, unsure herself. As if conjured by magic, Gavin's form suddenly crossed their paths.

Clara stopped at once but kept herself between Gavin and Holly, for which Holly was grateful. She wasn't sure what was worse, her brother making a scene or Gavin's betrayal.

"What's wrong?" he asked, but before either could answer, the commotion became more distant. Someone seemed to have led the arguing men out of the ballroom and into the hallway, though the voices carried through. Gavin frowned. "Was that Jasper?"

Holly wasn't sure what to do, much less say. She wanted to run after Jasper to settle whatever new issue he had created, but she knew it would be an empty attempt. She and her brother could not seem to cooperate on anything nowadays. A part of her wanted desperately to lean on Gavin, but the audacity of his betrayal for selling Felton Manor was too great. She tried to get away from him, from everyone in that crowded room.

Miserably, tears began to sting her eyes. She didn't want to ruin Katrina's evening, but she couldn't bear to stay, not when Jasper might be in the process of landing himself in a duel that could end in his death. She saw Clara and cleared her throat.

"Clara, will you watch over Katrina and see her home? I have to go."

"Of course—"

"Go where?" Gavin said, cutting his shoulder in front of Clara. "What's going on?"

She wanted to ignore him and pretend he wasn't even there, but she knew he wouldn't allow that—and she didn't want her family to be the cause of yet *another* scene. Instead, she inhaled slowly and stared him square in the eye, ignoring the pain she felt in her chest.

"Jasper is being tossed out and I've no doubt he's going to get himself killed in a duel."

"Stay here," Gavin said instantly, but her hand grabbed his sleeve, and he stopped.

"I don't want your help."

The weight of her words stalled him, and Holly was grateful that Clara had moved away. Holly could feel the frustration and hurt rolling off Gavin as he stared at her, his eyes confused.

"Excuse me?"

"I don't want your help," she repeated, her voice barely above a whisper as they spoke in the crowded room. "Mr. Mannion told me about the sale."

He had the nerve to appear confused.

"What sale?"

"Of Felton Manor. Do not deny it. He said you and Jasper had a conversation about it and papers were being drawn up."

Realization dawned on his face. So, he did know what she was talking about? A tiny part of her had hoped she was wrong and that Mr. Mannion had misunderstood somehow... but it appeared those hopes were in vain.

"You don't deny it?" she said, even knowing he wouldn't.

"Holly, let me explain."

She turned away from him, too hurt to be in his presence. She needed to leave, to find whomever Jasper offended and apologize to him so that she might still have a brother by morning.

She made it to the front entrance quickly and overheard a large, barrel-chested man with salt and pepper whiskers make fuming remarks on Jasper.

"Devil of a lad, that one," he huffed, brushing off the invisible dust off his sleeves.

"Who is he?" someone else asked.

"A pest. He caused some trouble at White's recently. Thankfully, he was thrown out."

"More like Clemet Club material."

"No doubt."

Holly bit her lip. Clemet Club was widely known as a troublesome place. Raids were conducted there almost weekly, and it was often reported in the *Times* that only the most desperate men would find themselves in such a place.

She moved past the gentlemen and quickly informed a footman that she wished for her carriage to be brought around. To her amazement, Gavin didn't pursue her, and by the time she was outside, waiting for her carriage, she had concluded that he hadn't ever really cared for her or her family. But then, why would he? Theirs was a marriage of convenience, a trick they both fell into.

A tear rolled down Holly's cheek as she set out on her search for her brother. She had foolishly let herself believe that some sort of fate or magic had brought Gavin into her life when it had simply been chance. There was nothing genuine between them, and as her carriage pulled away into the night, she prayed she be able to find her brother—and bury her broken heart in her search.

Chapter Eighteen

G AVIN STARED AFTER Holly as she left the ballroom. Every instinct screamed for him to go after her, but she was apparently eager to be out of his presence and he had no wish to upset her further. Not when she had already seemed near the point of tears when telling him that Jasper had contacted Mannion about selling Felton Manor.

Bloody hell. He would right this. If necessary, he would buy the bloody manor himself and gift it to her. But what was most pressing at the moment wasn't Holly's temper. No, it was her brother's life.

Turning, he saw Clara, who had done a fine job of pretending to disappear while he and Holly had spoken in hushed tones.

"What was Jasper doing here?" he asked, hoping he would have answers.

"I don't know," Clara said. "But he's caused quite a stir. I think I overhear him challenging the Duke of Gloucester."

Gavin groaned inwardly.

"Bloody hell. What is wrong with him? And what would give him the grand idea of challenging someone in such a public place?"

"Well, the duke insulted him. He called Jasper a child."

Gavin closed his eyes momentarily and pursed his lips into a line. He already knew that Jasper loathed being called a child.

"Splendid. Then I suppose he's gone off to prove himself the opposite. I've got to go after him, before he gets himself killed," he said, shaking his head as Derek and Silas appeared. "Holly's brother is causing a fair amount of trouble. I'm afraid I'll have to leave, though who knows where I should even begin searching for him."

"Ah," Derek said, his brow creasing. "I may actually know."

Gavin glanced at his friend. Derek rarely concerned himself with the seeder side of society... except when it came to gambling. Realizing this, Gavin knew where Jasper was going before Derek said it.

"Clemet Club," they said in unison.

Gavin turned to Silas. "Will you see to it that Holly, Aunt Marnie, and Katrina are conveyed safely home?"

"Of course," Silas said with a nod, before noticing Clara's wide-eyed expression.

"Is there something wrong?"

Clara shook her head.

"No."

But Gavin sensed she wasn't telling the truth. Curious, he wanted to question her, but Silas spoke first.

"We'll see everyone home safely."

"Thank you," Gavin said earnestly. Turning to leave, he found Derek by his side. "What are you doing?"

"I'm coming with you."

"There's no need for you to ruin your own night."

"Believe me, this is a godsend. Besides, you don't even know where Clemet Club is."

"And you do?"

"I know every gaming table in this city."

They were out the door and in a hired hackney within minutes, neither wishing to bother with waiting for a carriage. As they moved through the city, Gavin couldn't shake the image of Holly's angry face from his mind.

He hadn't meant to go behind her back, but at the same time

Gavin sympathized with Jasper, a young man aimless in the world. He had been that young man and had gone abroad for many years searching for something he hadn't ever genuinely found until recently.

A purpose.

Gavin had never felt tied to any person or place until fate had dropped him square in the middle of the Smyth family. It had been infuriating at first to come to terms with the fact that he had been hoodwinked into marriage with a stranger, but every day since being informed of his new life, he had felt grounded. As if he had finally found a reason for living—and it wasn't an endless pursuit of a hedonistic lifestyle. He found his only desires wrapped around the finger of a single woman who was furious with him.

But even her anger couldn't upset him. Perhaps it was his ever-mounting optimism, but Gavin was even grateful that she was upset with him because it meant that she cared about him.

Perhaps it was foolish, but Gavin was convinced that he could explain everything to Holly once he saved Jasper from whatever mess he had managed to get himself in.

Derek watched him with a confused expression, his arms folded across his chest.

"You seem... Oddly calm."

"Why wouldn't I be?"

Derek shrugged.

"If my brother-in-law insulted the Duke of Gloucester and was tossed out of St. James Palace after running up debts all over England's gambling hells, I'd be a touch more worried."

"He's a confused young man who will surely see the error of his ways in a few years. Until then, it's my job to keep him in line."

"Your job? Since when?"

"Since marrying Holly."

The earl stared at him.

"You seemed to have taken to the role of surrogate family

patriarch with ease. I would have guessed it would be stifling to a man who never had to worry about other people."

Gavin shook his head.

"That's always what you and Silas assumed—that I enjoyed my solitary existence," he said lowly. "But the truth is, it wasn't very fun for me. Not having anyone always left me alone, didn't it? And while I was blessed enough to have friends who always included me, there's nothing quite like being a part of something, irrevocably."

"So, marriage suits you?"

"It does, although I doubt I'll have the easiest time of it over the next few hours. Holly is perturbed with me."

"Why?"

"I made the mistake of informing her brother that I would consider helping him sell off Felton Manor, their childhood home."

"And she didn't want you to do that?"

"No."

"Well, save her brother from being drawn and quartered over gambling debts and she'll likely forgive you."

"I've my doubts."

"Then they are unfounded," Derek insisted. "She seems very fond of you. I noticed it at Combe's dinner party. She's very eager to please you."

"Ah, yes," Gavin said, smirking as he gazed down at his hands, flexing his fingers. "She told me about the candies."

Derek nodded before peering out the carriage window.

"We'll be there shortly. Kilmann's club isn't far now."

"How do you know about Clemet Club? I thought it was only a place for desperate men."

"I would be a poor host if I didn't keep up with my competitors."

"I thought you were giving up your secret gambling games?"

Derek shrugged.

"I will, eventually. The earldom has certainly taken much of my time, but I find I'm unwilling to let them go for some reason."

"Well, you should. I haven't been to a game in months and Combe refuses to go anymore, not since the last time," Gavin said, referring to the time Combe actually won his wife in a hand of cards. "I'm sure the time to let go is nigh."

"When something comes along to distract me from the game, it might. Until then…" he trailed off as the coach stopped. "We must be here."

Opening the door, Gavin was surprised to see a very plain brick building in an unassumingly quiet neighborhood. Though the cobblestone streets were barren, Gavin felt an unnatural chill. This wasn't like the gaming spots by the docks, where taverns and streetwalkers lined every sidewalk, creating a bustling nightlife of danger. Nor was it the pristine, wide windowed buildings he was used to, such as White's, where only the finest of London's elite went.

This place was dangerous.

Out of the corner of his eye, Gavin saw two silhouettes at the end of the street, standing there unmoving as he followed Derek up the steps, where another tall, dark figure lurked in front of the door. It seemed there were men at every turn around here, and Gavin suddenly realized just how perilous it would be for someone trying to escape with unpaid debts.

Derek spoke to the figure only to be rebuked immediately.

"Piss off," the thick cockney accent bellowed through the night at them while Derek squared his shoulders as if ready for a fight.

"Now, see here—" he started, but Gavin held his hand up and pressed it into his friend's chest.

He had been to similar places in Greece, where talk could do little to persuade people. The only thing anyone generally understood was a coin.

Pulling out a five-pound note, Gavin squashed it into the man's fist.

"We want in."

"Don't you dare give him that," Derek warned as the man tucked the money away.

"It'll cost you. Kilmann don't like wasting his time on pigeons."

The derogatory term for tight-laced dupes nearly made Gavin smirk while his friend began to shake.

"What's the buy in?" Gavin asked.

"Two hundred."

"Absolutely not," Derek spat, but Gavin nodded.

"Fine."

"No." The earl placed his hand square in the middle of Gavin's chest. "Don't you dare give him so much."

"You don't have to come in," Gavin told his friend. "But I do."

Derek seemed to think about it for a minute and then, sighing loudly, nodded as the man turned and opened the door.

Clemet Club was not a place of grandeur or splendid things. It was dark and smelled heavily of smoke and gin. While White's had all the decorations and magnificence of a fine establishment with tall walls and high ceilings, Clemet Club was decidedly darker, with few furnishings aside from several tables lined against the walls in a part-open ballroom, part parlor. It had been refurbished to accommodate gambling tables, and there, against the wall, near a black marble fireplace, stood Kilmann.

Wearing a vest and beaver top hat, Kilmann stood a foot above everyone, scanning the tables from his post as Gavin and Derek entered. Kilmann was older than everyone in the room but sharper than most of London. His wrinkled, worn face seemed to be carved from ice. Gavin saw several men he knew, all sweating and focused on the games at their tables.

And there, at the faro table, sat Jasper. He hadn't even realized that Gavin and Derek had entered; he was so focused on the cards in his hands.

The scent of desperation and greed filled the air, and when Kilmann approached, he noticed the flicker of a predatory gleam in his eyes. They were new meat for him.

"Ah, Lord Trembley. To what do I owe the pleasure of your presence at our humble establishment?"

"We're searching for—"

"A game to play," Gavin said, unwilling to drop any unnecessary connection between them and anyone else. It seemed dangerous to let this man know too much about them.

Kilmann's gaze flickered to Gavin.

"Indeed. Well, we've a faro table set up, hazards just over there and vingt-et-un if you're feeling daring."

"Faro."

"Very well. Two hundred, all in coin. No other form of payment is accepted."

"Is that so?" Gavin said. "No house deeds, or anything like that?"

A flash of suspicion came over Kilmann's face.

"Do you have any house deeds you wish to offer up?"

"None that I know of. Shall we?" Gavin asked, turning as he went to take a seat next to Jasper, who finally glanced up. What little color had been present on the young man's face disappeared at the sight of his brother-in-law, but thankfully he was too well versed in guarding his expression to let Kilmann know anything about anything.

"No, that table is full," Kilmann said slowly, moving his hand to an empty table. "We'll start another game here."

Tension snapped between the room, and Gavin was suddenly aware that everyone else was aware of their presence. He and Derek sat at the table and began to play a very unsettling game of faro.

Chapter Nineteen

Holly hadn't planned on following Gavin and Derek when they passed her in a rush, unaware that she had been standing behind one of the archways. In fact, she had only wanted a bit of fresh air, to collect her thoughts. But when she saw them rush past her and enter a hired hackney, a sudden need to follow them took over. Perhaps Jasper had run off to White's again, and they were pursuing him? Or maybe they would go to the apartments where Jasper was staying. Either way, she was going to follow them and find her brother so that she might give him a piece of her mind.

Holly found her carriage, thankfully loitering down the line, close to the street. Their driver, Mr. Hoss, was leaning against the vehicle, speaking to another driver when he saw her approaching.

He quickly straightened up.

"My lady?" he asked, concerned.

"Follow that hackney that just pulled off," she said with an authority she hadn't believed she possessed. He opened the door and helped her in. "And please, make haste."

Evidently when one spoke with conviction, people didn't ask questions, for the driver nodded and quickly climbed into his seat. They were on the road in mere seconds.

Holly held her hands tightly entwined on her lap. Perhaps she was being foolish chasing after them, but indignation swallowed her along with the need to demand answers. Felton Manor may not belong to her, but she wouldn't let it go without a fight. Jasper and Gavin owed her an explanation.

A small, annoying voice sounded in the back of her mind, though. It asked what she was holding on to so desperately—and why? It was Jasper's inheritance after all, not hers, and if he was fool enough to sell it, no doubt for half of what it was worth, perhaps she should simply stand aside and let him. He clearly did not care one way or the other about the property, so what did she hope to gain by forcing him to hold on to it? He'd been dying to get it off his hands for years. She thought it was foolish to give up a farm that could easily support him for the rest of his life, but if he made the decision to run through his inheritance, he'd only have himself to blame. Besides, she had plenty of resources to help Katrina. She didn't need Felton Manor. So what was she holding on to?

A former life? The reminiscences of her mother and father? Of a time where she hadn't been so burdened? She shook her head. It wasn't as if Jasper was selling her memories. She would never forget her mother or the simple, sweet life she had once upon a time.

Perhaps, if she allowed herself to let go, she'd find an equally sweet and peaceful future. With Gavin.

Still, the sting of finding out that it had all happened without warning... well, it hurt much worse than she would have expected. Had Holly kept Gavin at a distance, she might not have been surprised at his betrayal, but she hadn't. She let him into her heart and now she'd been forced to realize that it had been a mistake to do so. It was her fault for believing in him.

Despondent as the carriage turned down this road and that at a brisk pace, Holly was barely aware that they had come to a stop when the door opened, revealing Mr. Hoss.

"My lady, I fear we're not in the best of neighborhoods," he said tensely, peering over his shoulder. "I think it would be best if we returned to Bairnsdale Terrace."

"Where are we?" she asked, peering over his shoulders. "This isn't White's, is it?"

"No, my lady. The baron and the earl came down this way and entered that house," he said, pointing a finger across the way to a fairly normal looking brick building. "I watched them go in, not moments ago. But it is not a kind place. Pickpockets don't even come down this way, my lady. It's unsafe."

"Well, if there are no pickpockets, then I'm sure we'll fare just fine," she said, moving towards the door.

The driver blanched at her determination but stepped aside to let her out. It was a dark road with a decidedly eerie stillness, but Holly would not be deterred. If Jasper was in the brick house, she would go there, pull him out, and set everything to rights herself.

She took a deep breath and stalked forward, followed by Mr. Hoss, who refused to leave her.

"If you insist on going in there, my lady, I'm afraid I must accompany you."

"Very well," she said stiffly, though deep down, she was grateful not to be left alone.

Coming up to the house, Holly realized a tall man dressed all in black was standing in the shadows, blocking the door. As she approached, the bright orange circle of his cheroot illuminated the tip of his broken nose, the edge of his cheekbones, and the glassiness of his eyes.

Holly swallowed back her fear and cleared her throat.

"Sir—"

"Piss off."

Holly's mouth dropped at the vulgarity while her driver hissed.

"How dare you speak to a lady like that," he said, puffing out his chest. "I have half a mind to teach you a lesson." The tall man unfolded his arms, stepped forward, and glared down at the both of them. Holly heard the gulp in her driver's throat. "But I wouldn't want to insult the lady further by displaying such brutality in her presence," Mr. Hoss added, a little shakily.

The man chuckled evilly.

"Ain't no way you're getting in."

She frowned.

"Then would it be possible for you to bring someone out?"

He took a drag from his cheroot and blew it out above her head.

"No."

Silent tension followed as she tried not to inhale. Holly needed, at the very least, to get Jasper out of the house, but there would be no way to get around the guard. If only there was a way to get them to come out.

He took another inhale of his tobacco, and Holly got an idea.

"Might I have one of your cigars?"

He stared at her, as did the driver.

"Why?"

"Because I'd like to see one."

"Go away," he said, turning his back on her.

But Holly would not give up. Turning behind him, she reached for the doorknob, only to be gripped by his painful grasp.

"I said, get gone!"

"I will not," she said firmly, hitting the door with her other hand. "I demand to be let in at once!"

"Unhand her!" Mr. Hoss yelled as he lunged for the bully of a man.

Temporarily distracted, Holly took her chance as the guard turned his attention on the driver, but just as he fell into the front door, she was gripped by a pair of vise-like hands.

"Now, now, now, what do we have here?" a slick, dangerous voice sounded in her ear as she was put back on her feet. The man was tall, with a long, wrinkled face, an ornate vest, and a top hat, and he appeared mildly interested as he stared down at Holly. "A lady? Finkle, unhand this woman's driver," he barked over his shoulder, causing her to wince. Glancing back down at her, the man smiled, though Holly felt ill at the sight. "Now, my lady, how may I be of service to you?"

"I... I was hoping to have a word with one of your patrons. I know you mustn't permit women, but I insist."

"Ah, but I welcome all sexes to Clemet Club. Coin is coin, after all. But no one who enters this house who isn't themselves a patron. And if you can afford the two hundred pound entry, you are now one."

"But I don't have two hundred pounds."

"By the style of your dress, I say you've got plenty, but let's not stand out in this drafty hallway while we discuss it."

He held out his arm to her, and Holly felt she had no choice. She was now indebted at least two hundred pounds simply for entering. Giving him a tight smile, she barely rested her hand on his forearm as she squared her shoulders. He led her into a somewhat brighter room, though it was still very dark, filled with a thick layer of smoke and the scent of gin.

Several tables filled with several men were scattered around the room. No one appeared to be particularly interested in her arrival except a man in the center of the room. His hazel eyes locked on hers and the tension in his shoulders made her insides tighten.

Gavin.

He stared at her like she was some sort of apparition, but he didn't get up. In fact, Derek, who sat next to him, seemed purposely trying to ignore her. Something was very wrong, indeed.

"We were just starting a new game, my lady," the older man in the top hat said, escorting her to the table where her husband sat. He pulled out a wooden chair, and she sat as her nerves began to buzz. "Allow me to introduce myself. I'm Mr. Kilmann."

"V-very nice to meet you," she said softly, trying to keep her eyes off Gavin, whose expression was barely controlled. A slight vein pulsing at his temple told her that he was struggling to contain himself. She had never seen him so upset. "What game are we playing?"

"Faro," Kilmann said, turning to Gavin as he began to deal

out the cards. "Now tell me, Bairnsdale, what do you want? You know everyone who comes here is good for their coin."

"I am aware," Gavin said stiffly, trying not to look at Holly. "We were just searching for a friend. He insulted the Duke of Gloucester tonight, and unfortunately, he may be called out. We didn't want to see him killed before morning."

"Is that so?" Kilmann said, obviously uninterested. "Well, that is a situation. And you said Smyth was his name?"

"Yes."

"Hmm. Well, I don't know anyone by that name here," Kilmann said, his head turning to face the other table. Holly tried to follow his gaze without detection. She saw her brother, eyes down on a set of cards as a stream of sweat dropped from the side of his forehead. "But I do know someone who claims to be a cousin of yours, Bairnsdale. It's how he gained access here."

Kilmann dealt out several cards around the table.

"A cousin?" Gavin said as Holly picked up her cards. "Is that so?"

"But you don't have any cousins, isn't that correct?"

It would be foolish to try to deny it. Everyone knew that Gavin Winscombe was the sole heir to his uncle—the last of his line.

"Correct."

"So, I've been lied to."

Noting the dangerous turn in conversation, Holly opted to distract the man named Kilmann. She brought her forearms to the edge of the table and leaned forward. *Heaven help her.* She might die of embarrassment, but it would be better to die by her own humiliation than by a bunch of cutthroats. Pressing her upper arms against the sides of her chest, she tried to accentuate her breasts as she fanned out her cards and made her voice sweetly high-pitched.

"Goodness, is four kings the best hand you can get?" she asked, leaning towards Kilmann. "I always forget what beats what."

Kilmann gave her a double take, noticing the deep cut of her neckline, and her eyes flashed to Gavin, whose face darkened as his eyes flashed murderously. If humiliation didn't kill her, Gavin might.

"Is that what you have, my dear?" Kilmann asked, his tone suddenly flirtatious.

"Well, I can't tell you that, can I?" she said with forced lightness. "You might hold it against me."

"There are a number of things I'd like to hold against you."

"Play. The. Hand," Gavin's soft, furious voice bit out from across the table.

"Now, now, Bairnsdale. I'm sure the lady here is a reasonable creature," Kilmann said, turning back to Holly. "You know, at first I thought you were someone from the first ranks of society. But I think you've fooled us."

"Oh?" Her tone went slightly higher.

"Yes. I think you must be a very well-practiced courtesan, although you must be new to London." He tilted his head as he watched her, as if trying to remember her. "I've never seen you before."

"I'm out. If you'll excuse me," Derek said, standing up, dropping his cards. "I must visit the necessary. Excuse me."

Kilmann waved him off, waiting for Holly to continue.

"Yes, I am fairly new to town," she said, noting that Derek was heading towards the door. At least someone was thinking about their exit. "I've just come from Paris."

"Really?" Kilmann said. "What is your name? Surely I would have heard about someone of your beauty through my connection there."

"Oh, it's Madam Downs," she lied, placing two cards on the table. "You know, like in horseracing."

"I'm well versed in the term. Calling the turn," he said smoothly as he flipped over the cards before them. His eyes flashed with delight. "Ah, I'm afraid you won't win this hand, my dear. Lady Luck has blessed me yet again."

Laying down his cards, Holly realized this man had barely even looked at his hand but had still won with ease. Despite outward appearances, Holly had been taught many card games, but faro was not one of them. She followed Gavin's lead and dropped her cards in the middle to be dealt again.

For two more rounds, the same measured playing occurrence, and by the third round of losses, Holly felt herself begin to sweat. Derek returned and fared no better. The room was uncomfortably warm, and a footman kept bringing them whiskey but had no water available, which Holly found suspicious.

She realized they were losing a great deal of money. If they continued, surely they would lose a small fortune before the night was over. Especially if they included Jasper's losses, as well. All that money could have been used for something worthwhile instead of lining the pockets of a crook.

Trying to catch Gavin's eye to signal her desire to leave, she saw that his gaze was locked on the cards, the slight crease between his brow more prominent against the shadows that played across his face in the dark room. He appeared deep in thought.

"Lord Trembley, I expected better from you," Kilmann said, laying the cards out again. "I've only ever heard what a great player you are."

"I must be having an off night," he said lowly, displeasure cast all over his face. He turned to Holly fully and leaned towards her. "How goes it, my lady?"

Confused, Holly gazed down at her cards, unsure what she was seeing, but when she tilted her head up, she realized Derek was staring at her intently. The barest lift of one of his brows told Holly to play her part as a sultry courtesan.

She gave Kilmann her most seductive smile.

"I would say my luck has long run out, but I don't think I ever had any," she said softly. "Would that you could share some of yours with me, sir? I'd be very much obliged."

Out of the corner of her eye, she saw a movement on the

table. It must have caught Kilmann's eye too, for he frowned and was about to turn back to look when she reached across the table and touched his arm to distract him.

"My, for a cardplayer you've an exceedingly muscular arm," she said earnestly, earning a somewhat sloppy smile from the man. "Oh, but I should refrain from saying such things."

"Are we to play or are we to hear this babble all night long?" Gavin said, his tone low and furious.

Kilmann began flipping the cards once more.

"I win, again," he said, but quick as a shot, Gavin's hand came over the pot.

"Not so fast. Check again."

Kilmann's face scrunched with puzzlement for a moment. Then he turned several shades of red as he stood up, nearly knocking the table over.

"You've cheated!" he yelled, his chair kicking to the floor as everyone around them stood.

"Says the man stacking the bloody deck," Gavin accused. "This whole operation is a scam."

"One you'll pay for," Kilmann said, producing a knife from his pocket.

Holly froze with fear as the man lunged at Gavin, surprisingly agile for his age. She cried out when they collided and fell to the ground, rolling together on the floor. Before she knew it, she was pushed off into Jasper's arms by Derek.

"Get her out of here, now!" Derek yelled as he narrowly missed being tackled to the ground by a man who seemed to have come out of nowhere.

The entire house abruptly descended into chaos. Fights broke out at every table and the sickening sound of knuckles slamming into skin turned Holly's stomach as Jasper grabbed her and tried to drag her away. But she fought against him.

"I can't leave him!"

"You'll only distract him! We have to go now," Jasper yelled over the grunts and screams from the others.

Hating that he was probably right, Holly hesitated for only another moment before letting her brother lead her away as a chair flew across the room, splintering against a wall. They rushed out of the brick house to find Holly's coachman standing near the carriage as they came running up.

"My lady! Oh, thank goodness," the driver cried, helping her and Jasper into the coach. "Let us be away from this place at once."

"We're not going anywhere," Holly said firmly. "Not until Gavin comes out of that house."

"But Holly—"

"Jasper, if you ever cared an ounce for me in your entire life, you will not move this carriage," she said, her gaze locked on the brick house. "I will not leave him."

Jasper gave her a contrite look before conceding to her wishes. Nodding to the coachman, he waited with her as they watched the flood of people leaving the house. Holly thought they looked like mice trying to escape a burning barn. The men scurried away in every direction. After several long moments, Jasper spoke, his tone remorseful.

"I do care about you, Holly. I know it doesn't seem like it. I know I'm constantly disappointing you, but it's difficult. You don't understand what it's like, not ever having a choice or a say in one's own life. It's infuriating."

Holly turned to her brother.

"You think I have ever had a choice? Jasper, I've only ever done what was expected of me. Never did I even dream about my own life."

"No one asked you to give your life up."

"No, because it was never a question as to whether I would or not," she said. "Mama and Papa only asked that I watch over you and Katrina. I tried my best, Jasper, I have, but if you are set on ruining your life, then so be it. All I ask is that you have a care for Katrina. When you go about insulting dukes and running up debts, you give us nothing but heartache. I'm not asking you to be a saint, Jasper. Only that you be considerate. Katrina is a good girl and deserves to have a chance at a life without hardships and drama. Your reputation is ruining that."

Jasper bowed his head, seemingly unsure what to say in response. Holly turned her attention back to the brick building. It seemed the house had nearly emptied when two shadowy forms raced out. Feeling it in her soul that Gavin was one of the two men, Holly opened to door to the carriage and shouted.

"Here!"

Both figures stopped and turned in her direction. Then they came running. Within seconds Gavin and Derek were in the carriage. Derek fell into the seat next to Jasper while Gavin sat down next to Holly just as the carriage took off. Her husband was breathing heavily as he rested his head against the padded backboard while they charged forward, full speed ahead.

"My goodness, I didn't know...What?" Holly's hand reached for Gavin's arm, but he winced. Peering down at her fingers, she saw a dark, sticky liquid shining beneath the carriage lamps. Her stomach dropped. "Gavin?"

"It's only a scratch," he said, but Holly did not believe him.

"Take off your coat."

"No—"

"Take it off at once. I demand to see what's going on," she said before hitting the wall with her fist. "We need a doctor!"

"We don't need a doctor; the housekeeper can stitch this up."

"Gavin, I swear—"

"And don't you dare turn this carriage around. I refuse to go back in the direction of that hell hole. And also, I'm furious with you."

"With me?" she snapped, barely caring that Derek and her brother were in the coach with them, witnessing this spousal spat. "What did I do?"

"You practically crawled into the murder's lap for one."

"I did not—"

"Um, pardon," Derek said, causing Holly and Gavin to turn

on him.

"What?" they said in unison.

"If you aren't going to die, might I suggest dropping me off. I've never had a stomach for marital fights."

Chapter Twenty

GAVIN COULD NOT keep the shakes out of his body as he watched Holly enter the house. He had known anger before, but never known genuine fear until that night, which had unnerved him greatly. First, the fact that she had even come to Clemet Club had made him livid. She could have been hurt or killed. Then, to see his wife fawn over another man, even though he'd known full well that she was pretending, had nearly been enough to make him lose his mind.

It had taken every last bit of strength to pin himself to where he sat, which was perhaps why it had taken him so long to realize that Kilmann had stacked the deck and was cheating. Knowing an outright accusation would have had him tossed from the property, Gavin did the only thing he could do to retaliate.

Cheat *back*. Cheat better.

It was easy enough. Gavin knew how to count a deck. He and Silas had learned all the tricks to faro and wist and a dozen other card games from Derek. He had taught Gavin every way to cheat, so that he might be able to spot cheats at his own tables when he hosted his games. Derek was an honest player, but believed that the best way to spot a dishonest one was to know how they worked, and he had taught Gavin long ago how to count cards, or paint cards, or change bets beneath a dealer's nose. Gavin hadn't done so in a long time, but he still had a talent for it. Kilmann's reaction hadn't been what Gavin had hoped for, but then the fight had been distracting enough to get Holly and Jasper out, and as soon as they were out of sight, Gavin had unleashed his pent-up frustration on the man responsible.

But the fight hadn't quelled any part of his fury at the situation, which had continued to stew until he, Holly, and Jasper returned to Bairnsdale Terrace. Following his wife up the staircase, he let her order the servants to bring clean water, bandages, and whatnot to be stitched up.

His forearm had caught Kilmann's knife, but he hadn't even realized it until Holly had touched it in the carriage. The adrenaline was still coursing through his veins.

"And we need a doctor," Holly said firmly to Mr. Spieth.

"Very good, my lady."

"We *don't* need a doctor," Gavin hissed as he followed her to his bedchambers.

"Don't you dare tell me no," she countered.

"Here, see for yourself." He shrugged off his coat and rolled up his blood-soaked sleeve.

Though it was messy, the cut was only superficial. Holly shook her head, undeterred.

"I see nothing that would keep me from ordering a doctor."

"He may come first thing in the morning. I refuse to be poked tonight."

"But it needs to be cleaned."

"You can do that," he said as they entered the room.

"Fine," she said hotly, coming around the bed to wipe his arm with the hot water-soaked cloth the servants had just left.

She pressed against the wound, and he wondered if she was trying to make him wince. He watched as she made short work of tending his arm, even wrapping it in bandages like a skilled doctor. When she was finished, she sat back and stared at him.

He could not express the fury bubbling inside him since leaving Clemet Club. He felt as though he might choke on his words if he spoke, but the anger in Holly seemed to dissipate as she tended to his wound.

"I didn't want to make that dreadful man notice me," she said, her voice quiet, if not defensive. "But I didn't want him to know our connection, either."

Gavin stared at her, begrudgingly aware that she had done the correct thing. Regardless of her intentions, however, it still infuriated him.

"I wanted to kill him," he said slowly. "And throttle you."

She glanced at him, startled.

"Whatever for?"

"For going there in the first place. Not to mention making him stare at you so much," Gavin said, his hand gripping hers as he pulled her towards him. "I never want you to behave like that ever again. God save the next man who leers at you."

Holly's bottom lip dropped as she stared at his mouth, now only inches away.

"Gavin—"

But he wouldn't hear her explanations. Instead, he pulled her closer, kissing her with a heat he had only ever experienced in her presence. Never had he ever felt this sort of custody, as if he were possessed by some devil that commanded he care for her and only her.

As he pulled her on top of him, he knew that he was desperate to keep her. He had never known fear until he saw her enter that card room. All good sense had gone out of him, and he had barely been able to catch the tell from Kilmann. She was too much in his thoughts, too steadily ingrained in his life. He wanted her with him constantly, and it was a struggle to concentrate on anything other than her whenever she was in the room.

"You're an addiction," he whispered against her mouth as he broke their kiss, mad with desire for her. "I can't think properly when you're near me."

"Gavin," she breathed, kissing him back as she pushed what was left of his shirtsleeves down his shoulders, careful not to hurt his bandaged arm.

His hands dug into her sides as her legs fell to either side of him. He wanted her bloody dress off, but she was kissing him, moving her hands over him as though she needed to feel him, and he couldn't think straight. It was animalistic, but he savored every bit of it.

His hands slid down her neck and pulled at the bodice of her gown, tearing it slightly as she gasped against his mouth. She didn't stop or scold him. She was as possessed as he was. He dropped his head, sinking against the pillow as he took the tip of her bare breast into his mouth, eliciting a moan from her, which only fueled him.

Shifting, he undid the front of his trousers as she gathered up her skirts. Never had two people been more in sync and insane with desire, he mused as her hips came up and she sank onto his shaft.

Gavin's brow scrunched together at the painful pleasure of finally feeling her around him. It was devastating and brilliant. He knew there would never be another place where he would be more tortured or more at peace than in her arms.

God, how he loved this woman.

Holly shifted, grinding herself against him in a way that caused his mouth to drop open. He was her servant, her anything if only she would command him. Her gentle, shaking voice saying his name genuinely undid him, for the tremble in it proved that she was just as much at the mercy of him as he was to her.

"Gavin," she whimpered, her breathing shifting to short gasps.

He felt a rush of triumph, knowing he was responsible for the pleasure she was feeling. Her building orgasm was *his,* as would be every one that came after.

"Keep going," he said shakily.

"I... I..."

"Say my name," he whispered as his own body began to tense. "Holly. Oh god, Holly."

"Gavin!"

The convulsions around his manhood tore through his body at the same time as she shook, tense in his arms before dropping entirely onto his chest. Breathing heavily, Gavin wrapped his arms around her back and held her as tightly as he could, vowing silently to never let her enter any danger again.

After several silent moments, their breathing returned to normal. Gavin helped a prone Holly remove what was left of her gown and underthings while he kicked off the pants that were still wrapped around his ankle. How ridiculous that they hadn't even been able to get fully undressed, but then, laying naked together beneath the counterpane of his bed, Gavin could barely find fault with the moment.

Except that, as his senses returned, so did his worries about what had happened. Squeezing her, he spoke.

"I never want you to do something so ridiculous ever again. Do you understand?"

Holly pulled back, her walnut-colored hair shining in the firelight.

"Me? What about you?"

"What about me?"

"You could have been killed," she said with a frown. "I don't ever want you to be in a situation like that again either."

"I'm a man, Holly."

"And that makes little difference to me. Man or not, Kilmann could have murdered you."

Her worry for him did something to his heart. She cared about him, and while he doubted whether she could ever fully love him, due to the beginning of their marriage, it gave him pause.

"Promise me you'll never do anything like that again," he said.

"You're being unfair."

"Am I? It's unfair that I should want my wife to avoid cut-throats, gamblers, and villains?" he asked, noting the pink hue that flushed her cheeks at using the word *wife*. "What were you thinking, following us to that place? Surely you must have known how dangerous it was."

"I was incensed. After what Mr. Mannion told me, I didn't know what to do. But then you and Derek came storming out of St. James into that hackney, just as I was taking a bit of fresh air. When I saw you, I was overcome, so I had the driver follow you."

Gavin shook his head.

"Whatever Mr. Mannion told you was a lie. Your brother hasn't signed anything."

"No, but he's entertaining the idea. And you facilitated it, even though you knew I didn't wish for it."

Gavin had done that, but then he had only been trying to help Jasper figure out how to govern himself. He disagreed with Jasper's wish to sell Felton Manor but understood it. Still, perhaps his wife's feelings should have come first.

"I was trying to help your brother. He lacks a certain confidence in decision making and I thought it would be beneficial for him if I supported him, regardless of his decision."

"But letting him make poor decisions would only hurt him."

"A little, perhaps, but it would make him learn to think critically. If he never learns to fall on his own, he'll never learn to walk on his own either."

Holly bit her bottom lip, and he could tell that she had already considered this by the glimmer in her eye. Still, Holly wasn't the type of woman to callously toss her brother out into the world without any defenses. She had only wanted to protect him, and Gavin respected that.

"I suppose I should step aside then and let him make the mistake," she said meekly, shifting to focus on the hand on his bare chest. "I cannot stop it anyway."

Gavin's arm tightened around her. He should tell her his intentions about buying Felton, but sleep seemed eager to take her, for in the next moment, she drifted off.

Slumber quickly enveloped him, too. Visions of shapeless figures moved about a dark room, but Gavin couldn't find it in him to care. His only desire was to be with Holly and he awoke several times throughout the night, relieved to find her sleeping form pressed against him. Squeezing her tightly, he would fall asleep each time more settled than the last.

The following morning Gavin's arm stretched out over the bed as he woke, but he found to his displeasure that he was alone. The sun was high, and though he hadn't meant to sleep in, he guessed that his body had demanded it.

Dressing without issue, he was careful with his arm, though it really didn't hurt much. The wound was thankfully superficial, but he didn't want to undo the bandages Holly had done. Soon he was dressed, heading out the door and down the stairs in search of his wife.

It had dawned on him the night before, when he saw her enter Kilmann's place, that he was devoted to her. Though it had enraged him seeing her in a place like that, he knew his reaction was due to his deep-seated love for her. It was a bizarre feeling, as though he would never fully be at rest again, for fear of some harm coming to her, but he found that he did not care. He had never experienced this all-consuming need and it was almost too powerful to think about. He wanted to tell her how he felt, but worried how she might react.

Hearing voices as he reached the landing, Gavin followed the loud bickering that was going on in the parlor. Upon entering, he found Holly holding a length of paper, her face pale and drawn. She was standing next to a seated to a very pleased looking Mr. Armstrong, who had his papers spread out over the settee he was sitting on. To his surprise, Aunt Marnie, Katrina, and Jasper were arguing over something or other as he entered the room.

"What's all this now?" he asked as everyone stopped to face him.

But his eyes were only for Holly. She had a paleness to her cheeks that unnerved him, and he couldn't stop himself from going to her.

"What's wrong?" he asked as he reached her, but she didn't

speak.

Instead, she handed him the paper she held before dropping to the chair behind her. Gavin scanned down at the article and felt a sinking feeling drop in his stomach.

Petition for Annulment.

The words seemed to dance on the page. When he looked up, he saw a very happy Mr. Armstrong nodding to him.

"As requested, my lord," the lawyer explained. "It took a great many favors, and I'm certainly in several people's debts because of it, but I've managed to procure your annulment. I took the liberty of acting on behalf of both of you, as you are both my clients, so there is no need for even a signature. The annulment has been finalized."

A faint buzzing began in Gavin's ears. Finalized?

"You mean, we're no longer married?" he asked, his tone hoarse and strained.

"Correct, sir. Congratulations."

This wasn't possible. It simply wasn't happening.

"Is there no need for the courts?" he asked desperately. "Surely the law demands a lengthy review."

"Not necessarily, my lord. I've explained to countless members of parliament what the sixth baron did and while many thought it a sporting idea for their own sons, none seemed too pleased with the idea of it happening to them. Because your peers are sympathetic to your cause, I was able to convince the majority of them to sign off on the petition. So, you and the baroness—er, I mean, Miss Smyth—are free and clear to go your separate ways."

Gavin stood motionless as Mr. Armstrong's words fell over him. Free. Never had he detested a word more. He had been told he was free his entire life, that he should be grateful for being unburdened by family or responsibility. But never had he felt so untethered in his life. He finally had a family, and suddenly, they were to be removed from his life?

What about Holly?

Shifting his gaze to her, he found her head bent, the sadness emanating off her like a light in the mirror. Surely she didn't want this. They couldn't do this. They had consummated their marriage for god's sakes.

"Holly?" he said, only to be interrupted by Aunt Marnie.

"This is outrageous," the old woman squawked, coming forward. "An annulment would only bring shame to this family."

Gavin's brow creased, confused.

"Excuse me?"

"You heard me. Lord knows that this annulment is a lie."

"My sister was tricked into this," Jasper said defensively, stepping towards Aunt Marnie. "If she wishes to be free, we should support her."

Gavin's confusion only grew.

"*You* wish for us to get an annulment?" he asked, pointing to Jasper before turning to Marnie. "And *you* wish for us to remain married? Is that correct?" Both nodded stiffly. "Well, that's a change."

"But shouldn't we ask Holly?" Katrina offered helpfully as everyone in the room turned to face Holly.

"We know what she wants," Mr. Armstrong said, shaking his head. He seemed confused that everyone wasn't more pleased. "Miss Smyth was very clear. You both said to procure the annulment at all costs," he said, turning to Gavin. "That is what you said."

"Yes," Gavin conceded. "I did say that."

Holly's eyes shifted upwards as she glanced at Gavin. She appeared guilty but of what he did not know. All he knew was that he didn't want her to leave him.

"I suppose... We should..." She tried to get the words out, but they refused to come.

Taking a step forward, Gavin reached for her hands.

"No," he stated firmly.

"No?"

"No." His grip tightened on her hands. "Holly, I want very

much to remain your husband, for as long as I live, if you'll have me."

Her head snapped up.

"But… but you said an annulment was the only fair thing to do."

"I did, when I thought it was what you wanted, but if it isn't, well…" He paused. "I wouldn't mind living an unfair life. Would you?"

Tears shone in Holly's eyes as she shook her head.

"No. No, I wouldn't mind that at all," she said as he helped her to her feet.

He pulled her into his arms, and though they were surrounded by people, Gavin couldn't help but hold her closely as he kissed the top of her head.

"Um, excuse me," Mr. Armstrong said, leaning forward after an awkward moment. "Are you telling me that neither of you wants an annulment?"

Gavin turned to the lawyer and shook his head.

"I'm sorry for the inconvenience, Mr. Armstrong, but no," he said, facing Holly again. "No, we are quite content to be married."

"Oh dear," Mr. Armstrong said. "But I've already gone through the proper channels and everything. It's done."

"Well, if that's the case," Gavin said, gazing into Holly's blue eyes, "will you do us the favor of procuring a wedding license?"

The lawyer appeared frazzled for a moment and then exasperated. Gavin was sure he was unhappy with the turn of events, but Gavin couldn't find enough of a reason to be sorry. Holly was his wife, and she would remain so.

Forever.

Epilogue

HOLLY AND CLARA were huddled together in the corner of the Trembley family's parlor, waiting for the guest of honor to appear. The earl's youngest brother, Alfred, was set to arrive any moment, and rumor had it he was bringing a fiancée from America, along with a future sister-in-law.

"I cannot believe Derek has agreed to this," Clara said quietly as they moved amongst the small party that would welcome Alfred home. "Derek has always kept a tight leash on his brothers' propriety, despite their vices. To allow Alfred to propose marriage to someone the family hasn't even met yet is quite a testament to Derek's own development."

"I think Derek is eager to have his brothers settled down. Or at least that's what Gavin says," Holly said as they were joined by Katrina and Violet. "He says the earl has been quieter these days."

"The weight of the earldom lays heavily on him, or so Fredrick thinks," Violet said, with pity in her voice. "It seems as though he's eager to become his father."

"But wasn't the previous earl rather dull?" Clara asked. "I mean, that's not to say I've heard bad things about him. I never got to meet the old earl. But I've heard that he was a very quiet, proper sort of man. Derek is proper enough, but he's certainly not dull."

"Perhaps not, but maybe he wishes to settle down soon, too,

as his brothers have," Violet said, peering over the crowd. Holly watched as her fiancé, Fredrick, caught her gaze and winked at her. She smirked. "I believe it would do the earl good. He should find someone to marry. It's a very pleasant experience."

Clara smirked.

"Says the unwedded one."

"Do you disagree?" Violet asked, before adding. "And I'll remind you, you are married to my brother."

Holly smiled as Clara laughed.

"On my honor, nothing has brought me more happiness than my union with Silas, but I do have reservations when it comes to the Trembley men."

Violet shook her head.

"I assure you, the Trembley men are perfectly capable of being happy."

"Fredrick, certainly. But the earl?" Holly asked, gazing across the room to where her husband stood. "He doesn't seem like the type of man to allow himself much room in ways of love."

Gavin, Silas, and Derek were discussing something, but to her satisfaction, her husband turned, as if sensing her stare. Catching her eye, Gavin smirked at her, and a warmth Holly had begun to cherish filled her heart as memories of the night before played between them. She turned her focus back to the ladies.

"I'm sure the earl is capable," Violet said. "Now, let me tell you about Alfred's bride-to-be."

"Yes, how did they meet?" Clara asked. "And what of this sister who is accompanying her here?"

"Well, from what I understand it was all very fast, but according to Alfred's letters to Fredrick, he is besotted and she is supposedly as sweet and lovely as the morning dew," Violet said, her eyebrows raised. "It is quite humorous when the Trembley men turn poetic. It means they're truly in love."

"Has Fredrick ever spoken to you like that?" Clara asked, surprised.

"Of course," she replied. "Now, Alfred's future sister-in-law however, is another story entirely."

"Why is that?"

But before Violet could explain further, the footman announced the arrival of Alfred and his party.

"Mr. Alfred Trembley, Miss Leona Meadows, and the Comtesse de Retha."

Holly shared speculative glances with the others as a surprised hush fell over the crowd. Alfred entered the room, escorting a young lady whose beauty was as evident as the sun. Her honey-blonde hair was pinned back in an elegant style. She was dressed in a pale blue travel gown, and she carried herself with an air of grace most ladies strived for. She was breathtakingly lovely.

Alfred brought her to the center of the room, where she was introduced to his mother, the dowager countess, and the earl.

Before introductions could be completed, however, a woman starkly different from the first entered. She was dressed in mauve silk, with dozens of dyed feathers trimming the hood of her travel cloak, which she pushed back to reveal her near black hair. Silver-blue eyes glanced over the room, and a slight smirk caught at the corner of her mouth as all eyes fell on her.

"There's no need to use my title," she said to the footman before adding, loud enough for the rest of the room to hear, "My divorce was finalized well over a year ago."

A few soft gasps filtered throughout the room, and Holly stared wide-eyed at the American woman. She was bold in her style of dress, as well as her mannerisms, but there was a quality about her that made Holly curious.

The lady came forward, curtsying to the dowager countess.

"My lady," she said.

"A pleasure to meet you," the dowager said, somewhat startled as her gaze flickered to her son. "Alfred has written the kindest things about you, as has your sister."

"The pleasure is all mine," the dark-haired woman said sweetly, before shifting her focus to her soon-to-be brother-in-law,

Derek. "My lord."

"Comtesse," he said, his tone stiff.

"Miss Meadows," she said, her tone teasing, yet thoughtful. "Or are you hard of hearing?" Violet stifled a giggle, earning a glance from the American, who sidestepped the annoyed looking earl as she came forward. "You must be Violet. Judging from what Alfred has shared, I'm certain we will be great friends. Come, you will be my commencer."

The entire party seemed wholly focused on the American divorcee. Holly was somewhat fixated on the woman herself when she felt the warm touch of Gavin's hand at her elbow. With the entire room distracted, he could pull her away without much notice, which confused but delighted Holly.

"What are you doing?" she whispered as they disappeared from the parlor.

"Tending to you."

She smiled, though she was still confused.

"Whatever for?"

"You've been practically begging me to do so for the last quarter of an hour," he said, his mouth coming down to her ear.

She shivered.

"I h-have not."

"Oh no? Then why all the longing looks?"

"Longing looks, my heel," she repeated with humor. She shook her head. "I can assure you, I haven't been looking your way since the entrance of the new arrivals. In case you didn't notice, the entire room was rather taken with Alfred's guests."

He pulled back slightly, and she prepared to hear something about how exquisite the American appeared. But Gavin merely frowned.

"Were they? I hadn't noticed."

Unbridled glee went through her.

"She was rather pretty. They both are."

"If you say so," he said, kissing her again. "Now, let's find some dark place so that I may do wicked things to you."

Holly couldn't stop the smile that spread across her face. He was truly and wholly only aware of her, and her heart felt as though it might burst.

"I wish I could thank John for all he's done," she said softly as Gavin kissed down her neck.

Gavin and Holly had both read through John's journals together and while there had been some very salacious writings about members of the ton, there were far more interesting things written as well. For one, John had detailed the precise amount he had paid as a monthly stipend to his sister every year since he had inherited the title from their father. He had tripled it the year Gavin had gone to live with Marnie, for a total sum that was so generous it nearly qualified as princely. With those funds at their disposal, they should have been entirely comfortable... but evidently Marnie hadn't ever been able to keep it.

It seems she had a taste for gambling, and most of the money had been lost each month at the tables. She had barely managed to hold on to enough to keep them alive. While Gavin had been angry at the discovery, his grief had been even more profound when he read just how much John had wanted him. Apparently, John and Marnie had fought viciously over Gavin's upbringing, but upon the threat of exposure, John had given up.

Furious, Gavin had wanted to confront Marnie, but Holly had dissuaded him from doing so, reminding him that his aunt—for all her faults—truly loved him.

Another interesting thread they had discovered in John's journals had been his plot to bring Holly and Gavin together. Evidently he had tried several times to get the two to meet, but it had never worked out. When he learned that he was sick, he had devised a plan to marry them by proxy, self-assured that they would find happiness together.

And he had been right.

Gavin pulled back slightly to look at her.

"Me as well."

Holly smiled.

"I love you," she whispered against his mouth between kisses, and he moaned.

"Love, that's just the thing to embolden me," he said. "Come. Let me show you all the ways I love you."

He turned, leading her down one of the empty hallways of Trembley's London home, where no one would bother them for quite some time.

About the Author

Matilda Madison lives in the Pocono mountains of Pennsylvania. A history lover, she finds immense joy in knowing useless facts, exploring the woods around her home, and drinking copious amounts of tea. When she's not writing, she can be found researching obscured periods for her books, refurbishing old furniture, and baking.

Catch up with me anytime on my socials.
Website – www.matildamadison.com
Instagram – matildamadisonbooks
TikTok – @matildamadison